Her Kind

Her Kind

NIAMH BOYCE

PENGUIN BOOKS

PENGUIN BOOKS

UK | USA | Canada | Ireland | Australia
India | New Zealand | South Africa

Penguin Books is part of the Penguin Random House group of companies
whose addresses can be found at global.penguinrandomhouse.com.

First published by Penguin Ireland 2019
Published in Penguin Books 2020
001

Copyright © Niamh Boyce, 2019

The moral right of the author has been asserted

Set in 12.01/14.24 pt Garamond MT Std
Typeset by Jouve (UK), Milton Keynes
Printed and bound in Great Britain by Clays Ltd, Elcograf S.p.A.

A CIP catalogue record for this book is available from the British Library

ISBN: 978–0–241–98323–2

www.greenpenguin.co.uk

Penguin Random House is committed to a
sustainable future for our business, our readers
and our planet. This book is made from Forest
Stewardship Council® certified paper.

To my parents – Anne and Francis Boyce

KILKENNIE

WALL AND TOWERS

HIGH TOWN

HIGH STREET

LOW LANE

IRISH TOWN

Breagagh River

Grines Bridge

John's Bridge

The River Nore

① Kilkennie Castle
   and Gaol

② Saint Mary's Parish Church
   and Meeting Tower

③ Kytler's House

④ Watergate

⑤ Saint Canice's Cathedral
   and Round Tower

Kilkennie Castle

By first bell, a crowd had gathered beneath the trees. They wore cloaks lined with rabbit or vair, according to their rank. Despite the snow, they waited, watching the castle gates. They argued constantly – of the witches locked inside the Castle Gaol, which would be the first to confess? Which, if any, was innocent?

'These are serious proceedings, not a play,' Friar Bede told them. 'Go home until the cry is raised.' They went hungry, but they would not go home.

As prime was rung, figures appeared at the top of the hill. The prisoners had left the confines of the gaol, but no one could say afterwards how, or by which door. Had everyone looked away, to the sky, or to their feet, at the same time? The women moved slowly. Heretics' crosses had been stitched to their chests. Weighed down by their trailing gowns, the ladies were last. The maids, less burdened, led. One was unveiled, her hair straggling past her waist. As they neared, people blessed themselves.

It was a strange sight, the bent figures, dark against the snow, the yellow crosses on their gowns, the bright cold sky above. The crowd muttered their names, as if counting children who had been lost. *Helene, Esme, Lady Cristine, her sister, Beatrice* . . . but where was the one they had waited for, where was the maid of Dame Alice Kytler?

BEALTAINE

MAY

English rule is barbarising the Irish; the invaders have forced us to seek mountains, forests, bogs and barren places, even rocky caves, in order to save our lives, and over a long period have made us dwell in these places like wild beasts.

The Remonstrance of the Irish Chiefs

1. Petronelle

We were so frightened, my daughter and I, scurrying through a maze of alleys, nervous the gatekeeper's son would lead us astray. He surged ahead, his feet slapping the earth, his torch trailing sparks into the night. We came out into a narrow lane, and the boy stopped midway. He gestured to a stone house with large steps and an arched door. The lad strode off without speaking, whistling a soft tune, as he did so. As if without us in tow, the night was a much safer place.

I knocked on the heavy door then tugged my daughter close, terrified of being caught after curfew, strangers inside their walls. There was no answer. I rattled the nearest shutter till a light glimmered along its edges. The door swung open and a candle was raised towards my face. There was silence, and then, the sound of breath being released.

'Is it really you?'

'Yes,' I said.

Beckoning us to follow, Alice Kytler turned and walked into a vast room. Her skirt trailed behind her, blooming from her waist like a black flower. Embers glowed from the wide hearth, where two dogs were stretched out, a dusky mastiff and a white mongrel pup. The mastiff rose and growled. His mistress hushed him and he settled back down. His companion didn't stir beyond cocking a silky ear.

My daughter collapsed on a cushioned bench by the wall. She was trembling as if chilled. Alice fetched furs and blankets from a fireside box and handed them to me, taking in my every aspect. I became aware of my hands, cut and filthy.

Lines ran from her own eyes, but her skin was pale and unweathered. When I'd last seen that face, it had belonged to a different woman than the one who stood before me now.

'I thought you were Roger,' she said, 'else I wouldn't have opened the door.'

'Roger?'

'My husband – not yet home.'

'Well, I'm grateful for that.'

'Don't assume you'll have anything to be grateful for.'

Alice went over to the fire and stoked it a little. I carried the covers to my daughter and placed a dark fur about her shoulders. Instead of being thankful, she shoved it off. 'Take it,' I whispered, aware of Alice's gaze. I realized then that it was a wolf's pelt and understood my girl's reluctance. I offered her a wool blanket instead. She knuckled a tear from her cheek and took it. She suddenly seemed strange, flesh of my flesh, my constant companion – her skin white from exhaustion, her coils of red hair tar-black in the low light of the fire.

Alice dragged two stools to the hearth and bid me join her. When she spoke, her voice was sharper than before. 'You survived.'

'I did.'

'Are you here for revenge?' she whispered.

'I am not.'

'So, why my door?'

'We have nowhere else. I hoped Jose would –'

'My father is long dead.'

It dawned on me then that the Kytler people spoke of, the wealthiest moneylender in the country, was not Jose any longer, but the woman now taking in my hands and neck with quick assessing glances.

'What did you bribe the gatekeeper with?' she asked.

'A jewelled girdle, my dagger. We need shelter, we –'

'How do I know you won't steal my silver, my husband?'

Looking over at the bench, I saw my daughter had curled up and closed her eyes. I reached under my collar, lifted my necklace over my head and offered it to Alice. Taking it, she pressed an amber bead to her mouth.

'How dull they seem now, just mere conkers.'

'I'll pledge it to your keeping, I promise we'll leave next spring. One winter is all I ask.'

'A winter bride,' she laughed, weighing the beads in one hand, then the other.

'For my girl's sake.'

She looked over at my sleeping daughter, took a purse from the deep folds of her dress and slipped my beads into it.

'I do need servants.'

'Servants?'

'Yes' – she had lowered her voice again – 'and there must be no mention of past acquaintanceships, for servants are all you will be. Understand? The roof over your head depends on it.'

'Yes.'

'Good. You'll have new names, English ones, if you're to stay on in Hightown.'

I felt careless with relief. The moneylender could call us anything she pleased.

Someone had left smocks as thin as gauze across our beds. I placed an amber bead beneath the pillow. Unable to part with them all, I kept one back. My daughter's pallet was alongside mine. She could barely stay awake long enough to climb into it. I didn't rest as easily. The wolves. I'd drift off only to be awakened by their calls. Sometimes they all howled, mournful and low; sometimes it was just one. I imagined their eyes in the

7

darkness; pictured them circling the house, nudging an unlatched door. Nonsense, I told myself. Every entrance was locked, every window secure. After a time, the howling ceased, but I still couldn't sleep. I opened the shutter over my bed. Outside, the orchard rustled; there were pale blossoms on the trees. Beyond, the river glistened. We were safe, I told myself, strong city walls stood between harm and us. To survive here, all I had to do was serve Alice.

She had set out my duties earlier. I was to dress her, undress her, arrange her hair, take care of her gowns, mend, embroider, carry messages to her friends and debtors. I was to oversee the hives. I was never to speak of my life before: there was to be no Gaelic, no native ways or tales. For this, my daughter and I would be safe. It seemed a fair exchange, but it was my due and Alice knew it.

The next morning, we rose with the tolling bells. There was a knock on the bedroom door. I opened it to find a neat pile of clothes in a wicker basket. We swapped our cloaks, tunics and loose hair for maid's smocks, kirtles and neat coifs. My daughter was silent as I untangled her curls, combed till gold glittered amongst the red and plaited it neat. I pinned the coif in place and kissed her forehead. 'See,' that kiss tried to say, 'we are as we always have been, mother and daughter, new names don't matter.' With the white linen framing her sulky face, she looked pure as a novice. We hurried downstairs for our instructions. Our time is not our own any more, I reminded her, our time belongs to Alice Kytler.

The mastiff barked as we entered the hall. My daughter sidled towards him, and he quietened. She scratched his head; the brute was meeker than he looked. The windows were glazed with thick glass, sallow as pondweed, making the lane outside appear green. Seeing it in daylight, I realized the room was even larger than I had thought. Rush mats were strewn about the earthen floor. Some stools and a bench were set by the fire, along with a carved wooden chair. A folding screen stood behind it, its green panels closed like a fan.

I noticed a huge tapestry on the far wall. Thinking it familiar, I went closer. A border of golden suns surrounded panels of hunters, beasts and angels, woven in reds, oranges and blues. I caught my breath. The last time I'd seen it, the angel's wings and hunter's tunic were still bright skeins in my mother's basket. I remembered the snippets of thread clinging to her cuffs, her bandaged fingers raising the warp, shuttling thread through as the pattern grew. Líthgen was a wonderful weaver. I was not as gifted but loved working the loom. I had carried my shuttle with me when I fled Flemingstown as a girl, my smooth little boat, its bobbin fat with crimson thread.

'After father died, I meant to have that tapestry taken down . . .'

Alice stood beside the screen, draped in a violet gown. She was more ornate, less homely, than the previous night. She had not changed as much as I had thought.

At her bidding, we followed our new mistress behind the screen. There, wide steps led down to a rough-hewn door. She pushed it open on a smoky, sunlit room. A cauldron steamed on the crook in a huge hearth. Leverets hung from its lintel. Herbs and onions were strung from the beam above a long table where two servants sat preparing a meal. Beyond them, a door opened out on to a courtyard where hens pecked the ground and a thin boy brushed a stout piebald. Alice led us to the doorway and bid us to look out.

'Herb plot, latrine, stable, vegetable rows, rose garden, orchard, hives . . . and the land down to the river? All mine. And the latrine seats three at a time.'

The servants had risen to their feet; they both wore white

kerchiefs on their heads. The elder was dressed in a brown kirtle and a linen apron. Tall, stout and tidy, her brows and lids were completely bald, her eyes grey. She was the cook, Alice told us, and her name was Esme. The younger maid was slight, with eyes too dark for her complexion. The string of her apron went twice around her narrow waist. She was called Helene. Alice gestured towards us.

'This is my new maid, Petronelle de Midia, and her girl, Basilia.'

Helene dipped into a crock and offered my daughter an oat cake. She didn't answer, just stared at the glossy strand of hair that spilt from the maid's cap and down her neck. I realized then that it had been some time since my daughter had spoken.

The rest of that day passed swiftly, with much pounding up and down the stairs behind Alice. She chanted instructions as she mimed the way a lady's gown was laced, her wimple pinned, where and how her clothes were to be stored. I was shown which tray to carry up for each meal, for, unless there were guests, the dame dined in her chamber. I was shown how to wait discreetly, with my back to the wall, at those times that I would not be needed. The sun set without my seeing its face.

That night, I joined the servants in the kitchen. At the very least it would be warm. In truth, I wanted to be apart from my girl and her silent brooding. They sat at the table, which had been dragged near the hearth. Half a dozen tapers gave a dim light. The boy I'd seen brushing the piebald sat on the floor paring a whistle. No one had seen fit to tell me his name. 'Milo,' he answered when I asked, going back to his whittling with a blush. Helene was splitting peas into a bowl and popping every second one in her mouth. The cook wore filthy white gloves; she was chopping mushrooms and adding them to a saucer of milk.

'A sauce?' I asked, as I joined them.

'Yes,' she laughed, 'for the flies.'

I didn't understand.

'The mushrooms are venomous, see.'

Esme pointed at the windowsill, and then at a nook of shelves in the corner: on each were saucers, with flies floating on the surface. She peered at me.

'So, what brought you to Hightown?'

'This is a good place,' I answered.

'If you don't mind being tamed, and named like a pet,' said the cook.

'There are worse ways to keep warm,' I said.

'True, true,' she said, shrugging.

'Has Alice's husband come home yet?' I asked.

'Yes, he finally showed his face. You should've heard them arguing, the tongue on Alice.'

'She was worried perhaps,' I said. 'She must've been, to sit up so late.'

'The mistress only waits up to make sure Sir Roger locks the door,' interrupted Helene. 'She wouldn't care if he never came home. "Let monks, poets and fools sing of love, I'll measure my life by silver" – that's what Dame Alice says.'

The Alice I knew used to mock merchant wives who slept with their silver. This woman they spoke of – she didn't sound like the girl I remembered.

'What were the two of them fighting over?' asked Helene.

The cook recounted the argument with much arm waving. '"Go join your kin," Sir Roger roared, "those clods from Flemingstown." "At least my people toiled hard," Alice answered. "Yours exhausted themselves gorging and fornicating."'

'What happened then?' asked Helene.

'Oh, he laughed, roared laughing. And she did, too.'

'What's so funny about fornicating?' Helene seemed confused.

'Nothing my dear, nothing. I've said enough, maybe too much.'

Esme gestured towards the door. It was ajar and an eaves-dropper's black skirts swung briefly in the gap.

'Who was that?' I asked.

'A spy, I wager, paid by Alice to keep an eye. There's much wealth under this roof, many things of value. We often feel ourselves being watched; sometimes hear footsteps, or glimpse a shadow . . .'

'I think it's a spirit,' added Helene.

'I'm aware of what you think.'

There was a smile growing in the corner of Esme's mouth. Was she teasing the young maid? Was the girl light-fingered, and in need of tales to keep her from pilfering? I thought of my daughter upstairs, staring at the ceiling with her hands clasped. Her skirt was dark; most likely it was her.

'Mór, that's my real name,' said Esme. 'What's yours? It's not Petronelle. I see your pale skin, the red at your daughter's temples. You've Irish blood.'

'I doubt that,' Helene said in her sing-song voice. 'A lady like Alice, having a native combing her hair, fixing her dress? A lady like Alice? I doubt that.'

'This native prepares every morsel that enters said lady's mouth,' said Esme.

'You're different.'

'Am I?'

'The Gaels are meant to keep to Irishtown, you know' – Helene looked at me – 'and are forbidden to trade or mix with *us*.'

I did not like how her mouth twisted on the 'us'. The cook wasn't letting her question go.

'So,' she said, 'what's your name, your real one?'

'The one I hear from my mistress's lips,' I insisted.

'An droch bréagadóir,' the cook muttered. She had called me a liar, and a bad one at that. Yet the glance she gave, as she unpeeled her poisonous gloves, was one of kinship.

2. Basilia

My mother undid her kirtle and tugged on a nightshift that made her look like a ghost.

'Was that you? Were you spying on us?'

Her voice was tired, different to the one she had used downstairs. Let her wonder – I'll not answer. I had seen her down there, chit-chatting with the servants, like nothing had happened in the woods.

As if hearing my thoughts, she spoke. 'I wasn't myself.'

She sat on her bed, her hands open and dead on her lap. *Not herself.* Had my mother and her soul become parted in the woods? Could it still be there, caught in high branches, dark from the distance like a crow's nest?

'Please speak, Líadan.'

I stayed silent. I decided to answer if she used my new name, the one the dame gave, but she didn't. She just sighed and lay down. I was sad, then angry. How dare she beg me to speak, she who kept so much to herself? Some winters we had almost starved to death on that mountain, and all along she could've brought us here, to this place – a house of plenty. Instead, she never even mentioned Kytler's or Dame Alice. Our new mistress was a sight to behold: her veil hemmed with beads, her tight gown filleted at the sleeves to show a brightly dyed kirtle beneath, the satin bulging forth like guts from a belly. Her fingers were jewelled, her nails pointed. She wore her girdle belt low on her hips, weighed down by keys of all sizes, and her eating knife, scissors, file, comb and tweezers. They hung from chains she called a 'chatelaine'.

Dame Alice chimed through her house, silken trains whispering in her wake.

As the days passed, I found that living in Kytler's was like being at court, or what I imagined a court must be like – one where Dame Alice said yes or no from her oak throne. There was an alcove near the hearth, where the maid Helene slept at night. I crouched there on a bed of old blankets and watched the dame move coins across a board to count them.

The dame spent most of her time bartering with a trail of visitors. They bartered with silver bits here, not just food or skins. People brought their precious items – a chair, golden thread, an embroidered mantle, a silver ewer and a stuffed parrot . . . If they didn't repay the loans, she kept them. She explained all this while slicing notches in a tally stick, the splinters spinning on to her lap. The valuables were brought to a locked room, she said, called the Pledge Room.

Alice knew everyone, and everyone knew her. Like most in Hightown, she said, her people were not from this country: they were Flemish. It sounded like an illness. *Flemish, Flemish and owning half of Kilkennie.*

After a week, Helene was instructed to chaperone me about the town. She linked my arm as we left the house, warning against thieves and beggars. She didn't understand why her mistress had taken in strangers and allowed them such freedoms. I didn't either, but was glad of it. She spoke slowly, as if not being a town dweller made me a half-wit. As we stepped into the heat of Low Lane, a stench rose from the dung heaps. I clamped my hand to my mouth. Helene laughed. 'At least it's dry. Wait till it rains and all that filth turns to soup.'

Across the way from Kytler's, steep steps led up to a paved alley where a milkmaid sold butter from her cart. It looked dark in there, cool. It would've been nice to feel those chilled slabs beneath my feet, but Helene pulled me on.

I heard noise before we even turned the corner. The shambles was rowdy with pigs, sheep and chickens, penned or tethered. A pup lapped a pool of blood. Shit spilt from the haunches of frightened beasts. The air was full of flies and feathers. Meat hung on hooks from the butcher's house front. He was a winky smiler. Helene elbowed me and grinned. 'I'd marry him on the spot only for the sound of those knives sharpening.'

We came then to a wide road where houses stood shoulder to shoulder. Shutters were propped like tables beneath each window, laden with bolts of cloth, medicines and bright spices. 'Paprika. Ginger. Cinnamon . . .' Helene chanted, waving her finger, mimicking Dame Alice's habit of listing her treasures. Traders shouted their wares, boys pushed barrows of offal, swine ran riot.

Beggar children were everywhere; scrawny little creatures that tugged at my sleeve and darted about our skirts. Helene growled and slapped them away. One grabbed my hand, a curly-haired, brown-eyed girl. Her plump wrist was wound with plaited bracelets, grubby red threads. She tugged me forward. Helene smacked the child, who released her grip. I swayed backwards, almost knocking against a barrel. The child's figure blurred as she skipped off. Helene steadied me. 'You're so weak,' she snapped, 'and much too thin,' as if it were something I had chosen.

Helene had a vain walk, returning many of the glances thrown her way. We passed cobblers, bakers, furriers, a barber scraping a young man's jaw. All the men in Hightown kept their hair cropped and the women kept theirs covered. I felt a stab of loneliness for my own people. Helene led me off the street and through a warren of passageways: Asylum

Lane, Blind Boreen, Red Alley, Garden Row . . . She slipped ahead, almost at a run. Trying to lose me or get me lost. As if I cared – roaming was second nature to me.

We came upon a smith at his forge, a large man, his flushed face close to the glow of the rod. He looked up, wiped the sweat from his forehead.

'Good day to you, Ulf,' Helene called.

The man nodded and turned back to his work.

'He loves me really, just hides it well.'

As we strolled on, the sound of a river came closer. At the foot of a small stone bridge stood a gate tower topped with a turret. Its iron gate was shut to us.

'Watergate,' Helene said. 'It guards the walls that keep Hightown and Irishtown apart. You might as well muzzle a pair of cats.'

A keeper leant out of the tower window. His hair was slick as an otter's and his beard dripped, darkening his white tunic. He waved at us and Helene waved back. She called up to him in a foreign language. He laughed before disappearing again. We heard a loud creaking as the gate began to rise. A group of clerics rode their horses over the bridge, and Helene pulled me backwards till we were standing in the long grass.

'Don't gawk!'

She lowered her head and shut her eyes – as if the men couldn't see her if she couldn't see them. When they were out of sight, she spat.

'That was the bishop, off to tour Hightown like a sheriff.' She looked at me crossly then, annoyed by my silence. 'Do you've a tongue in your head at all?'

Helene led me back to the house. When we arrived, she pestered my mother with one question after another. Why does your daughter not speak? Did she speak before? What's it like outside the walls? Are there heads staked at every crossroad? How did you escape the wild Irish? If you came from so far, how did you know to come here, right to Alice's door?

'She followed a scent, you Welsh whelp' – Dame Kytler had appeared on the bottom step of the stairs – 'that's how she knew. Now leave us in peace.'

The following day, the dame sent word down to the kitchen that I was to accompany her to a meeting of the Greater Twelve, once dinner was over. My mother laid down her spoon and wondered who the Twelve were.

'Men of quality, skill and standing,' Esme explained. 'They run this city, make laws, set tithes. Sir Arnold will be there, too, seneschal of all Hightown and loyal friend of our mistress.'

As we ate, my mother complained about the waste, how I could be helping mend Alice's linens instead.

'And why,' added Helene, when my mother had left the table, 'should a maid's daughter attend the court of the Greater Twelve?'

'She's not attending the meeting, she's attending her mistress,' said Esme.

I followed Dame Alice through Low Lane, trying not to darken her train with my sweating fingers. I felt guilty, having such a light load while my mother worked hard at home. Though it was summer, Alice's feet were shod in kid slippers. The stone felt warm beneath my own bare ones. We climbed the steep steps that curled about Saint Mary's Church and led us to the meeting tower.

When we neared, the crowd parted to let Alice through. Inside, people lined the stairs, and again we climbed. I kept dropping her train, and tripping on the hem of my own gown – it was much longer than anything I'd worn before.

'Where's Sir Roger?' someone asked.

'Taking care of business,' Alice said.

Whatever that business was, Roger was doing it in his sleep. He had been still in bed when we left. The higher we climbed, the louder the noise. People were pressed against the wall along the stairs. Once we got to the meeting room, Alice told me to stay by the doorway. I watched as she joined the men in the benches. She sat next to a bearded one I guessed was Lord Arnold. A dark man with a trimmed black beard, his tunic was brightly embroidered and his puffed sleeves were tied with ribbon at the elbow. The men in our settlement would've sliced him free of such fine threads, once they'd finished laughing. A bell was rung, and the babbling died down.

A small child stood before the bench. His hair was feathery at the neck, babyish still. An elderly nun stepped forward and explained that the convent was placing him at the mercy of the town. Sir Arnold and Alice were talking to each other. One of the Twelve questioned the nun. The boy's name was Jack, we heard, and the Sister who cared for him had just died.

'I remember this case,' the official said. 'The convent was paid a great amount for his keep some years ago, were they not?'

'No, no, most of it went to Canice's Cathedral,' she said, rubbing her knuckles. 'It paid for another bell.'

'Why so?'

'I cannot say – it is a matter of decency.'

The official smoothed his beard. 'Who owns the child?'

'Some nun's misstep,' the man behind me whispered.

The old woman looked to the ground and made no answer.

'Did he spring from *your* loins?'

There was great laughter as the nun shook her head. Sir Arnold suddenly raised his hand, and the crowd quietened.

'Father?' he asked the nun.

'We do not know.'

'Is the mother dead?'

'Dead to *this* world.'

'Ah, I see.' Arnold nodded as if everything were clear. 'And you would turn out her child?'

'We've no money . . .' added the nun.

'Ah, so she's looking for money. You'll get none here. Care for the child,' snapped Arnold, 'as your deceased Sister once did.'

The nun left, the boy trailing after her, his eyes searching the crowd. All stared back but none stepped forward to offer him shelter. I looked over at Alice, but she and Arnold were chattering between themselves again.

There were many matters next, mostly tithes, fines . . . a baker condemned to the stocks for weighing down his bread with grit. My mind wandered to the mountain, where people were too busy living to gather in stone towers deciding who should care for stray children. If children were there, they were cared for.

When at last the meeting was over, everyone pushed against each other to leave. Once outside, Alice pulled me over to meet Sir Arnold.

'This is Basilia.'

'Oh' – he looked at me – 'I see.'

What did he see? He didn't say. They turned their backs to me and continued talking. I liked the name Basilia, and how my mistress said it. I noticed the boy Jack: he was sitting cross-legged on the ground nearby. The nun was nowhere to be seen. When I looked again, the child was gone. Alice finally shook off the last of those who wanted to wish her well and we returned home.

Inside the house, Sir Roger was perched in Alice's wooden chair, picking his teeth. He hopped to his feet and wrapped his arms around his wife when we arrived. He was ruddy-faced and seemed in the best of humours, but she whacked him away for crushing her veil and urged him to put on his hose. I watched my mother as she helped Alice rearrange her head pins. She seemed so dull compared with everyone else in this place, her skin, her voice even.

'Líadan,' she said, 'come to the hives in a while?'

I fled to the kitchen without answering. Let her call me Basilia, like the rest of the household.

3. Petronelle

I like to be the first awake, always did. So, by our second week, I became the one who let daylight in, the one who unlocked the shutters, drew the bolt on the front door and shooed the dogs from the hearth. That morning the pup bolted as usual but the mastiff moved slowly, stopping at the doorway. Prince, they called him, though he was an old wreck of a beast. The dog was about to raise his leg, so I ran at him. He hopped out with a yelp. The floor needed sweeping, and ash had spilt on to the hearth, but those were Helene's tasks not mine.

I walked over to my mother's tapestry, studied a panel bordered with acorns. In it, a hunter reached towards the burlap of arrows on his back. One look at his face and my heart tightened. My mother had woven Otto. I pressed the threads of his red tunic, and dust rose. A tear came. I wanted to show Líadan, but remembered my promise to Alice. The past must not be mentioned.

At that, I heard my mistress's bell. She kept a small brass one by her bed and when it rang, I ran.

I climbed the stairs to her chamber and found her already at her mirror, fixing rings into her ears. The gold glinted, as with a twist of her wrist she slipped a hoop through her lobe. On their bed, Roger dozed with his night cap over his eyes.

'Hurry, my son Will's coming.'

'Will he be staying?' I asked.

I had yet to meet Alice's son, for he lived in the Le Poer household.

'No, no! We're off to court. Today, we elect the new seneschal.' She laughed then. 'I could save the town crier his breath and announce it now; for the new seneschal will be the old seneschal: Arnold, the loyalest ally anyone could wish for.'

I combed her hair and Alice talked about needing allies more these past couple of years, with the bishop on Irishtown hill getting crankier and crankier. 'Completely ignorant of how things are run here in Kilkennie. He hasn't even the decorum to remain absent like all the bishops before him. This Easter' – Alice's neck flushed – 'he condemned a certain moneylender – "A female," he said, "prone to usury." Everyone turned and tittered in my direction.'

'How awful,' I answered, holding back my questions.

No matter how much we chattered in the kitchen, I'd noticed that, around Alice, servants were required only to listen.

'Since then, I attend Saint Mary's Church. It's far closer than the cathedral, and besides my William rests there. I'm funding an altar in his honour.'

Alice remembered her first husband fondly as I buttoned a sleeve to her gown. How different this woman was towards the girl who had galloped on an invisible horse with her dagger raised, who had come bursting through the thickets, crying, 'Have no fear!' Maybe that change was no bad thing, for young Alice could be as cruel as she was reckless.

'You'll see him for yourself tomorrow.'

'Who?'

'Don't you listen? Bishop Ledrede, when you attend cathedral mass.'

'It's swarming season; had I better not watch your bees? I have a feeling –'

'No, you'll go to the cathedral. And be sure to stay awake – Esme kept falling asleep and missing the best bits.'

'Of course.'

I would've much preferred to check the hives, one of the few tasks permitted here on a Sunday. Though town walls meant safety, I was also learning that they meant rules, many rules.

I began to pin Alice's wimple into place. She was impatient with my slowness. My fingers were more used to soil than the folds in a lady's veil. There was a commotion on the stairs.

'Will has arrived. Oh, wait till you see him. Did I mention he was fostered by Le Poers, of all families?'

'You did.'

'He's soon to receive his accolades and will be a knight before long.'

'That's wonderful,' I answered.

I did not think it wonderful. Had I a son, I would keep him as far from battle as I could. I thought of Otto, his likeness stitched into the tapestry downstairs, his bones somewhere under the earth.

Will strode into the room then. A young squire used to servants, he didn't acknowledge my presence. At fourteen, he was already tall and broad of shoulder. A battle scar ran from the corner of his eye to his chin, tugging his mouth downwards. His mother doted, kissing him on both cheeks and pressing her hands over his. They left with great excitement for the seneschal's election.

I decided to visit the Altar Room. Esme had shown it to us the day before. A small room off the hall had been turned into a chapel with a simple altar and one pew. Alice created it shortly after the bishop accused her of usury. It meant she could hold mass under her own roof if she pleased. He was furious at her arrogance, as were some of the merchants. 'They needn't have concerned themselves – Alice isn't at all pious. There hasn't been a mass here yet,' laughed Esme.

I entered the sweet-smelling silence of the Altar Room and knelt at the pew. After a while, Otto's face came to mind. Seeing him woven as the hunter had startled me at first, but now I was glad he was there. I remembered the two of us, our feet dangling from the banks of the stream. How we dipped our toes but did not swim, because the water was moving fast and floods had torn away the bridge.

Since I had to go to church the next morning, I prepared an old recipe for the bees. Esme watched with her feet up as I mixed foxglove, tansy, honey and a dab of butter in a crock. She was delighted not to have to attend the cathedral, so took a great interest in my recipe and was very encouraging. I carried the concoction down to the orchard till I found a place not far from the hives, in what I hoped would be the path of their flight. I coated the hollow of a large oak there in the paste. A sweet snare. With some luck, any bees that swarmed would settle there to build their kingdom, and not on another's land, gifting someone else with honey, wax and mead.

I called my daughter, and we set out for the cathedral. I was over-warm; Alice had insisted I wear a lavishly embroidered cloak of hers. The furred cuffs alone could keep a family for a year. I felt ashamed passing the clutch of beggars by Watergate. A gaunt woman, her belly swollen with child, stared at me with hatred. The gates had been raised to let worshippers into Irishtown for the sermon. A watchman sat in the window of his tower, precariously close to the edge. He saluted us grandly. As we passed under the arch, I looked up and saw the teeth of the black gate overhead and said a prayer that it was more firmly secured than its keeper.

As we crossed the bridge, Líadan stopped and gazed into the river. I tugged her on, drawn by the huge building on the hill. Just like Hightown and Irishtown, the cathedral itself was behind walls. Kilkennie, it seemed, was a riddle of walls, a stone honeycomb. We climbed steps to yet another archway and entered the grounds. Before us, stood the highest, narrowest bell tower I'd ever seen. Its door was set off the ground, with no stairs or ladder to reach it. The cathedral huddled behind it, like a giant child. I walked towards the church, taking in the coloured-glass windows and enormous oak door. Heads were carved above it, watchful monkish faces, peering down. We wandered amongst the grave slabs and yews that surrounded the building. The grass was speckled with buttercups, daisies and piss-beds.

I felt someone's eyes on me, as sure as if they had reached out and touched the side of my face. I looked about; there was no one else here. Yet the feeling didn't go away. I noticed a path worn to a narrow wall that jutted from the cathedral. There was a slit in the stone, a dark cavity. From there, an eye met mine, blinked, then disappeared. A hermit within the walls. No one had said. I knew it was a woman who watched, but I couldn't say why. I wondered what it was like, to live within the walls of a church. I longed to go closer, to kneel by the opening and beg a blessing for my daughter. The prayers of an anchoress had great power.

A light laugh distracted me from my thoughts. Two ladies approached. One waved. From her manner, I knew she had mistook me for Dame Kytler. I had almost forgotten I was wearing her cloak. 'Besides,' whispered one, as they came closer, 'she's much too tall to be Alice.'

The women stopped and introduced themselves. Annota Lange and Lucia Hatton. They had heard Alice had a new maid for they were both very good friends, they told us, of the dame. Annota was a kind-faced woman with pocked skin, plainly garbed for a merchant. Her powdered companion was short, with soft brown eyes and a sharp nose. Lucia was a neighbour of ours, she said, looking at us from head to toe. She clutched a lapdog and did all the talking.

The grounds began to fill with people who milled towards the cathedral doors. The bells rang, with one toll running into another, urging us inside. We followed the ladies, stopping as they did at the entrance to dip a finger in a white marble font. The burgesses settled into pews, but I noticed our kind stood in the centre aisle, so that's where we went. It was a far cry from our mountainside church, with swallows in the eaves. Gold-painted angels in loin cloths blew trumpets from the beams. There were carvings on the stone columns. Directly above my head, leaves sprouted from the open mouth of a river god, as if a song he'd been singing had come alive.

My daughter stared at the tiles and shuffled her feet. The smell of church wax and incense mixed with that of wool and sweat. I would've much preferred the apple blossoms in Alice's orchard. The bees would swarm, I felt it in my gut. If they settled on another's land, we'd be obliged to share the honey. Worse, if I couldn't find them, a season's harvest would be lost.

The hum from the congregation ceased as a neat robed figure appeared on the altar. I rubbed Líadan's shoulder, and when she looked up her eyes were as dark as slate. They'd taken an offended expression recently, just like the one she'd had as a new-born.

With a voice befitting a town crier, the bishop reeled off a Latin mass. The morning brightened, the windows behind him becoming lances of light that dulled as clouds passed.

When the mass was over, Ledrede spoke to us in English. Someone worthy had drawn the bishop's attention to the lepers in Magdalene House, someone fearing contagion, who wanted the hospital to close its doors. Ledrede announced Kilkennie had no need to fear the lepers, for many citizens were as unclean as they, just as malignant and diseased.

'Heresy is the worse contagion; you must be vigilant. Those of you who know of a heretic, whether neighbour or kin, must tell.'

Heretics, he went on, worshipped demons, performed obscene rites, spat on the Holy Cross. How could anyone spit on the Holy Cross, I wondered, on Christ in his Passion, sacrificing his life so ours could be saved? They also committed sodomy, bestiality and necromancy. There wasn't a whisper; the bishop had them in his thrall – denouncing acts I hardly recognized.

I thought of the anchoress kneeling in her cell, pictured a soft face and dark woollen hood, beneath which braids must be coiled over each ear. I imagined them as conch shells echoing the waves of distant shores, drowning the bishop's words.

His voice rose a pitch. He knew how to weed them out, for he, Richard Ledrede, had been at the papal court when the pope rounded up the Templar monks, each one. Now you'd not find a Templar anywhere, not in Avignon, nor in the Holy Land, nor in Ireland . . .

The bishop stood there, staring into the congregation, letting the silence linger. Líadan was swaying slightly, light-headed from standing so long. I laid my hand on her back.

The bishop carried on. 'The pope lives under constant threat of revenge. His enemies are everywhere – even now, in the sanctity of Avignon. You, too, must keep your eyes open, and be brave in Christ's name. Be vigilant. Disobedience is everywhere. Look about you! There are clerics here, in this very town, living as common men do, siring children.

This very morning, a priest tarried down Dean Street with his child on his shoulders! Singing!'

There were no gasps from the congregation this time, just a rather meek shuffling, and a few laughs.

'You snigger? I tell you this. Any priest who keeps a concubine should put her away. Shun the woman and her offspring, or be suspended.'

There was a snort from behind us. The bishop spoke in French then; he went on for some time. I thought my legs would buckle.

'Sodomy', 'bestiality', 'necromancy' – I committed the words to memory as we left the cathedral, wondering what on earth they meant. It was drizzling now, and rivulets of swill ran on to the street from between the dwellings.

Back at the house, I went up to Alice's chamber to give my report. She was propped up in bed, her tray of food untouched. She made much of my return and, with mock appreciation, thanked me for not running off with her valuable cloak.

'The last maid did. Hard to blame her, I suppose.'

'Yet you got it back?'

'Oh, she didn't get far,' Alice said, tapping her eye tooth.

I was humiliated to learn my trust had been tested, but perhaps that was the point. I relayed Ledrede's sermon and Alice listened. She explained what sodomy and bestiality were. I knew of these acts, but not what they were called. That there were names for them made them seem worse somehow.

'He has said some of this before, but not as vilely. The congregation's becoming conversant with a great many intriguing topics,' Alice said. 'Is the bishop entirely sure of what he's doing?'

Yes, he is, I thought, but did not say, for Alice was not really asking.

'There is a cell there, a hermit?' I asked, removing the heavy cloak.

'Yes, Agnes has a good reputation – she cured one of the lepers through fast and prayer. Bring Basilia to her: she might cure her silence.'

'Perhaps,' I answered, irked by the name Basilia. 'Where will I put your cloak?'

'Antechamber. Where else?'

She glanced over at her counting table, frustrated at being kept from her accounts. I hung the cloak in the small room set off from the chamber. It was stocked with various chests and hung with cloaks and hoods. The air tasted of pelt. I quickly left.

'Might Líadan remain here next Sunday? I'd rather she didn't hear such sermons?'

Alice corrected me for calling my daughter Líadan. She sensed rebellion, and she was correct. I had named my child; she couldn't change that. There was only so much Alice could control: my tongue and my daughter were my own.

'And that's nonsense; the sermons won't do her any harm. Our Basilia is no frail poppet. She survived those savage mountains well enough – I heard you ate each other up there, that last famine winter.'

I remembered the baby I saw suckling from its dead mother, and I longed to slap Alice. What would she know about anything, safe here in her stone coop, fed and watered like a prized pet?

I finally got to the hives. Seven glorious skeps set on low tables, surrounded by apple trees at the end of Alice's orchard. I was just in time to catch a swarm leaving. A smoky buzzing cloud, it veered in the direction of the river. I gathered my skirts and followed a while before tripping. I damned the overlong kirtle I had to wear. As the cool blades tickled my face, I remembered being breathless and a child, racing unhampered through the grove towards the giant tree in Flemingstown. I rose to my feet and called out the charm to keep the swarm close. 'Do not fly wildly to the woods, be ye mindful of my good.' After some time I found the oak. My snare had worked. Smoky and silver-winged, the swarm hummed from inside its breast.

4. Cathedral Hill

The young clerics formed a solemn row and left the choir
stalls; once outside, they raced across the green, flinging
their psalters in the air and catching them. Inside, the bishop
strolled from the altar, satisfied with his morning, despite
the distraction of the anchoress's voice trembling along with
the hymns. High and out of tune, Agnes's voice irritated his
very bowels. He had briefly envisioned jumping from the
pulpit, and driving his staff through the slot in the wall and
into her warbling neck. Instead, he called on the Virgin Mary
for strength and rallied on with his sermon.

His words had had the desired effect: the congregation had
shuffled out afterwards, not gossiping half as much as usual.
They were unnerved, and that was how it must be. Otherwise
they would never betray the heretics amongst them.

He had presumed the woman wearing Kytler's cream cloak
was the moneylender. When she ignored the pews and stood
amongst the commoners, he briefly thought the dame had
repented. But then the woman looked up. For a horrible
instant, he thought it was the anchoress – she had the same
oval face and dark eyes. As if by some perverse miracle Agnes
had been transported from her cell to torture him further.
But it was someone else, some stranger garbed in the moneylender's robes, an impostor whose mouth reminded the
bishop of the sour whores in Italian frescoes.

Ledrede made his way down the aisle to where Bede bent
over his tablet, scoring the wax. He was in the burgesses'
section, tallying the morning's head count. The names of the

wealthiest merchants were carved into the oak pews: Out-lawe, Le Poer, De Valle, Hatton ... some had followed Kytler's lead and stopped attending in person. They worshiped instead in Saint Mary's of Hightown; a glorified oratory where the corporation held its cackling assembly. The bishop ran his finger over the fat *K* of Kytler at the end of the bench.

'Seems Dame Kytler's stout servant has been relieved of cathedral duty,' he said.

'I saw – a new maid came instead. Wore that sinfully lavish cloak, and was accompanied by a girl.'

'Where did they come from?'

'Well, r-r-rumour says –'

'Who is "rumour"?' The bishop was impatient with Bede's pride in his flock of spies.

'One of my boys, a new one. He says they came from the Leix Hills.'

'Gaels?'

'Claim to be English. Mother and daughter.'

'Since when did any English live in the hills?'

'That's what I thought.'

He waited as Bede finished his tally. One hundred and forty-two. That was all – a quarter less than last year, and half the number that had attended his very first sermon.

One sting reminded him of another. That first year of his bishopric, the sheriff came from Dublin to welcome him, to inspect the churches' taxes and, of course, collect his portion. Ledrede had the best wine ready, eager to share a bottle or two with his guest. A lamb was roasted and a feast prepared, but the sheriff wouldn't stay. 'You'll not journey to Dublin on an empty stomach?' Ledrede had asked. He could recall the answer word for word. 'Ah, but we always stay in Kytler's; the dame's hospitality is famed. Surely you'll be there yourself later.'

No invite came from the dame. Ledrede drank the red himself, while ruminating on the frank way the sheriff had refused his invitation. Had he guessed at Ledrede's humble origins? Was it in his speech, in his walk, was it etched into the lines around his mouth? However they knew, they always knew – that breed of people. He never did get to sit at Dame Kytler's table, though officials from all over Ireland were said to sup there.

The bishop and Bede left the cathedral. They found some of the congregation lingering in the churchyard. They had lined up, in a rather snake-like arrangement, to speak with the hermit nun. On walking further, they saw a young man kneeling by the aperture in the cathedral wall, whispering and nodding.

Not for the first time did the bishop consider sealing Sister Agnes in. Through two small chinks, one by his altar and this one in the outer wall, the anchoress endlessly annoyed him. Why did the people confide in a mere flesh and blood woman – petitioning their prayers, bringing babies to bless, limbs to heal? Had she not sworn to leave worldly concerns behind, to devote her life only to prayer?

The woman was lucky even to be here. She had once been a concubine to an Irish chief. 'A lowly abductee,' the man's wife had called her. No trouble, till she gave birth in the middle of the night to a longed-for boy child. The wife paid a high price to have the girl walled in and her baby taken by the convent. Ran away, she had apparently told her husband – *what did you expect?* If only these people petitioning the hermit's prayers knew that, the bishop thought, wondering then if it would make any difference at all. Their sense of shame was not strong.

'There's something in all this fervour, something heathen,' the bishop muttered.

'The lepers come, too. They arrive at sunset, shaking their rattles, but still – it's rather unclean,' said Bede.

Ledrede suddenly felt invigorated. Antagonism often had that effect.

'Pope John showed wonderful foresight in allocating Ossory to a man like me, Bede,' he proclaimed. 'It must've been divine inspiration.'

He remembered his first sighting of the city of Kilkennie. Beggars had lit on them as he and his company neared the gates, but that didn't distract from the sudden warm tug in his chest. It wasn't as if he had arrived in a foreign land, but as if he had come home. He had almost forgotten that sense of purpose, the certainty that his fate was connected to this place.

He must chronicle his progress as bishop, plan further work . . . First, a new roof for the cathedral. It often rained on the congregation. He thought of the moneylender, that gemmed white spider, Alice Kytler. She resented his very presence in Hightown. It seemed previous bishops had dwelt elsewhere and were more interested in siring offspring than in writing sermons.

Her new maid was an odd woman. Seemingly reverent, she had not chattered or whispered. Yet her lips had moved. It was disconcerting – was she praying, or could she be mocking? Just as he had raised the host, she seemed to buckle. When the sacred is raised, the profane will fall.

One day soon, Kytler and all her ilk would fall, would no longer impose their will over Hightown, set their own laws, nurse wealth rightfully owed to the Church. Kilkennie was full of avaricious merchants like her, mere usurers and gluttons – their bellies protruding as vulgarly over their belts as their houses did on to the street. Arnold, their seneschal, was interested only in power, wealth and reputation. The bishop knew his sort well.

MEITHEAMH

———

JUNE

A settlement of Flemish artificers took place not long
after the English invasion. Fullers, cooks, brewers
and weavers of linen and wool; they inhabited a
suburb of Kilkennie, built a town of forty-five
orchards and gardens, and fortified it with gates
and towers.

'Ancient Flemish Colony in Kilkenny',
John G. A. Prim

5. Basilia

We were almost three weeks in Kytler's, when Dame Alice summoned me to her chamber. I opened the heavy door to find her perched on a canopied bed, her pale hair fluffed like a dandelion clock. One side of the room was strewn with Roger's high boots, cloaks, furs, poulaines and damp hose. The other side was tidy except for the large desk in the corner, which was laden with scales, weights, scrolls, loose parchments, inks and quills. Alice smiled, showing tiny sharp teeth, and beckoned me closer. The bed cover was embroidered with gold-and-red branches swirling around tiny bluebirds.

I sat waiting for instructions, but Alice said that all she required was company and folded her hands on her lap. I looked at her bright rings, the mauve veins beneath her pale skin. One fingertip was stained black from ink. I felt, as I stared, that this, whatever it was, had happened before. I had seen it all – the neatly stitched bluebirds, her jewelled ink-stained fingers – once before. The dame, noticing how I stared, thought I liked her rings and began to list the precious stones.

'Garnet, amethyst, ruby, pearl . . . I earned these, every one. You must not think my father sailed from Flanders with caskets of finery. It was hard work, some luck, but mostly hard work that brought our family wealth. Jose taught me to write but, more importantly, to stay alert, be watchful, and let no opportunity pass. "Do not rest," he always said; "you can rest in your grave."'

Though Alice kept busy, her work was far from hard. The servants claimed Jose Kytler left Flanders in a ship so laden it had almost sunk. Maybe both tales were true – I didn't really care. The dame leant forward and gently tugged a lock free from my cap. She peered closely but didn't mention the colour like most would.

'I might even teach you your letters, what say you? Yes, perhaps I will.'

She placed her hand over mine then – it was dry as parchment. I wanted to take mine away, but I didn't dare. Dame Kytler seemed to be thinking, or maybe she was drifting off.

After a while, she spoke about her physician, a learned man. He might visit sometime – might he 'examine' me? I shook my head. I'd had my throat blessed, tied with red ribbon, anointed in fat. It made no difference. Her doctor couldn't help me speak, for I no longer wanted to. Most people didn't like the silence that followed their words to me. After a while they didn't even see me any more – people like Lucia Hatton and Alice's husband, Roger. Even my mother had stopped urging me to speak, but she had always preferred quiet to clamour.

When Alice dismissed me, I slipped from the house and wandered the town. The Hightown Gates were shut, though it was not yet curfew. The keeper eyed me sourly from the turret, the armour on his chest glinting. The gate was gridded and barbed. A gaunt, bearded man stood upon a dunghill, tugging a carcass from the mess. With much swearing, he wrenched up a ribcage that might've once belonged to a deer. I followed as he carried it down through Hightown and towards Watergate.

The keeper waved him through the gate. 'Show me your wares?' he jested, as I approached. He knew I'd no wares and no business there, but he seemed less strict than the keeper who guarded Hightown. On Sunday, he had just left the gates open, perched on his window ledge, and saluted the prettiest girls making their way to Saint Canice's. I passed over the low bridge, a few steps behind the man and the carcass. I had to run to keep up. He didn't climb the steep steps to the cathedral, but turned off on to Dean Street and ducked down a muck lane, where he entered a lone hut.

The door was open, so I peered in. The man glanced up; he didn't seem annoyed so I sidled in and leant against the wall. He said he was a comb-maker, and his name was Fiachra. Had he not such a hooked nose, he would've been handsome. He dumped the carcass into a steaming cauldron and added more turf to the fire beneath.

There were tools and blades on a table. Baskets lined the room: they were filled with cleaned bones, some smoothed into shapes, some already turned into loom weights, knife handles, dye stones or beads. I sat on the ground; it was covered in bone dust, so I drew with my finger. The clay beneath was red. I drew a moon. I drew a bird. A small bird like the one on Alice's bedcover. A bird of earth and bone.

The comb-maker stood over his table and fixed a pale disc into a clamp. He began to saw teeth into it, one by one.

'Gabh go mall. Go slow and careful,' he said, 'that's the trick.'

He spoke as if to an apprentice but didn't look for answers. His tunic was stuck to his back with sweat. He pulled it over his head and hung it on a nail. A line of fur ran from his belt up to his navel; a pendant hung around his neck. A wolf's tooth. I rose to my feet. He lifted it to his mouth and kissed it. 'For luck and a long life,' he said, and something else, but I didn't hear, for I left as quickly as my feet could carry me.

The wolf fang stayed in my mind as I walked towards Watergate. I shivered. I thought of the wolf that had circled me and my mother. I leant over the bridge and gazed into the ferny water. The keeper was shouting down at someone; I wished he'd cease. I wanted to listen to the stream and forget about the wolf, but I kept seeing us there, crouched behind the cairn. The wolf had been rib-thin, head low to the ground, ready to pounce. My mother gripped her dagger so tightly her nails whitened. Was she about to stab the wolf? She locked her arm about my neck. I couldn't breathe. A pack howled in the distance then, and the wolf just flipped away. She released me and I touched my neck. Blood came away on my fingertips. My mother hadn't lifted her knife against the wolf at all – it was me she'd been about to kill. The blade had sliced a raw notch at my neck. In my fear, I had felt no pain.

Afterwards, my mother hoisted our bag on to her shoulder and began walking. She hurried down a slope. I remember her slashing through a thicket, till she found the low, black mouth of a cave. She led me inside, her back bent, bidding me to follow carefully, to take just one step for each of hers, to place my foot in the very same spot – 'There are drops so sharp . . .' It was dim, yet she was sure of her way. A thought came then – that before there was mother and me – there was just mother, a girl unknown to me who knew of caves like this.

The narrow entrance opened out into a great stone room. Above us was a huge fang. I grabbed her cloak. 'It's rock, only a spear of stone.' We veered to the side for many paces and heard running water. There was a small spring, I cupped the ice-cold water and drank. A rabbit ran past, in the direction of the entrance. Mother left me to gather kindling for a fire, dry grass for a bed.

I sat in the dark and remembered watching her making sparks as a child. I had three years, maybe less. She was crouched over a nest: it was woven with hair, grasses, and down – she admired the magpie's delicate work. She struck her hands together till stars sprang out and the nest singed and smoked and flames rose up. I didn't know what a flint was, or that she held one. I thought my mother could make fire from her fingers.

In the cave that night, I slept beside my mother, hating that I needed her warmth, that I was too ignorant to survive alone. I thought of our horse, Finn. Did the pack get him, is that why they howled, did his death prevent ours? When morning came, mother found us a road to follow; we were going to Flemingstown, where she'd lived as a girl, where she'd last seen her own mother. She never mentioned Finn, or what she had done to me. That's when I decided to hate her, and it was a relief, so much easier than what I'd felt before.

We walked for one day and arrived at dusk to find a stone arch that led to nothing but wilderness. Her Flemingstown no longer existed. Beyond the arch was waist-high grass, bushes and stones. There was no sign that anyone had ever lived there. Set high on the arch was a woman's stone. My mother reached up and rubbed the worn place between the hag's legs. Now you cry, I thought, as I watched her, for a place called Flemingstown, for a somewhere I've never known.

We should've stayed on the mountain, hidden till the raid was over. We were abroad in a strange place and night was falling. I was growing scared. I'd heard all about the robbers and cut-throats of the roadways. I knew by her face that my mother longed to pass through the arch but she didn't. She led me off the road and towards a river instead.

We were heading to a place called Kilkennie; only one more day's walk. She said a man called Jose Kytler would be there, a moneylender famed for his wealth, and he was known to our family. We followed the river all night, past a watermill churning in the darkness, creatures entering and leaving the water, till we reached a moonlit moat and a huge castle. My mother tugged me on as I stared. Where were we going, I thought, if not there? Then I saw the lit rushes, the shadow of two watchtowers and the city gate between them staked with skulls . . .

The bells rang, bringing me out of my memory and back to the bridge and the grasses in the riverbed beneath, rippling back and forth like the pelt of some sleeping beast. I longed to swim in it, to feel more than the breeze coming off its waters. Instead I headed back to the house, slipped into the kitchen and sat by the hearth. Esme handed me a bowl of broth and patted my head. What happened in the woods seemed far away then; almost like a tale, but not one for telling.

Mother didn't like my spending so long away from the house. In our room that night, she chided me: 'It's different here; you cannot wander any more. From now on, your time is to be spent helping in the kitchen.' The next day, I found myself cleaving capon while Helene made crumbs and sang Welsh rhymes at the top of her voice.

'That girl gets on my goat,' she said, when Esme arrived, 'the way she never speaks; the mad eyes on her. Why on earth does Alice favour her so?'

Esme didn't answer; she was late and flustered. She just sent me to the garden to gather lemon thyme.

On my fourth day of life as a kitchen maid, Helene had ceased to speak to me, paid me no heed and gave no instructions. Delighted, I slipped out the door, past Milo, who was busily weeding. He was a hard worker, not like the other helper, Ralph. There was no sign of him. He was probably idling about the stables. He groomed his own black hair more than the mares. I passed through the orchard and down to the coiled straw skeps. I sat and watched the bees fly in and out of the tiny doors. Soon they'd be smothered, and small silver dishes would be filled with honey. One landed on my hand but I didn't worry. I was rarely stung. Bees picked up the scent of fear, the way other animals did.

I wandered on down to the river bank and watched some boys wade for pearls. One of them waved, a dark-skinned, sandy-haired boy I'd seen sometimes in the lane. He kept looking. I turned around to see if he was smiling at someone else but there was no one there, only me. I watched him move further out into the river, the sun on his shoulders. Even my breath felt happy. If fear had a scent, I wondered, did love?

That night my mother noticed the muck on my gown. I was surprised, for, though she denied it, her eyesight had started to weaken. As she picked off the briars and sticky tendrils, she chastised me again for idle straying. 'This isn't our world; our place in it has to be earned.' I didn't agree: the house was my world; there was nothing to earn.

Alice instructed my mother to take me to the anchoress. It was said her fasts were powerful. If anyone could find my voice, she could. When we got to the cathedral grounds, a small group was gathered by an elm. They were lowering a body into the ground. It was bound in a white sheet. There were only two people besides the priest: the young gravedigger and a decrepit nun. We stood back, heads bowed, until the slab was fixed in place, and the rites were finished. The gravedigger stayed on after the others left, praying with his head bent.

We went over to the anchoress's cell and my mother knelt on the worn patch of ground beside the cleft in the wall. It was only then we noticed that the chink was blocked. The gravedigger approached, moving as if his feet were made of mortar.

'She's not there – she lies beneath the earth.'

For someone used to burying bodies, he seemed troubled. My mother blessed herself and rose to her feet.

'What happened?' she asked.

'She starved.'

He peered at my mother's face.

'Were you kin to her?' he asked.

'No, no, we are just maids, seeking a cure.'

He walked away from us backwards, all the time looking at my mother. He pointed at her then. 'You,' he shouted, 'are a liar!'

Startled, my mother grabbed my hand. She held it as he returned to the grave. He lay on the hermit nun's slab, his cheek pressed against the stone. I let go of my mother's hand – her grip hurt.

'The poor man has gone mad,' she said.

We slipped away. Once home, my mother told Esme and Helene what we had seen. The cook wondered why Agnes was buried so swiftly. The townspeople, who had worn a path to her cell these past five years, would have liked to have paid their respects one last time.

'A young gravedigger was there,' said my mother.

'Jasper.' Esme didn't seem surprised.

'He was half mad with sorrow. He shouted at us.'

'He got fond of her, that's all. Lots of people did,' said Esme.

'Jasper's always in love,' added Helene.

'A talented boy, though: there's not much he couldn't turn his hand to,' said Esme. She held up her own hands, and we all looked at them. Rough-skinned, and large, they could've been a man's.

Late into the night, I heard muffled footsteps outside my door, then the rustling skirts of women. They seemed to be rushing down the stairs, frightened and wanting escape. While my mother slept on in her bed, I quietly left our chamber and followed the sounds. At the bottom of the stairs, I entered the hall to find nothing but shadows and the glow of low embers – yet I could almost taste the fear.

The next thing, it was morning and I didn't know which part was dream and which real. Had I gone downstairs during the night? I looked at the shut door of our chamber and did not know.

Dreams had always troubled me. It was a dream that had set us on the road here. In it, I was standing in the centre of our settlement. Everyone was asleep in their huts. I could barely see but every sound was louder than ever: the snoring of the men, the animals shifting in their pens, the creak of the trees outside our staked fence. Then came a sound that began soft and slow: that of grass being crushed beneath a careful foot, then another foot, and another and another, till it became like rushes being whipped by the wind. Before I could take one step, a hail of lit arrows swooped from the sky and each hut became a bonfire so swiftly that no one could crawl out.

It terrified me so much I woke my mother to tell her. She believed it was an omen. She told Donagh, but her uncle didn't listen – no one did. We left the next day, just the two of us. At the bottom of the mountain, we almost ran into the troops, but hid in the thicket while their horses drank on the other side of the stream.

You have foresight, my mother whispered. I thought of my friends, of the newest baby, Áine, and her clear cries that morning. It made me never want to sleep again. If only it was as easy to stop dreaming as it was to stop speaking.

6. Petronelle

Bells rang from dawn until dusk here – telling us when to rise, when to pray, when to work and when to stop. The latrines overflowed and the dunghills grew, for the night-soil man had been found smothered in one of the pits and no one had taken his position yet. The place was in a state of high stench but that didn't stop Alice from venturing out. She wanted to inspect the altar mural in Saint Mary's, and visit Sir William Outlawe's grave. She liked to consult her late husband on business decisions.

A sedate priest met us on the church porch, casting his eyes to Alice's purse and pressing his hands together in reverence. An old man rushed forward and practically kissed her hem. Going by his soiled tunic and paint-spattered legs, I took him for the artist. They praised Alice, and the weather, and she admitted that both were indeed wonderful. I was not spoken to or required to speak. Together, we entered the cool of the church. The workers all turned and bowed the best they could, allowing for the brushes and pots they held. The fresco was incomplete, showing bright painted robes from which finely drawn hands and feet emerged. There were three workers: two were strangers, but the third, and the one most covered in plaster, was Jasper. Seeing him, I felt nervous. He was standing on a ladder, drawing with chalk on the wall behind the altar.

Alice conversed a little with the artist, before slowly counting out some coins and placing them in his hand. My mistress walked to the front of the church to inspect the mural more closely. I followed as she went up the aisle and in behind the altar. Jasper reluctantly stepped down from the ladder, his eyes not leaving his work. He was chalking a face framed in dark braids.

'Her hair should be golden, not dun,' she said. 'Brighten it up.'

'Mary wasn't blonde,' he answered quietly.

'My Mary is,' she snapped.

Alice stared up at the face on the plaster. She looked from the image to me and back again. I stared at the blur of chalk and wondered what annoyed her so. The artist, sensing strife, had joined us. He smelt wonderful, of some rich sweet musk. It had become rather crowded behind the altar.

'Whose face is this?' Alice asked Jasper.

'Why, the Virgin's.' He seemed mortified, yet also slightly angry at the attention.

'Don't be insolent – you know what Dame Alice means. Whose likeness is this?' said his master.

'Agnes.'

'The anchoress?' asked Alice.

He nodded.

'I don't believe you. I see plain as day who that is.'

Alice launched herself up the ladder. She reached towards the face and smeared her palm across it. Jasper swore an oath beneath his breath. She put out her hand and I held it while she climbed back down.

'The Virgin should have the features of a noble woman, not a noble woman's maid.'

I hadn't time to catch up with my thoughts, for I was dragged from the church by Alice. She held my hand aloft, as if we were about to dance. Out in the churchyard, she released her grip. It had become a beautiful clean blue day, the sky as bright as the robes on the images inside.

49

She looked across at me. 'That face was like yours,' she accused.

'Not a bit,' I said, though I hadn't really seen it.

'Perhaps. It was smoother; not as weathered and aged.'

'Ageing I may be, but I'm younger than you by half a decade.'

I ducked then, knowing she would swipe, which she did. It was just like when we were young.

'The audacity!' she laughed. 'So few dare speak the truth to me nowadays.'

She linked my arm, and we were somehow friends again. Alice marched in the direction of a mausoleum. The priest, who must've been watching, appeared. He shuffled ahead with an enormous key.

'Don't encourage Jasper's attentions – he's a foolish boy,' said Alice.

'You are mistaken,' I answered.

A shield nailed to the wall bore a coat of arms. The priest opened the padlocked door. My mistress stepped down into the crypt, which as far as I could see was a crowded place, with monuments stacked in each other's shadow. I stayed put as she recited her prayers for William Outlawe's soul, and then added some private soft petitions of her own. She came to the door after a while and beckoned. I took my place beside her. The tomb was a waist-high table, and I was shocked to decipher a figure lying upon it – the corpse of her husband had been carved into stone, with every feature represented, from his rings to the fine details on his codpiece. I wanted to cover my eyes, but Alice seemed so proud.

'The same mason will create my effigy. The drawings will soon be ready.'

She cupped the square jaw of the stone corpse and kissed his mouth. Thankfully, she began to sneeze and we had to leave.

7. Basilia

It was Midsummer's Eve, and I was as far from mountain bonfires as could be, snug in a hammock in a merchant lady's chamber. My mother was tacking Dame Alice's hem. The gown had even more cloth than usual, so the task was taking an age. She rubbed her eyes often but didn't complain. Dame Alice looked over at me and smiled. She liked that I was wearing her gift, a heavy necklace. It was not precious but it was beautiful.

'Why don't you wear the pretty things I give you?' Alice asked my mother.

'I keep them for old age; I may need to sell them for bread.'

She said it in jest but I knew it to be true.

'But wear some, till then.'

'Oh, they'd just get in the way.'

'Stop pretending you like to be plain. Wear trinkets, oil your hair, laugh more often – maybe then you'll find a sweetheart.'

Our mistress seemed to find amusement in that notion.

'I have no wish to marry again.'

'Again?' Alice asked, suddenly harsh. 'And in which church doorway was that?'

My mother did not answer.

'Ah, what difference does it make . . .' said our mistress, touching the top of my mother's head. 'You're good to me. Petronelle.' She drew my mother's new name out slowly.

'No more than any maid.'

'Ah, but you have my trust. Few have that.'

Sir Roger bounded in then, kissed his wife on the forehead and almost tripped over my mother. He was searching for a pair of poulaines for the feast day celebrations. Oxblood, he said. All his silly pointed shoes looked the same to me. He thumped about the room hunting for them. I looked at his bulging belly and his hose in slack creases around his thin ankles and wondered how Alice could lie with him. Had the dame a gift for finding something to cherish amongst us oddments? Me, with my voice still trapped in my throat, him with his beetroot complexion and bandy legs.

When I woke the next morning, it was Midsummer. My mother was already in Dame Alice's room. When our mistress finally appeared, she looked a wonder in her pearly gown. Her sleeves were embroidered with crimson and she waved a black feathered fan. As Alice made her way across the hall, I noticed specks of blood on the hem of her train. If the dame had known, she wouldn't be so full of smiles. My mother must've pricked her finger as she'd sewn the dress. She was upstairs still, exhausted after working through the night.

Dame Alice turned around and slipped me a shining coin. 'Freshly minted in Kilkennie Castle,' she whispered. 'Don't let on I gave you that, or every servant in the house will want a handout.'

I crossed my heart. I wouldn't tell a soul. I had never held a coin before. It was cool, and light. I imagined two little men, working side by side in a castle turret stamping King Edward's face into coins as the room about them filled with silver till it spilt out the door and down the winding stairs. Dame Alice left, swishing her fan. Ralph and Milo followed in her wake, carrying her train between them. Dressed like squires for the day, they wore gloves, piped hose and stiff tunics. Their necks were puce from embarrassment.

I heard Lucia Hatton going into raptures out in the lane, then glimpsed her flushed face as she joined the dame, fussing and complimenting, yap, yap, yap. 'Oh, Alice' this, 'Oh, Alice' that. 'Silk! Swan feathers! And such threads!' I did not like that woman. I was the one age with Lucia's daughter, Sofia. I had overheard Alice suggest that we might become companions. Lucia had laughed and said, 'With a servant? I think not!'

Mother, Esme, Helene and I went out together a little later. Hightown was full of traders, jugglers, fortune-tellers, dancers, hagglers, pipers and rhymers for Midsummer. There were pies, crubeens and cakes for sale. The alewives were doing good business. By noon, I was lost from the others, and happy with it. I bought a pastry, and a carved frog so polished he looked wet. I had heard a parrot talking, seen a man gobble fire and watched part of a play. It ended with Saint John's head on a plate and Salome dancing her seven veils off. I watched as she spun, her arms in the air, ringlets as red as mine, the tiny bells stitched to her skirts chiming.

I became queasy from the pie and let a beggar child take mine. There were more than usual about, half naked and half starved. One scrambled after a piece of fallen crust, a boy so skinny I could see each rib. I glimpsed his face before he ran off: it was Jack – the orphan the convent had forsaken.

Near dusk, the drummers began to play. The beat slowed, sped up, stopped and began again. A youth was vomiting yet holding his mug of ale steady lest he spill a drop. There were many outsiders about, some in rich colours and some in rags. Most of the musicians were Gaels, and it wasn't just their long hair that made me know this – there was something about their faces. I wondered about mine and my mother's. Did our faces tell on us, too?

Some harlots paraded by, stripped to the waist. One had

got a smack for her efforts if her split lip was anything to go by. A couple rutted against a wall. I thought of last Midsummer in the mountain: sitting around the fire pit till dawn, listening to old songs and making up new ones, and how, if a girl met a boy, they'd walk hand in hand away from the flames and into the dark together, not fooster against a wall, his paws gripping the cushion of her behind.

It was almost dark now. The patrollers blew their horns and began to rally outsiders towards the gates. It was time for them to leave. I saw my mother: she stood at the corner of Red Lane, at the edge of a small crowd. I went over. A woman sat on a low stool, a kerchief half covering her white hair. She untied a leather pouch and removed a cloudy glass sphere. A maid from Hattons' stepped forward and asked a question. The soothsayer held her amulet at arm's length and it began to swing in a small circle, then a wider one. A large woman patted my shoulder.

'Get back, little one: too close and you'll lose a tooth,' she laughed.

The soothsayer looked up at the Hattons' maid. 'The woods beyond Irishtown; search there . . .'

'But those woods are strange – all the women say so.'

The seer shrugged; the maid handed her a small parcel and left.

'Are you here, my girl?' The seer peered about suddenly. 'Are you here?'

My mother stepped forward and crouched before her. They hugged then. It went on so long the other women began to elbow each other. Eventually, my mother rose to her feet and called me closer. I went, and the soothsayer reached out and touched my cheek.

A patrol man stepped near and frowned. 'It's the other side of the gates for you,' he said to the seer.

'Mo leanbh. Come see me,' she said.

'I will,' answered my mother.

The patroller began to guide the soothsayer away. My mother made as if to follow, but I caught her by the elbow. She stopped, but she did not stop staring. We watched them leave. Despite his rough talk, the patroller guided the woman towards the gates as if leading his own mother home. Mine stood beside me, weeping.

'Even now, you don't speak, not even to ask who she is.'

I didn't need to ask, I knew. I had heard of her many times as a child. She was Flemingstown's finest weaver, Líthgen, my grandmother. As she disappeared, my mother hugged herself and sighed. Then she noticed the frog I was carrying.

'Where did you get that? You can't just take things here; everything has to be paid for.' She gestured at the dancer. 'Look, look what happens to light-fingered girls.'

Salome was dancing slowly now, her arms weaving above her head as her body swayed. I saw then what my mother wanted me to see. On one of the dancer's hands was a thumb of flesh; the rest of her fingers were pewter. My mother snatched my carved frog and flung it into a ditch before marching me back to Kytler's.

Everything being topsy-turvy for the feast, Esme and Helene sat at the table like men, nursing ale and sharing their day. It lifted my mood, to see them like that. I imagined them in doublets and hose. Alice, too, was there: she swung back and forth in her cloth cradle, which had been strung from a beam in the middle of the hall. She didn't care that her silken trains were sweeping the floor, or that the pup was excitedly snapping in their wake. My mother went to her and asked to retire, but Alice said she should remain 'at hand'. Sir Roger stumbled in then and felt his way to the stairs like a blind man. The women did not laugh till he was gone, and then they couldn't stop.

My mother sat on a stool and stared into the fire. She had wanted me to show feeling for Líthgen, but none was there. My grandmother had haunted us all my life, but she was my mother's ghost, not mine. I wondered if the soothsayer could tell us if Donagh had survived the raid, if Áine had lived long enough to crawl? They were the people I cared about, not her. Shush crying, my mother had said, as we left the mountain. She told me to pray for their souls and keep walking.

Esme and Helene were chatting loudly about the people they'd met at the fête. My mother didn't join in. Her eyes were closed. Had she gone back to the mountain, too? The tilt of her head said yes. The mountain path was white with elderflower the last time I'd looked back.

There was a sudden change of mood. I looked up. Helene was saying something about the teller with a crystal amulet. Alice had stopped swinging back and forth.

'The one called Líthgen?' asked Esme. 'She came last year, too.'

'That wretched creature was inside these walls?' cried Alice.

'Oh, was she banished? What was she banished for?' asked Helene.

Helene couldn't imagine anyone not wanting to live inside Hightown – that Líthgen wasn't banished, that she chose to live somewhere else. No one answered, so Helene tried some answers herself, dragging her thumb through the spilt ale as she did. 'She has her limbs, so not thieving. Maybe she was a silly thing with men, maybe she was love-struck –'

'It's a pity you aren't dumb-struck,' said Alice.

'But what could be the wretch's crime, to be kept outside the walls?'

'Enough, Helene,' my mother said, 'or you'll soon find yourself cast out.'

Alice jumped down, flung her skirts over her arm and strode over to my mother. 'I give the orders here. You are not, nor will you ever be, mistress of this house.'

I did not understand, or much like, Alice's words. My mother rose and left. We heard her stomping upstairs and banging her door.

'Trollop,' spat Helene.

I skipped over and smacked the maid with all my strength and prayed it hurt her well. Alice stared at me then. 'Oh,' she said in a silky voice, 'the kitten has claws.'

8. The Bishop's House

After days of stifling heat, the rain fell. It fell on Hightown and Irishtown, on the haymakers, on the sheep in the bishop's pastures. It turned the cathedral from grey to black; made a mire of the graveyard, swamping the offerings on the anchoress's grave – the reed crosses, rosary beads, scapulars and an infant's coral necklace – till they floated away. Inside the bishop's house, Ledrede sat at the head of his table and ate with his clergy. There was some excitement amongst the new recruits, who kept staring up at the bishop and whispering. What were they saying? What had they heard? Ledrede raised a heavy goblet to his lips. The wine didn't lift his mood.

Agnes. He saw her small hand reaching through the chink in the wall of her cell, beseeching. He was glad she was gone. Five years of those eyes watching from that hole. The squint, they called it here.

The wine felt like swill in his stomach. Where was the usual warmth, the vigour? He had added quite a few drops of Aqua Vitae to his cup. The tonic had no potency. Proper preparation was another lesson he must teach them. He cleared his throat and began to address the clergy regarding the virtues of Aqua Vitae. Friar Bede was especially attentive; perhaps he had a good mind, it was hard to tell – at times his speech was a nuisance to decipher.

'If you moisten a piece of cloth with Aqua Vitae and place it on your tongue, Bede, it will prevent your stutter.'

On seeing the other monks look up with interest, the bishop continued: 'Its properties are useful to alchemists.

Aqua Vitae can cure all passions. It's lethal to worms, toads, spiders, it cures snakebites –'

'How miraculous,' interrupted the archdeacon. 'Were there many alchemists around your last table?'

'There were plenty of alchemists at Avignon.'

There was something snide in the archdeacon's manner. A bald, wax-faced man with a disconcertingly vivid mouth, he smirked whenever Ledrede spoke. Did he perceive poverty in the bishop's vowels? Did he despise those who earned their positions through diligent education?

The bishop suddenly heard his mother's hoarse voice. *Richie! Richie!* He was briefly convinced she would waltz in carrying a serving of pottage.

'Tell the boys of life in the papal court at Avignon, Brother Richard,' said an elder scribe.

The bishop told the youths about the huge fortress that was Avignon, of Pope John's battle against evil, particularly against the Templars, whose forked tongues spoke prayers by day and summoned demons by night. How his holiness was not even safe in his own palace and had to use a magickal snakeskin to test his food for poison.

He watched the entranced faces of the younger clerics; they wished to hear more of these sins, of the kissing of goats' behinds, of illicit rites. He spoke instead of his own learning at the feet of Pope John, of the vigilance which was needed in these times, the rewards available to those who kept their eyes open – like Jacques Fournier, for instance, who was currently ridding Pamiers of the heretical Cathars.

'In fact,' he told them, 'Jacques just received a sheaf of indulgences from Pope John.'

'Straight to 'eaven for him so,' quipped the archdeacon.

'You dare to sneer at my accent – you who couldn't even begin to comprehend the legal canons I've memorized?'

The archdeacon bowed his head and all were silent. Ledrede rose and made his way to his private chambers. Halfway up the spiral stairs, he stopped to catch his breath. Voices rose up from below. The bishop peered down the stairwell.

'Snakebites!' said the archdeacon. 'The bishop promises us remedies for ills that do not exist. How little he knows – there has never been a snake on this island.'

'There hasn't,' the old scribe answered, 'but Brother Richard will find one.'

The bishop would ensure the scribe would be illuminating serpents till he saw them in his sleep. The Garden of Eden perhaps, in miniature, and in triplicate. *May the old scribe go blind inking their fangs.*

He entered his chamber and sat at his desk. The serving boy refilled his goblet and stoked the brazier before disappearing again behind the curtain of his alcove. He sighed. Until he arrived, the clerics here had never even heard tell of Fournier, so sealed were they in their own petty world. And they certainly had no idea of perils he himself had endured travelling across land and sea, just to bring salvation to Kilkennie.

The bishop decided to write to Jacques Fournier. He would compose the letter in his own hand. There were indications that Jacques would be made cardinal soon. Ledrede and he had studied at the papal court in Avignon; had both been given bishoprics by Pope John; and had both risen from humble but honest beginnings. No doubt, their futures might be similarly linked. *Cardinal Ledrede.* He wrote to Fournier of his own ambitions as Bishop of Ossory. 'I hope to distinguish myself here,' he wrote, 'as you have done in Pamiers.'

9. Petronelle

I woke to the apprentice bell and wondered where my mother was waking this morning. How quickly Alice had turned when she heard mention of Líthgen. It was a side of her I'd almost forgotten, one Líadan hadn't seen before. I looked over to my daughter's cot, where she slept on, arms thrown over her head, her fingers curled. There was a leather thong around her neck, strung with beads of coloured glass. Where had it come from? She had taken on a secretive air. I almost wished she was four again, crawling into my lap and playing with the ends of my hair. I felt an awful grief, as if the child I'd known was gone and a changeling had taken her place. One who adored Alice, just as I once had. Perhaps it was only natural – she had been good to us. But I worried. Our mistress liked to acquire things.

I went to Alice's chamber. She was seated at her mirror, her face crumpled from sleep and her hair in a frizz. I set warmed water on her table and handed her a cloth.

'*I'm all alone in the world!*' she said, as she wiped her face.

She used a thick accent meant to be mine. Was that how I had sounded that night I had sought shelter?

'We *were* alone,' I answered.

I hadn't lied. How could I know that Líthgen had survived when I saw Flemingstown gone?

'*Sixteen years,*' I had whispered to my mother. '*Sixteen years and you didn't seek me out?*'

'*I knew you would return some day.*'

What did I expect? A mother who would've left everything

61

and ridden through the Leix Hills till she found me again? Yes, I suppose I did.

I began to lay out Alice's various combs and pins, and knocked over her favourite flask of scent. Nothing was spilt; it was well corked.

'Perhaps I need a defter pair of hands. Maybe Basilia would be better suited to this position? At least her mouth is unsullied by deceit.'

I combed Alice's hair, and she began to talk about Líadan, of curing her silence. On and on she went, about the muteness. Waging that if the girl were capable of speech once, she could be again.

'Isn't there something pure about our silent one?' Esme had said. That I found comfort in those words made me uneasy.

'My physician will see her. He's an unusual man, but good with his hands.'

The idea of a physician examining my daughter, bleeding her, cutting some part of her body . . . I felt sickened. I had done it myself – I would've cut her throat to spare her being torn apart by wolves. Had I been wrong? What if the wolf had not turned?

'I long to hear her speak,' said Alice, 'to say my name.'

To say my name. As if my daughter were her poppet. Alice had no idea who my daughter was, who I was. I suddenly wanted to tell Alice what I had done in the woods.

'She'll speak in time; you see our journey here was difficult –'

Alice interrupted and began to rail against Ledrede and his taxes. Our journey did not interest her. Perhaps there was room enough in her dry head only for measures – of clothes, skins, spoons, grain, silver . . . All must tally. Alice gave nothing away, nothing in her house, nothing in her heart – not without reason or reward.

As she babbled on, my mind travelled outside the walls to

build a shelter beside my mother's, wherever it was. I was not plaiting Alice's hair; I was weaving new skeps for the hives I'd tend there. I could almost hear the dry grasses flick.

Sir Roger had been poorly of late. His sickness had taken our master by surprise. 'A man like me – taken ill like this!' All professed to share his shock, though corpulent old sinners such as Roger suffered bad health sooner or later.

The physician came to bleed the master. A slender figure in a grey tunic, he mounted the stairs as we followed behind, with Helene carrying his medicine chest. Roger lay low in the bed – there was a yellow pallor to his skin. Dame Alice sat beside him, holding his hand, giving it little squeezes. She had taken off her rings so she would not hurt him. The physician studied the contents of the chamber-pot and advised more bleeding. Poor Roger sighed, and sank further into his bed.

While everyone was distracted with the patient, I sought out Milo. He was a steady boy, not prone to gossip. I found him by the stables with Ralph. They were throwing horse shoes. I took him aside and asked him to find a certain sooth-sayer; that she was outside the walls, most likely near the ruins of Flemingstown. He looked up at me with his round serious face and said he had never heard tell of such a place. I was saddened. I thought of the busy town, its weavers, houses and bells. To think that to some it had never existed. I told him where it used to be. My description of Líthgen made him laugh.

After all that, the boy made me wait for an answer. He came when I was at the hives a day later. He'd go on his next day off. All he wanted was a parcel of food. For that, he said, he would find my mother's whereabouts.

'How do you know she's my mother?'

'You said.'

'Did I?'

'Yes.'

Milo left that Saturday evening. When a full day and night had passed, I became worried. Had the wild dogs got him, had some blaggard killed him for fun? Before supper I went to check and was relieved to find the boy had returned, asleep in his loft. I climbed the ladder and tapped his back. He uncurled from the straw, eyes drunk with sleep. Why had I sent one so young outside the walls? Yes, he'd found Líthgen, but she wouldn't let him travel back in the dark – that was what had delayed him, nothing more.

'She has a shack all to herself,' he said, impressed.

'Where is it?'

'Between the ruined arch and the Black Woods.'

He must have meant Flemingstown Woods.

'Is that what you call it? The Black Woods?'

'Yes, everybody does.'

'Did you tell her who sent you?'

He nodded.

'What did she say?'

'Not much.'

I handed him the covered basket. I'd filled it with plums, hard cheese, warm bread and a slice of pork. As I walked through the orchard, I heard the boy yell with joy. He had discovered the meat.

I stopped and sat on the wicker love seat. The garden was alive with flowers and bees. Blossoms formed circlets beneath the trees. I thought of my mother. The settlement had fallen, but she hadn't budged. I should've ventured through Flemingstown Arch that night with Líadan and searched the land beyond it. I had been afraid. Any woman would be, on the savage roads with darkness falling.

*

Early the next morning, I opened the front door to an elegant lady in a blue gown. Holding a baby, she was very pale and rather flustered.

'Where's your mistress?' she demanded. 'I need to speak with her.'

She stepped inside, handing the child to me. It was a newborn, wrapped tightly and asleep. Oh, such a beauty, and barely the weight of a feather.

'Alice!' I called, and the baby's arm jerked as he woke.

'I meant you to fetch her! My Lord, the whole world will know my business.'

I tickled the baby's damp chin; it grabbed my finger, pulled it into its mouth and clamped its gums down.

'What's he called?'

She looked hurt by the question. 'Let's see if he lives first . . .'

Alice entered the room, and at the sight of her the lady released a sob.

'My priest has thrown us from him; we've nowhere to go. How could he do this to the children, when he loves them so much?'

'Are you squabbling again, Sabina?'

'No, it's Ledrede. He's forcing priests to shun their families. Some protested, but he said anyone who speaks against their bishop is either a lunatic or a heretic.'

'You take him too seriously.'

'And so should you. Look what happened to the anchoress: she displeased him and now where is she?'

'She was too vigorous in her fasting.'

'That's not what my priest said. He heard her cell was sealed and her food stopped. Oh, what am I to do, dear friend, with no roof over my head?'

'The bishop is just giving a display. Let him strut around,

declaring all he wants to declare. Things will still be run as we wish them to be run. Move from the house you share with the priest; find somewhere, wait a few weeks and then go back, and go on just as before.'

'Find somewhere?' The lady's words were dealt quick and cold. 'My baby is not strong. Are there no beds here?'

'No, no, there are too many happenings in this house. My husband is ailing – it cannot be done.'

The baby was snatched from my arms, and the lady trounced out.

'She's upset, but it can't be helped,' said Alice. 'It's not a good time for lodgers, not with poor Roger.'

My mistress didn't wait for my response but hurried from the room, the train of her gown catching in her rush through the door.

The real reason Alice didn't want visitors wasn't her husband's illness. An extra pair of eyes would not be welcome, especially not a woman's. Our mistress might be tending Sir Roger by day, but she had begun to tend someone else by night.

A few nights earlier, I had been woken by a clatter and sat up in bed. I opened the shutter slightly and peeked down on to the courtyard. Her clothes were those of a man but I knew my mistress's shape. She mounted her steed and rode in the direction of the river, leaning tight to the mane as she galloped, neither human nor animal but both, as if she had become one with the horse. Morning found her in a blissful mood. She had even forgotten to take off her sapphire necklace. There were two things Alice was never too tired to do: one was to check the doors were bolted; the other was to lock up her jewels.

Late the next night, I heard the stable door creak open, hoofs hitting the mud and then nothing but my own breath.

I wondered who Alice's lover might be – could Arnold be her secret sweetheart? It was said he always acted as if Alice were a queen, kissing her hand, lighting up when she spoke. And she married to Sir Roger, who, though very pleasant, didn't think much of her at all.

'Why is Sir Arnold so smitten with Dame Alice?' I had asked Esme once.

'By all accounts, she funds his battles.'

'So, is his admiration genuine or flattery?'

'We'll never know, will we?'

While not tending her ailing husband, Alice was primping like a girl. She had begun to order warm baths, something she had never needed before. I wasn't afraid of toil, be it at the earth, the hives or the loom, but I was not a born maid. It was wearying doing everything for a person with healthy arms and legs of their own. I scattered blossoms in her tub and prepared her flesh for some lover's touch, all the while promising myself: soon, we'll leave here and join Líthgen. I had whispered as much to Líadan, who stamped her feet and hurled herself on to her bed. I endured no suffering in Kilkennie, no hunger, no pain, but I felt penned in by it all – by the walls, the bishop's sermons, the curfews and Alice's demand that my every waking breath be spent in her service.

Unhappy with the greys, she decided her hair must be brightened. I mixed the bowl of paste; added a drop of vinegar to loosen the ash. As I worked it into her hair, I reported on the most recent sermon, or as much of it as I had grasped. The bishop was fond of phrases no one understood. Rather than confuse, the strange words seemed to enchant the congregation with all their endless possible sin-filled meanings.

'Well,' she asked, 'any slurs cast in my direction?'

I told her what I remembered.

'He said the cathedral hasn't enough candle wax and the mean light casts shame on the town,' I told Alice. 'A church at night should reflect the generosity of God's light by day. Oh, and he mentioned the other thing again, moneylending, where there's profit, there's sin.'

'I predict the birth of another tax we've never heard of – he'll kill three birds with the one stone. Keep us sinless, keep us profitless and fund his expensive wax.'

I massaged her roots and smoothed her hair up into her crown. Alice became coy, oversweet then, as if her words were morsels laid out to entrap.

'I envy your hair,' she said, her own piled in a mustard hillock.

'It's just a dull black.'

'It's no special colour, but it's a colour none the least. Now Basilia, bless her, has hair as bright as heaven's gold, like Lithgen's was once . . .'

'I haven't seen her since the fair,' I answered before she could ask.

I had no intention of revealing any more. I never understood the bad feeling between Alice and my mother, but it had not waned with time. I watched the tight-faced woman and tried to match her with the careless girl who had tied knots in her skirts, splashed in streams and dug fire pits. I wiped paste from Alice's neck, remembering how we climbed trees, pretending the highest branch was the crow's nest of a pirate ship. Ahoy! Savage, pillage, plunder! I had followed her everywhere; she said I was like a little sister. We built our own shelter, sharpening sticks, pushing them into the ground, skinning saplings, weaving them together. Our handiwork looked like a giant unfinished basket. She laid an old black fur on the ground. We crawled in and lay staring at our wicker roof. We fell quiet then, and after a while the bird-song outside grew louder than we'd ever heard before. 'So this is what it's like when no humans are about,' I had whispered, forgetting what we were.

'So two knives,' said Alice, 'one for the fish, one for . . . what's the matter with you? Have you been listening at all?'

'Yes, of course, do go on.'

We had a special name for Flemingstown Woods, Alice and I – but, for the life of me, I couldn't remember what it was. Not the Black Woods, as Milo had called it, not that.

Sir Roger's health worsened, and he was moved to Jose's old chamber. After a few days, he ceased answering and hardly opened his eyes. On the last day of June, Roger reached out his hand and asked for his letter of indulgence. Alice went into the anteroom off her chamber and opened an old black chest there. She reached in and recovered what looked like a codpiece. It was a leather pouch, and inside was the tattered letter that would secure Roger his place in Heaven.

That night, the household gathered around his bed to pray, and he was given the last rites. Sir Roger de Valle died before dawn, clutching his letter of indulgence. Just after his passing, an anguished wail came from outside.

'Oh, Roger, of all the women you could've chosen,' sighed Alice, standing up.

At her instruction, the crier was ushered up to the chamber, already wearing a mourning sash. 'Margaret Dun,' someone whispered, 'Roger's mistress.' The girl sat by Roger's body and began to sing. Her keening filled the house – wailing, chanting and a recitation of utterances that went on and on, in a voice that seemed centuries old. She lamented Roger's death, easing the way for his soul with blessings, cautions and praise. I hadn't heard such a caoineadh since Líthgen had mourned my father's death by wolf. I hurried from the room and went downstairs into the hall, and then down into the kitchen, but I could still hear her. I lifted the cellar latch, picked up my skirts and went down into the darkness, almost tripping on the steps. I stood there amongst the caskets and barrels and wept.

IÚIL

JULY

I tie a knot to seek my love, wherever he may be.
I bless the knot to draw him close, and fasten him to me.

Old love spell

10. Basilia

The house was in mourning. Alice wore a gown the colour of nothing. She sat in her wooden chair at the top of the hall and a long line of people queued to console her. Most spoke of their sorrow at Roger's passing; some just pressed their hand over hers. I joined them but Helene called me down to the kitchen. I was needed to help feed the throngs.

In the kitchen, there was whispering and gossip. Alice was unhappy: she didn't want Ledrede to say the funeral mass, but word was sent that he would do it, or no one would. Roger's family vault was in the cathedral – his family were interred there, under the floor. It was his wish to join them. I wondered which slab was the De Valles'. I was always tripping over them, crammed as they were into the church floor, edges rising up to catch your toe.

Esme handed me a tray of carved meat to bring up to mourners. I went up to the hall. Alice looked so sad; she kept pressing her palm against her heart and sighing long sighs. She looked nothing like the red-faced woman who had leapt from the hammock and almost spat at my mother on Midsummer's Day. I gave the tray to Ralph, who was indoors for a change. He seemed quite at home, weaving through the crowd. I stepped into the queue of mourners: servant or not, I would put my hand on my mistress's hand.

The next morning my mother brought me up to Alice's chamber. We were to pack away Roger's possessions. Too many people were passing through the house to leave them scattered around. She bustled about, shaking out Roger's cloaks, folding them and handing them to me to put away. I opened his chest and saw his poulaines were there, the oxblood ones he had searched for. Everyone else in the house was moving like a sleepwalker, their faces sad, their voices quiet, but my mother hummed as she worked. She had swollen eyes the morning after he died, but now she seemed refreshed, cheered. She began to sing 'Lollai, lollai, litil child', then turned to me, held my face between her palms and kissed my forehead. I smelt cinnamon from her warm skin, heard my old mother in those words – the one who was called Bébinn and told tales by the fire, tales that got wilder and sillier with each telling.

'Close your eyes and open your hand,' she said.

I did as she said and felt something heavy and cold in my palm.

'Now, look.'

It was a crystal sphere, one like Líthgen had.

'It is hers; she wanted you to have it.'

I felt a terrible dread then and threw the crystal into Roger's chest. It lay like a glass apple amongst the woollens.

'You should accept your grandmother's gift.'

It was hard to believe that woman was my grandmother. She didn't feel like blood to me and I didn't want her gift.

I escaped the funeral preparations and set out to the comb-maker's. Settled cross-legged, with my back against the wall, I felt content in myself. I loved the clutter of the workshop, the patient way Fiachra made rough bones into delicate combs. He was on his high stool, carving something small. Often, he'd get lost in his work and pay me no heed. My mother's uncle Donagh was like that. With him, I was always at ease.

The door was open as usual: outside, the rain fell and

some monks passed with their hands tucked inside their sleeves, drenched heads bowed and eyes cast down.

'There they go,' said Fiachra, 'the shower of Latinizing, gluttonous, lecherous wife stealers, and they don't stop at wives, my Lord, they do not . . . they torment everyone, so they do – the sodomites.'

So that was what Ledrede meant. It made me ill to listen to the bishop speak. It wasn't what he said; it was how he looked when he said it – his mouth relishing each word. *Heretic, heathen. Sodomite, demon.*

Fiachra took to whittling with vigour; he was working on a slender handle. Holding it between finger and thumb, he carved for a while longer, then he blew off the dust, licked his thumb and rubbed the surface.

'A miniature,' he said, holding it up.

I saw then that it wasn't a handle – it was the trunk of a tiny body, with a nick for a navel. I noticed several tiny limbs laid out on the worktable. He fixed them to the body with fine pins. The head was bald and blank faced. He flicked a blade back and forth, scoring a mouth, a nose, a pair of eyes. He laid the doll on the table; I reached up.

'No! It's not a plaything. It's a charm, for protection. The mother will bind it with her child's hair or nails, or whatever other nonsense Margaret Dun has told her to. Why people give weight to her opinion is beyond me.'

I remembered Margaret Dun keening for Roger. It was like being at a mountain wake. I had almost felt the mists close around me.

He spoke about Margaret in such a cantankerous fashion that I suspected he was fond of her, nonsense and all.

11. Saint Canice's Cathedral

As the noon sun lit the coloured windows, Roger de Valle's coffin was laid beside the open vault on the floor. Incense failed to conceal the tang of decay from the grave. The top coffin had caved in, revealing a fragment of skull and some threads of hair. The bishop watched from the altar as the pews filled with Kytler's tithe-shy cronies: merchants in skimpy tunics and coloured hose, followed by their fidgeting wives and coddled lapdogs.

Dame Kytler had assumed the pose of one in prayer, wearing a pale gown and ruby necklace; she fed crystal beads through her gloved fingers. Her allies gathered behind her – ladies in gemmed girdles, flicking their gauzy veils, wetting their animal mouths. Her son, Will Outlawe, conversed with a dozen other men, all wearing the blue livery of Arnold le Poer – of course, young Outlawe was fostered by the Le Poers. Lastly, there stood a clutch of mournful servants. The bishop stepped on to the altar and waited for a lull. The moneylender was finally on his territory again; she would have to listen.

'Using a common trick of the tax evader, the deceased, Sir Roger de Valle, bestowed all his goods upon his wife before his death. He has thereby defrauded the Church, Christ and his own soul.'

The widow showed no emotion. A decent woman would've trembled, thought the bishop, fainted even. But she wasn't a decent woman; she had let De Valle sign every single thing over to her, leaving nothing for the Church. The bishop had expected a sizable sum from the estate, but now, in the eyes of the law at least, De Valle might as well have died a pauper. The items in his will amounted to no more than a few clothes and a shoe horn.

'It has been ordained,' he added, 'with the unanimous consent of the chapter and clergy, that Roger de Valle will not receive an ecclesiastical burial . . . unless immediate reparation is made.'

Now, Kytler would have to pay her dues.

The dame lifted her skirts and strolled down the aisle. She stopped by her son and whispered something, before heading towards the door. At the marble font, she dunked a gloved thumb, blessed herself and left the church.

Some of the congregation moved forward to remonstrate with the bishop. He raised his hands to silence them. Will Outlawe drew his halberd, but the choir surrounded him, brandishing their own knives till he made his retreat. A slight girl cast herself across the coffin and wept. The young grave-digger, Jasper, came forward and grasped her waist lest she slip headfirst into the vault. Eventually, De Valle's mourners carried his coffin from the cathedral.

Once they were gone, Ledrede approached the open vault. The stench rose up and filled his mouth. Something glinted from the shredded fabric. He knelt, rolled up his sleeve and reached down into the grave; the object felt cold and came away quite easily. It was a sizable opal, set in gold. He slipped the ring into his purse. He was entitled; it was worth only a fraction of what was due from De Valle's estate. A splinter protruded from his knuckle, he bit it free and spat. Blood ran from the puncture.

'A war wound, your holiness?'

It was the gravedigger. Where did he appear from? Was he mocking the bishop's courage?

'Replace that slab. No burial. No payment.'

The bishop left the cathedral, and crossed the grounds, growing more furious with each step. Kytler had so much wealth; the Church's portion of Sir Roger's property was a drop in the ocean. According to Bede's young spy, everything the moneylender owned was silver – from her buttons, to her spoons, to her chamber-pot. The dame thought she was above being taxed or penalized. Only the poor were punished here – and it was no different all the world over. No matter what their crime, the likes of Kytler would never be chastised, let alone fined or flogged in the marketplace. He imagined the moneylender tied to a whipping post, her rich silks lashed to shreds, blood instead of rubies glittering on her skin.

12. Petronelle

The townspeople lined High Street and lowered their heads as the coffin passed. We followed in its wake, reciting the rosary. All except Esme, who was ranting: 'A curse on the bishop's greed,' she said for all to hear, 'a curse on his grabbing hands and on his stinking sandalled feet.' We were heading towards Saint Mary's cemetery. At Alice's request, Sir Roger was to be interred along with her first husband.

Our mistress was waiting for us by the crypt, standing still as a marble angel. She appeared calm, but I knew by the set of her jaw that she was enraged beyond speech. We all stood for a bit, looking at Saint Mary's priest, who didn't seem to know how to proceed. Alice swung her fringed purse back and forth, and nodded at him. The chink of the coins must've eased his fear of Ledrede, for he stepped into the crypt and the mourners followed. The prayers for the dead drifted up from inside. The priest led the ceremony well enough, if rather hastily. We returned then to the house, where the boards were bending under platters of beef, veal, salmon, trout, pies, breads, pastries, cheeses, dainties – all draped in muslin, to the frustration of the hovering flies. Basilia and Helene served ale and wine, their kirtles laced with black ribbon. After no time the house was packed. A bard from Cork was there, one I'd never heard tell of. Roger had supported him over the years. Alice's mood had lifted.

'It's better,' she announced, 'that my husband's buried some place I'll visit, that I feel blessed visiting, rather than somewhere I'll never set foot in again. Now, celebrate the life of a hearty man – drink until you cannot stand!'

Margaret Dun, red-eyed but more composed than earlier, drank a mether of ale in one draught. She patted Helene's arm and whispered something. The maid giggled. When had Helene become so familiar with Roger's mistress? And was I the only person who had not known of her existence?

After we'd eaten, Lucia Hatton cornered Alice and was cooing with false sympathy. A waste of an arsehole, Roger used to call her. A little uncharitable but not far off the mark. A recitation was about to begin, and quiet was being called for. I decided to slip away. I brought Líadan with me, for she seemed rather giddy and was casting flirtatious glances at one of the Hattons' workers. I questioned her on the stairs. Had she been sneaking snifters? Who was that boy she kept sidling over to? Of course, I got no answer but at least she slept well, better than I did.

I tiptoed into the kitchen just before dawn. The funeral party was not long over. Men dozed under benches and around the hearth. Will was curled under the table, asleep with the mastiff. I'd heard Alice up talking until a while ago; she wouldn't rise till late. I wrapped a parcel of leftovers and took a small bladder of wine. Out in the stables, I found Milo still asleep. I woke him and, bleary-eyed, he led our mares through the yard. I took the dappled white. The other had a glossy dark coat and was a better horse, but it reminded me of the one I'd left to the wolves.

We cantered through a silent High Street, and at the town gates I showed the keeper the Kytler crest on my cloak and paid our due. We rode across the moat. The horses' hoofs on the wooden bridge beat loud enough to wake the town, and they certainly woke my heart – how good to be on the other side of the town walls. As soon as we were out of sight,

I straddled the horse properly. It was a hazy morning. The road to Flemingstown was swallowed by hedges, and leafy branches formed a canopy above our heads. The dawn chorus was as rowdy as any shower of drunkards. Midges bit so often, I stopped waving them away.

After a time on the road, we spotted a figure in the distance, on foot; he was carrying something. Milo and I drew our horses together as we neared. It was a blond youth, his head shaven a palm's-width above each ear. 'Irish,' Milo said under his breath, as we slowed to a halt. We had no need to fear. It was not a weapon he carried but a bodhrán.

'Dia duit,' he said, squinting up at me. 'An bhfuilimid i bhfad ó Chill Chainnigh?'

'Níl ach ní cheadaítear na Gaeil ar an mbaile,' I answered.

'Ná bíodh imní ort,' he said, smiled and bowed.

He strolled off in the direction of Kilkennie, drumming lightly on his bodhrán.

'You speak Gaelic?' asked Milo.

'I learnt from a servant.'

'What did he say?'

'He wanted to know was Kilkennie near.'

'But they don't allow Gaels there.'

'I told him. Why on earth would he even try?'

'He's in love with someone inside the walls.'

'Nonsense!' I laughed.

'Did you not see his eyes?'

I had noticed those bright eyes. Milo had guessed right. I looked at him; perhaps he was older in years than I'd assumed. A thought came as we trotted on – although I was dressed as a lady's maid, the youth had addressed me in my native tongue. My gown and wimple hadn't fooled the Gael.

The sun was high when we reached Flemingstown Arch. It was a lonely sight, that huge stone arch stripped of its walls.

81

I reached up and rubbed the woman's stone. As if someone had dragged me back, I felt the same shiver of fear as when I'd passed through sixteen years ago, a child in my stomach, its father dead. There had been no time to stop then. I'd just twisted my fingers deep into the horse's mane and galloped from the place.

I got off the mare. She whinnied and halted; it took some nudging before she'd go through the arch. The meadow was a wilderness, as if there had never been lanes or plots. Milo followed; he was sprightly here, different to the timid lad in Kytler's stable. I saw a heap in the distance and we went over; it was the remains of stone walls. And there was the giant oak tree. This had been the site of the common hall. A broken bell, rusted orange, was half in the earth. I could almost hear it toll. We tied the horses to the tree and walked the land. Now that we were here, Milo couldn't recall exactly where he'd found Líthgen's hut.

'It was different last time,' he said, confused.

'It's always different when you return.'

I stepped through a gap in a hedge – and there they were, the woods. I drank in the dense dark trees. I had been so free here. Alice and I had beaten a track through that long grass, cutting our own zigzag path to the woods. *Paradise*, I suddenly remembered. That was what we named those woods as children. Paradise. Milo called out. I looked behind – he was standing by a shelter of sturdy wattle.

I lifted the blanket draped across the doorway and went in past him. The walls were hung with skins – hare, squirrel, badger. There was a narrow crib, a handloom leaning against the end and a row of flints on a ledge. Rosemary, sage, thyme and yarrow were strung from the eaves. Milo gave a short whistle. I went outside in time to see a figure coming out of the woods. Her hair hung in a heavy white rope. Her back

82

was bent but she walked strong, hands swinging and her catch in one – a glittering fish. She didn't speak till we were face to face.

'You didn't bring the girl?'

'Not this time.'

In the bright of day, I saw what I hadn't that night. How her eyes were hooded, and her skin was webbed with lines. Those eyes were pale, mossy like a pond. She stroked my cheek. There was blood under her nails. An old feeling surged up inside. She was the mother I had not wanted. I would've preferred Alice's – a wistful memory leaving copious furs and tales.

'I missed you,' she said.

'So you said, but you didn't follow.'

'I stayed with my man.'

'He was dead.'

'Would you want him to return and find me gone?'

Líthgen believed my father would return from the other side, that souls close as theirs could not part for ever.

She built a fire outside the hut and then gutted the salmon. I watched as she sliced it lengthways and fried it in an old, long-handled pan. Every now and again, she would turn a piece with a flick of her wrist. Silver scales drifted from the fish, glinting like stars in the blackened pan. It brought me back to being a child, watching the skin crisping, knowing I would soon taste it.

We ate the salmon with the wine I'd brought. I watched my mother gulp it down and decided to bring more next time. She rarely used to drink but when she did she relished it. She would sing and outstay the moon. Milo lay on his back, chewing bread and surveying the sky.

I told Líthgen about my daughter and her silence.

'What can I do to make her speak again?'

'What did you do to make her stop?'

I turned from her gaze, watched the smoke twist up.

'Ah, your silence . . . our silence. And you're surprised she carries it, too, and uses it like a weapon? Why did fate take my clever daughter and leave the pretty one?'

'Time has passed, I'm no longer that.'

'So you're clever now – are you?'

'Never as clever as Dervla.'

My sister had been my mother's favourite. Losing Dervla had bewildered her. *Stolen?* she might ask in the middle of a task. *In the earth?* she might ask on waking. I became used to those whispered questions. For all her second sight, when it came to her daughter, Líthgen was blind. She never knew where Dervla might be. She was last seen by the stream but all we found there were horse tracks. *Come back.*

'What happened to this place?' I waved across the wilderness and fallen walls.

'The O'Tooles: they raided and burned till there was nothing left. I fled to the other side of the woods. You remember the cave?'

'I do. The townspeople – did many survive?'

'No one who lived inside those walls.'

'But Alice and her father –'

'They left the day before; took their most valued possessions with them.'

'That's more luck than is natural – were they forewarned?'

'Of course they were.'

I closed my eyes. The midday sun warmed my face. I removed my veil; the hair beneath it was hot to touch.

'This silent daughter of yours, is she content?'

'Content enough. She's never hungry, seldom cold and worships Alice Kytler.'

'Keep her apart from Alice.'

84

'She has been good to us.'

'Do as I say.' Líthgen rose to her feet, quenched the fire with her wine. 'Alice has no heart. Haven't you learnt that?'

Already we were at odds – disagreeing over Alice, just like years before. I sighed. There was no point in talking on; there wasn't the time. We had to get back to Hightown. I told Milo to fetch the horses.

We had mounted and were ready to leave when Líthgen reached up and grabbed my ankle.

'Promise you'll come back. Promise.'

'I will, don't worry. I'm going to Hightown, not battle.'

'Battle. Why say that?'

Why did she always have to be so contrary? She knew exactly what I meant.

'You know well why. Those who go to battle seldom return – Otto didn't.'

'Oh, foolish daughter,' she said, as she clouted my horse. 'A dead man can't ride to battle.'

With a jolt, my horse began to canter. I glanced back at Líthgen. She was standing there, watching us go, her hand pressed flat to her heart.

Milo and I trotted along in silence, each in our own world. I could not stop thinking about Líthgen's final words.

A dead man can't ride to battle.

Otto had been mourned as a felled warrior, by his family and everyone in the town. I had grieved over the years, but had grieved for a man cut down in battle.

A dead man.

Had Otto died before going into battle? If Líthgen was right, he had not even made it outside the walls. I kept churning it over in my mind. What had happened to Otto?

At the city gates, Milo got off his horse and handed me the rope.

'I'm not going back to Kytler's; I'm going to stay with Líthgen.'

With that, he ran off in the direction we'd come. Of course, I thought, as I watched him, of course he would prefer living alongside Líthgen to his coop in Kytler's. The keeper trotted over, set his arrow into his bow and aimed in Milo's direction.

'Escaping?' he glanced up from his quarry.

'On an important message,' I said, gently touching his shoulder for fear he'd release the bow, 'for Dame Kytler.'

He looked up at me, slight interest in his brown eyes, flicked the arrow back into his burlap and returned to his tower.

I smiled to see how Milo kicked up dust as he moved further into the distance. I hoped he'd be happy by Flemingstown Woods, as I'd once been. Though they would be alone, and we had been far from alone. There were many shelters back then, built outside the town, leaning against its walls. A few hadn't the means to pay tithes; others weren't welcome inside. Some were like my father, who just couldn't bear rules and curfews.

'Let the burgesses have their plots,' he used to say; 'we have the world outside it.'

In truth, we had next to nothing. Jose Kytler was like a merchant king and all either wove for him or owed him, and often both, like my mother. Alice ran as wild as I did; we used to rush into the woods together, shrieking like owls. It worried Líthgen. 'If anything happens to that girl,' she'd say, 'Jose Kytler will have our heads.'

'I've never heard a word of complaint from his mouth,' said my father.

'He doesn't even know you're alive,' my mother replied.

'Well, if I don't live, he can't have my head,' Father said, squeezing Líthgen's waist and kissing her neck. But he was long dead now, the outlaw who had eased his arms so contently around his wife.

13. Basilia

Though it wasn't very warm, Dame Alice wanted to be fanned as she worked at her desk. She kept pulling out the front of her gown and damning the heat. She scratched a line under a name.

'Damn King Edward, too; so much for my five hundred pounds. Perhaps Ledrede's latest sermons are spreading across the kingdoms. Since poor Roger's death, he's been ordering that no one pay the moneylender till she's paid her dues to the bishop.'

It was commonly said that even the king was in debt to my mistress, but I was startled by the amount. Was she jesting? Dame Alice seemed very serious as she twisted the thick gold band on her thumb. She always wore her father's signature ring while doing accounts. The seal was small, but it was the old Kytler one. She sighed loudly, and finally looked up.

'There are nicer things to think on. Come here and see this likeness for my tomb.'

She lifted a scroll from her drawer and unrolled a drawing of a sleeping woman. It was her effigy, the dame explained. The drawing was like her, but with a smoother, rounder face. The mason had even included the line of her parting, the neat coils of hair on each side of her head. *Her face in death will not look like that.* I saw Alice crouched: she was in pain and her hand was raised as if to defend herself.

'Whatever's wrong, Basilia?'

She glanced impatiently – I had dropped the fan. The vision came again. It was clearer. My mistress's silken skirts were speckled with earth. Each breath that left her mouth hung in the air like smoke. Embers crumbled from a nearby brazier. It was night, and the only other person awake was about to end her life.

I went over to the window, and looked out over the orchard. The vision was a warning. My mistress was in danger. I thought of the poppet Fiachra had carved for some mother; could a charm like that protect Dame Alice?

The day after the vision, my blood came. Esme was grinding cardamom seeds and Helene was on the stool by the fire binding kindling. There was a bowl of poached plums on the table, sitting in their dark juice. I had just spooned one into my mouth when the cramps started. I gripped my belly and bent over. The women fussed about how I looked.

'She's green in the face,' Helene said, smirking. 'It must be her time.'

Esme pressed her knuckles into my back, which eased the ache for a bit. I caught her raising her eyes at Helene as they shared some meaning. It vexed me, it was all so womanly, and they were trying to include me.

Upstairs in my chamber, I found that they were right. There it was between my legs, the bright blood. It'll only be a little, my mother had said when she told me about the curse: 'Nothing to worry about; it won't hurt.'

When she came into the room later, I was curled on the edge of the bed. She didn't offer tonic to soothe the pain.

'Stop crying – it's an honour, and about time, too. I was getting worried.' She handed me a wad of rags. 'Rinse these afterwards and reuse them, and on heavy days stuff them with moss.'

Heavy days – what on earth were heavy days? She took her scissors from her belt and snipped a corner from my blood-drenched smock. Folding it into a square of black felt, she sat on her bed and stitched shut her tiny relic of my moon blood. She looked up as I groaned.

'Ah, shush, it's only a little.'

It was not a little, and it hurt like Hell must. How was anyone meant to live like this?

Early the next morning I was summoned to Alice's chamber. The dame wore no veil – I was startled by the primrose yellow. I had forgotten my mother had coloured her hair. It made the skin beneath her eyes look like lavender bruises. An extra desk had been placed in the room, just under the window. She pointed to it and bid me sit. I was going to learn my letters, she told me; it would keep me from roaming.

She set a tablet in front of me and demonstrated how to inscribe letters into the wax with a stylus. She spoke the letters, as she drew them ... *A. B. C. D. E* ... When they were put together, she explained, they took on a meaning. This carried on for ages; over and over she sang the sounds. Then she put a piece of parchment alongside my table. On it was a list prepared by a scribe. *Bell, Vespers, Alb, Prayer, Dog* ... Alice recited. She was not pleased with the words. They were not, she said, the kind I would need. She watched over me as I began to copy. The parchment was stained yellow with pollen. The monk had drawn little creatures in the margins. Alice left me to practise while she made a better list at her own desk. The words might as well have been insects crawling across the page, but the curls, slopes and flicks were nice to copy.

At first, I rested my wrist as I wrote, but the wax kept softening under my touch. Keeping my hand aloft made it ache, but I kept on going, making loops and strokes ... *Dog, Sun, Crocus*. After a while, I got distracted by the view from the window. I could see over the orchard and all the way to the river. There, the boys were harvesting pearls in the shallow bend. Wearing only their braies, each with a satchel strung across his shoulders, they waded out, holding forked rods aloft. Piotr Hatton, Lucia's husband, was barking orders from the silt bank.

Alice came over waving a page. She read aloud from a list of newly inked words. *Due. Paid. Man. Woman. Child. Beef. Lamb. Capon. Ale. Pelt. Spice* . . . and on and on. She looked out at the Hattons' workers and tutted.

'Of the mussels, only one in a hundred holds a pearl, often not a pearl of any worth.'

Alice worked at her counting table while I inscribed wax. I envied the scratch of her quill, wished that dry whisper for my own writing. It was hard not to drift when sitting by an open window. Almost without realizing, I had drawn a blackbird from the tree outside. He was perched on a large red apple, spearing the fruit. I watched as the flesh split, and he stabbed and stabbed with his beak till the apple dropped to the grass.

Across the room, Alice stacked groats, pennies, ha'pennies and farthings on her casting board. Sometimes she would fill cloth bags, which would quickly disappear from sight. She spoke as we worked, flitting from subject to subject, with no expectation of an answer. She said she missed Roger, for talking to at night, those nights he stayed home. She ranted then about Ledrede: he was costing her business; as sure as if he'd put his pious hand in her purse.

'A foreigner dictating ridiculous laws from a hill built high with the bones of our ancestors.'

She said Ledrede spied on the good citizens of Kilkennie from the ancient tower, and had every merchant burying their coins for fear of his pouncing and demanding a portion for the Church.

'It's a surprise,' said Alice, 'that he isn't attending the

births of our citizens to tax their first breath. The view would do him good, I'd expect; that fresh wound might send him galloping back to Avignon.'

I thought of the rags stuffed between my legs, the braies I had to wear beneath my skirts.

After a week, I became better at shaping letters and words in wax, and Alice set me to work with ink and a quill. I leant too hard at first, and the nib crushed. It took time, and a few damaged quills, to make the shapes I wanted. I liked the rounded letters best, loved the gloss the ink had before the parchment drank it up. I preferred the monk's first list, and sometimes copied from it. I began each day by pumicing yesterday's letters from the page, wiping the grain away and then dipped my quill to begin. *Abbot, Bee, Beauty.*

Alice talked freely each time I wrote in her chamber. She didn't mind that I didn't answer. Sometimes I didn't even listen; I'd watch the pearl-divers. Near the end of the day, they'd come out of the water and gather around a brazier for warmth. Then they opened mussels and flung the husks to the ground. There was a song they sang as they worked. It was a slow but lively air in which no one led and everyone followed. It was sung over and over, till the bank was festooned with dark blue shells.

As the month passed, Alice's mood grew lighter and lighter. She even slept late sometimes. One day she led me down to the cellar and opened a heavy door I had not noticed before. We had to roll a barrel out of the way to get to it. She took a key from her chatelaine. 'This is a copy, just for you.' She unlocked the door, lifted her candle and went down some steps. There, in the middle of the crowded floor, was a bull's head. In the flickering candlelight, its horned shadow darted about the wall. I jumped backwards.

Alice set her candle on a table laid with silver ewers. She lifted a pole and opened a shutter high on the wall and weak light spilt in. The room was thick with dust motes. My nose itched as I stepped amongst the treasures. I almost tripped on a rug showing a tree woven in an unnatural shade of blue. Baskets were stacked with embroidered cuffs, dyed threads and gilt-handled scissors. There was an entire wall covered in pelts. Alice caressed each one, naming as she went. Miniver. Sable. Vair. She stroked against the nap, rippling and darkening the fur before smoothing it down again. Beaver. Rabbit. Wolf.

'Aha, you are paying attention now,' she said.

Stuffed hawks were stationed on the floor, wings outstretched as if they were about to fly. I wasn't to gawk, she declared, I was here to work. She unrolled a scroll; it was a list of items, their owners and their debts. 'An inventory,' she called it, 'such as a lady makes before she marries.' Knowing I wouldn't recognize some words, she had drawn pictures beside them. A tiny hawk. A squat candlestick . . . her drawings were poor but true. I had to check everything was accounted for, and in order. Alice alone added to or subtracted from the list, no one else.

When Alice left, I looked about the room. So this was the Pledge Room. I thought of the people who owned these items. Did they long for their return? I selected a pale shimmering box, placed a green velvet cushion between two trunks and made myself comfortable. The box was mother of pearl and contained pouches, rings and silver bracelets, most of which were tagged and numbered. Some were cut-off pieces, silver hacked from bracelets, armlets and collars. One piece was worked with spirals. Dame Alice's dislike of the Irish didn't stop her doing business with them. I selected a ring and eased it on: it was shaped into the tiny figures of a man and a woman, who reached out and embraced at the centre of my finger. Did the girl who once owned it still wait to be wed? I sensed a great loss as I twisted it off.

I loosened the mouth of a large velvet purse, poured out a necklace of amber beads. It was my mother's. Why would she pledge it to Dame Alice? I held the beads up. Their shine was not outwards but into themselves. If you looked long enough, their honeyed centres crackled with gold. I held them and felt warmth seep into my heart. 'They are all I have of your father,' she always said, 'besides you.' What had my mother pledged the beads against? Or were they just here for safekeeping? I was loath to return them to the purse, but I did. I locked the door and hung the key on my girdle. It rested on my hip as I walked. I felt like Dame Alice – keeper of keys, guardian of locks, chests and rooms stuffed with valuable things.

That night, Dame Alice returned from some meeting very pleased with herself. When only she and I were left in the hall, she ordered me to drag the screen around us. We sat close to the fire, her in her special chair, I on a stool. Alice decided to tell me a tale she had learnt as a girl. She sipped wine to wet her throat before she began. 'Fadó, fadó, a long time ago' was how my own mother always started a story, but Alice did it differently.

'Once,' she began, 'in a forest far from here, dwelt Lord Halewijn. His voice was deep and haunting and he sang a magickal song. Every maiden who heard it fell under its spell and was drawn into his woods.'

What song could be so strong as to make a person lose their senses? I couldn't imagine.

'One day, a girl heard Halewijn and mounted her steed to follow his voice. This girl was a princess, and wore a red skirt stitched with pearls. As she rode into the forest, she met a white bird who warned, "Those who go there, do not return!"

But the princess galloped on. The trees bent and their rustling said, "Those who go there, do not return!" But she could not stop, driven mad as she was with longing. She entered the clearing where Halewijn stood, tall and dark, and the wind lifted her veil and whispered, "Those who come here, will not return." Still, she dismounted and walked towards Lord Halewijn as if in a trance.

'"Welcome," he said, "come, untie your hair."

'And so she untied her hair, and as it fell so did her tears, for she stood in a gallows' field and women hung from every tree. Lord Halewijn gave the princess a choice of death. She chose a beheading, for its swiftness. "Sir," she said, "first take off your shirt, a maiden's blood spreads far." The lord laid down his sword to remove his shirt. As soon as it was out of his hands, the princess used it against him. She sliced off his head and it landed by his feet.'

I giggled. It struck me as startling, to have your head and feet beside each other. Alice got in a huff and refused to tell me the rest of the story. She waved me away to bed, but I sneaked down to the Pledge Room instead.

I unlocked the door and set my candle on a table. I didn't care about a silly princess who didn't listen to warnings, but the story nagged like a bad tooth. I curled up on my green cushion, flicked open a peacock fan and pretended to be the empress of a large kingdom, who rode to and from her ivory palace on the back of a magickal swan. But it was dark, and there were shadows growing up along the walls. The objects seemed to glare and gloat. I rubbed the scar on my neck, and pictured the princess in red, pearled and crowned. Down went her arm, down went the blade, like the beak of the blackbird, again and again – she kept cutting off that head. Then I saw the wolf's yellow eyes, his bared wet teeth, felt the edge of my mother's knife.

94

14. Petronelle

I was on my dead father's horse, my possessions tied across my back, a child swelling my stomach. The lackeys and their axes were catching up. Flemingstown Arch was close – if I could just pass through. If I could just . . . I woke in our small room, my child a grown girl and only an arm's reach away. My damp shift stuck to me like a second skin. Alice's bell sounded from down the corridor, an impatient trill – how long had she been ringing? Shivering, I dressed and rushed to her chamber. Alice sat at her dressing mirror, her face already powdered, her cheeks rouged. The shutters were open, and the sky outside was red.

'Sleepyhead,' she said.

I fetched a comb and stood behind my mistress. There was a small smile to her lips, and shadows beneath her eyes. I wondered if she had been to bed at all. I unpicked threads of straw from her hair. Our fine dame with her canopied bed was courting like a peasant.

I longed to ask about Otto, but didn't know how to begin. I lifted her yellow hair gently and brushed the length, untangling each knot as I went, for lately her scalp was easily hurt. I looked at her pale neck. There was a red mark there, the shape of a clasp. She'd lain in her necklace all night. Is that what her secret lover was after? Her wealth? It wasn't her beauty; not any more. Though Alice was still fetching on occasion, it took work to achieve the effect. Even then, there was no hiding the lines and loose skin. How I would've longed to see Otto age; to hold his hand, to argue even. We never argued then; we'd lie on the forest floor and watch the red leaves swirl slowly towards the ground. It must've been cold, but I don't remember any cold. What was Alice saying? She was holding two pretty combs. Ivory.

'I'll gift these to Basilia, when I'm old and no longer need them.'

When I'm old, indeed, as if that day had not already arrived. Oh, Alice.

'I think also that she should have at least one presentable gown.'

'For what?' I asked.

'For courtship, of course.'

'My daughter wishes to remain a virgin; she wishes to become a nun.'

'No, Petronelle, you are confused,' Alice answered. 'The one who wishes to be a nun is you.'

Her eyes met mine in the mirror. Now was the time . . .

'I wanted to ask –' I began.

'What?'

'It's been said that Otto didn't go to battle, that he was killed before he left Flemingstown.'

She reached to touch the necklace that was no longer there.

'Who told you such lies? It was Líthgen, wasn't it? What else did she say?'

'Nothing else.'

'My brother rode through Flemingstown Gates. It was the last time I saw him; now never distress me with this again.'

She put her hands over her face and released a sob.

'I am sorry, so sorry . . .' I said, until she stopped weeping.

Alice let me finish fixing her hair. As I worked, she avoided the mirror and studied her rings. Afterwards, I realized her face powder had remained completely dry.

*

Alice thought it was a secret, but I wasn't the only one who had seen her ride out at night. There was much whispering about it. Most guessed it was a man she was meeting, but some, more ill-disposed to Alice, said it was a faerie, or worse. Then, mere weeks after Sir Roger's funeral, she announced plans to remarry. The house was buzzing with the news that Alice's betrothed was due to visit that Saturday. We'd finally meet the man who had drawn her like a moon-struck girl. Cleaning began at dawn. The tapers were replaced with beeswax candles. By even-time, the hall smelt of rosemary and sweetly smouldering turf.

We lined up to meet our future master and Alice entered, her arm linked with that of a tall man wearing a short blue tunic and black hose. Sir John of Callan had a lean face and a full mouth. Helene let out a low sigh; Esme chuckled. He was younger than our mistress. We were surprised to see two girls following on their heels. Alice introduced them as Cristine and Beatrice, her stepdaughters to be. I watched my mistress carefully. Her smile was too wide to be natural. Had she known of the girls' existence before this, she would have mentioned them. Had Sir John not told her?

A little older than Líadan, the knight's daughters were twins. Both had budding rose lips and darting fingers decked in false gems. Their flaxen hair was braided into ram's horns and dressed in silver netting. Most striking was their skin, pale as pearl dust. Their father told us how wonderful our mistress was, how happy they would be as man and wife. There was something about his eyes, and the uncertain curve to his mouth, that made him appear insincere, mocking even.

The sisters fidgeted with their sleeves as if unused to such swathes of fabric. As one touched her cuff, so did the other; as one straightened and smiled, so did the other. I thought of mirrors, of trickery I saw once at a fair. But the girls were just twins; it was that simple, nothing magickal. The four went off to Hattons', where Lucia was throwing a supper in their honour.

'Lucia will have to set some extra places, for the twins,' said Alice as they left.

'Lucia will swallow her tongue when she sees those thighs,' muttered Helene.

'He seems a little young,' I added.

'Far from young – he's well over thirty,' Esme answered. 'Alice told me.'

'A lady her age,' said Helene, 'what would she want with a fine man like that?'

'The same thing as any woman,' I said without thinking.

I found out later that Alice had known nothing of the twins until the very day they arrived. I asked her directly.

'Surely he mentioned his daughters, all that time?'

'We didn't do much talking – you wouldn't understand.'

She wasn't pleased but consoled herself that the girls lived in Callan. They dwelt in their late mother's house, over a day's journey away, and there they would stay.

On the morning of Alice's wedding, while out fetching water, I found a glass bead by the well. Dark blue, it was the shape of a bird's head, with a yellow painted eye. I slipped it in my purse and carried the bucket to the kitchen. I was to prepare whitening for Alice's skin. I enjoyed the quiet, the crackle of the fire, wished I could stay longer, but she was waiting upstairs with her jars and bottles lined up in front of her. I mixed the whitening powder with more rosewater and went up.

I daubed Alice's skin till it was like ivory. I braided and wound her plaits into two plump ram's horns, using oil infused with ambergris and musk to smoothen the kinks and stray hairs. I tweezed her brows till they were almost gone, then greased her lips with beeswax and lightly rouged her cheeks. Alice dipped her finger in the pot and dabbed her mouth.

'Do not look at me like that, Petronelle.'

'Only harlots redden their mouths.'

'It's for my husband I make myself handsome. When did you get so unbearably pious? I wager you, too, would pretty yourself for a man's embrace, if you had half the chance.'

'The only embrace I long for is Christ's,' I said to irk her.

'That wasn't always true; Basilia didn't fall from the clouds, did she? She came from somewhere else entirely. Oh, look at you blush.'

She was very giddy; that kind of talk was unlike her. She opened a small pouch then and took out a phial. It held shimmering brown powder. The shape of a tiny beetle was burned into the stopper.

'Spanish Fly,' she said, 'otherwise known as Aphrodite's Assistant. I'm going to slip it into his wine –'

'It made Esme's sister vomit blood. She said that only for –'

'Oh, stop fussing. It's all in the measuring: a little lends itself to lust, too much sickens. The poor fool should've known that. And she's not Esme's sister – I don't know why we all go along with that charade.'

'Why, who is she, then?'

Esme often spoke of her sister but I had yet to meet her.

'Her love.'

Alice looked up then. She was hoping I would blush. She liked to think she was more worldly than me, and I suppose she was.

She jabbered on as I dressed each ram's horn in a pearl-bead caul. The veil was so fine you could barely see it fall down her back. We had laced her chemise tight to push her bosom upwards. Alice lifted her hand mirror and went over to stand by the window.

'So many lines.' She frowned, touching the side of her mouth.

'You only notice them now?'

'Could you not lie to me?'

'I prefer truth.'

'The first time I wed, I was fourteen. I hadn't a blemish, not a mark. I still recall that night; Sir William was like a flabby goat, passing wind as he spent his seed. It makes me sad somehow to think on it, though he was a good man.'

He might have been a good man, but Will was their only living child. And he came after a decade of sharing a bed.

'And Roger, the poor beast, was never cruel. I've been blessed.'

Alice didn't mention her second spouse; she never did. It was said he struck her more severely than a husband should. She shook her head as if she, too, were thinking of him. She requested her cloak then. I unfolded the royal-blue mantle from her armoire and fetched the Gaelic brooch from her jewellery box. Both were gifts from Sir Arnold, who had as many Irish allies as Irish enemies. She smiled as I pinned the cloak closed, her eyes hatched with lines; and there was happiness in them. She wasn't marrying for silver this time.

Sir John and Alice exchanged vows in the doorway of Saint Mary's Parish Church. 'I take you as my wife, for better or worse, to have and to hold to the end of my life,' promised Sir John, and they kissed each other full on the mouth for a very long time. Kjarval, the finest musician in the country, played the sweetest, lightest music. The ladies outdid themselves, every cuff and collar was furred, every gown was slit to show the rich fabrics beneath.

The house was lit like a cathedral. As well as the chandeliers, there were candles in every nook and corner. The heavy scent of beeswax gave the hall a church feeling. The harp was magnificent, painted, as it was, in red, blue and gold, and carved with mermaids. When I reached out to touch it, the harpist waved me away, shushing and hands fluttering, as if it were a baby that shouldn't be woken.

The party ate course after course and townspeople filled the lane outside, waiting for the leftovers. Wan faces gazed in, as Prince gnawed a meaty joint by the foot of Alice's chair. I wondered if such a large feast was a good idea – the drunkenness, dance, music, all the flavours of celebration spilling out into the street when so many were hungry.

After the feast, the wedding company, with the exception of young Will, who stayed on drinking with his manservant, trooped up to Alice's chamber. Our mistress sat up, her skin flushed, her hair still coiled and jewelled. She was now wearing a brazenly yellow chemise. Her husband lay on top of the covers; he was bare-chested in a gilt buckled belt and hose. The priest approached the bed.

'Keep it short, Father,' laughed Sir John.

'Let us pray, blessed Christ, O Lord, thou who watched over Israel, watch over thy servants who rest in this bed, guarding them from all phantasies and illusions of devils.'

The bed cover darkened as he sprinkled it with holy water. The party raised their cups to Alice and John and proceeded back down to the banquet hall, chattering and giddy. When the dancing began, I excused myself and retreated to the kitchen, where Esme was turning hens. The grease from the birds dripped and hissed into the fire.

'It's not long since we fed Roger's funeral company – could she not have waited for another month or so?' she said.

'Look at him,' said Helene. 'Who could wait?'

'Stop being so lustful – go up to the hall and replenish their ewers.'

The boisterous singing went on most of the night. I went to bed but lay awake, turning the glass bead between my fingers. I examined the bird with its yellow dot eye. I'd thread it along with some other beads and make something pretty for my daughter. I held the lone amber at my own neck as I watched Líadan sleep. She was curled on her side as usual. There was a flickering beneath her lids. She travelled far in her dreams, and was always startled on being woken. Her eyes would be empty, as if her soul hadn't caught up, was still off travelling. I leant over and lifted a strand of hair from across her mouth. We used to talk about the meaning of dreams. They were sealed away now; she no longer told them to anyone.

That morning, I found Helene and Esme stumbling about, repairing the damage to the dining hall, both with bad tempers and sore heads. The pup whined and whined. Prince was nowhere to be seen. Everyone had searched but not a trace of the mastiff was found. Alice entered the hall, draped in nothing but her mantle, her hair loose about her thin shoulders. She was parched – had no one heard her bell? Helene served her some ale, showed her a wedding gift that had not been opened. Pleased, Alice unwrapped the pale ribbons and muslin to find a carafe. She uncorked it and sniffed, and her smile left.

'Honeywine,' she said. 'Who delivered this?'

None of us knew who had delivered it, but we all knew someone was taunting Alice, mocking her age. All the honeywine in the world wouldn't bless this bride with a child. As if to distract from bad news with worse, Helene told her then that Prince was gone, taken most likely by the beggars who had crowded Low Lane last night.

'Murderers,' Alice guessed. 'How could they? And one of God's creatures.'

'Maybe another of God's creatures might live to see another day,' said Helene. 'Maybe a starving child has a belly full of meat.'

'Oh, you do not mean that!'

'No,' Helene agreed; 'I do not mean it, of course I don't.'

Helene did that often – they all did. Said what Alice wanted to hear, not what they really thought.

I ventured out for some peace. It was drizzling. I walked to the end of the garden and found my oak hive, the one I had snared myself. The bees were calm. I lifted out a small honeycomb and stepped away from the tree. I thumbed the creamy surface, breaking open the small pools of gold. There were some eggs, too, curled pearls in their cells. From one, a young bee began to emerge. I felt a sharp pain in my cheek, a sting. I scraped my skin with the side of my knife. Held the blade to examine the barb, thinking how quickly the venom had entered my flesh.

Later in the kitchen, I was mending with Helene and Esme. I picked a needle, held it close, licked the thread and fed it through.

'Oh, look at your face – you were bitten,' said Helene.

'Bees don't bite, they pierce. The barb's like a tiny sword, you see, a narrow spike with a sac of poison.'

'Sir John can sting me any time, as long as he doesn't leave anything behind.'

'You turn everything sinful,' I said.

Helene was very mischievous of late, reckless with her words. I prodded my needle into her arm. She cried out.

'Was your mirth worth the pain?'

'Yes!'

'One more word,' I warned, 'and I'll tell Alice how you swoon after her husband.'

She sobered then, brought her stitching closer. 'He's only her husband because of trickery. She cast a love spell, that's what Cristine said.'

'He's her husband because he wants to be,' I answered.

That silenced the maid, though I wasn't sure that she believed me. *Cristine said.* What else did Cristine say? The sooner those twins were back in Callan the better for all of us.

15. Basilia

Alice was all the time in her chamber with her new husband. My mother ran back and forth, with bowls of warm water, soft towels, lavender douches, and sticks of cinnamon for her breath. There were calls for sweetbreads, chicken legs and wine, and oh, empty the chamber-pot again. The new husband was a tall man, a strutter. Worse, he was a widow with daughters. In the days after the wedding, the twins slept in a chamber we called the coffin. There was no window, so it was pitch without a taper lit. 'Don't go up in flames now, girls,' smiled Helene as she handed them a candle. They were not pleased, but no one really wanted them to be. After a week, those horrible sisters – 'Can she not speak? How funny,' they giggled. 'What if we gave her a pinch?' – trotted back to Callan.

Not long after, Lucia Hatton called for news and a tipple. As she and Alice made themselves cosy by the hearth, I tucked myself into the alcove to eavesdrop. They talked about John, Lucia's own husband, Piotr, the twins, and then my mother, who, Alice said, had become dour. My mistress thought she resented all the care she herself needed, now she was married again, and this time to an attentive man. Or perhaps the maid was jealous? Lucia speculated, though Lord knows why. She was free, after all, from all that poking and pulling, and, worse, some babe swelling your stomach, then ripping you asunder trying to get out.

'You only see the bad side – have you forgotten the good? Has it been that long, Lucia?' laughed Alice.

'Not long enough. Your maid should count her lucky stars.'

'I pity her lonely flesh, her skin that will go untouched till death.'

'Maybe she prefers it that way.'

'Maybe. Still, it must be difficult to prepare another for loving when you'll never know it again yourself.'

'Since when did you care what anyone else felt?'

They gained great amusement from their wonderings and now I was trapped listening to them. For if I stepped out I would reveal myself. When Lucia came over, Alice became a lesser person. I couldn't understand why, other than to pass the time with a very boring woman. Even so, they had no right to talk about my mother like that.

Sir Arnold and his nephew Stephen came to feast with Alice and John. Piotr Hatton was there, too, and lost no chance to make sly bids for various loans. He was as painful as his wife, Lucia. Sir Arnold did not behave like a lord – he nodded when served and listened as well as spoke. He had brought Alice wine from France, an almanac and a small pouch of tiny diamonds – 'To fill the gaps in your teeth,' he said, smiling. Stephen was a younger, paler version of his uncle – an apprentice Arnold. He sat close to him, but did not speak much except a few words to Sir John about his stables in Callan.

After supper, John announced he was going for some air. Piotr said he'd join him. Alice glanced at Sir Arnold. 'You, too?'

'No, I'll stay here, where it's warm and cheerful.'

When the two men had left, the conversation turned to property. The nephew just sat listening. The Hattons held a plot across the river. She was eager to get hold of the land, to build her own bridge across the Nore. If it meant humouring them, well, let it be so. Arnold lowered his voice and began to speak of the bishop. It was said, he told Alice, that Ledrede was garnering spies. Merchant or wretch, she needed to be careful. Children swarmed to and from the bishop's house-hold, the kind that would do anything for bread.

'I just want him gone, captured, whatever it takes.'

Arnold said not to worry, that he had good relations with Ledrede's superiors in Dublin. They would soon stunt his growth. I could not hear much of what followed, for they leant very close.

At last, the ewers were drained and the esteemed visitors readied to retire. Jose's chamber had been prepared. Arnold explained to his nephew that the gable chamber was famed for its vantage point. From one window you could see High-town drawbridge; from the other the castle. It was rumoured, he said, that, by a system of secret flags, castle officials used to send messages to Jose Kytler, and he back to them. I would've loved to have slept in it, even once – the bed was as big as a boat and canopied in red – but staying there was an honour reserved for special guests or those near death.

After the men retired, my mother and I tidied the hall. Dame Alice stayed on, warming herself by the dying fire, swaying and humming a tune. She looked well in one of her best gowns: creamy velvet with heavily embroidered cuffs and neck. She sat at the table and called us over then, to admire the almanac Arnold had brought. It had a picture for each sign. She read our horoscopes. I was a Gemini, Twins. 'He hath two sides,' was all she said. My mother didn't know the month of her birth. 'Winter,' she said, 'sometime in win-ter.' Dame Alice was Leo, the Lion. Leo was a good sign, according to the book – 'They that shall be born are likely to live, he who takes to his bed is quickly healed, he who takes to flight shall get through.'

We carried on clearing the hall, stacking the rush mats along the wall. My mother kept glancing at the curtain to the Altar Room, as if it were hiding cake. She had been thrilled when shown it. 'A place to pray!' she had cried. She just loved to be alone. I couldn't bear that poky room. Perhaps I wasn't my mother's daughter; we were nothing alike. She was dark and I was red; she was tall and I was short. Perhaps she found me beside her spindle one day. Sometimes I wished I was Dame Alice's daughter. If I was Alice's daughter, I wouldn't be cleaning past midnight, and I falling with tiredness.

'What's wrong with our Basilia?' called Alice from her place by the fire.

'How can anyone know when she never speaks?'

'Is it the story, Basilia?' said Alice. 'Maybe she's cross I told her the beginning and not the end. I left her with Halewijn's head by his feet. Old Halewijn, you remember him, don't you, Petronelle?'

'It's not a nice story, Alice.'

'None of the good ones are.'

Later in our chamber, just as I thought she was asleep, my mother turned to me and began to speak.

'After the princess did what she did – because she had to, she had no choice, for she was about to die – Halewijn's head spoke from the ground, pleaded with her for a pot of salve to rub on his neck. She guessed it was magick salve. "A killer's advice – I will not heed it," she replied. She lifted his head by the hair, washed it clear in a well and galloped off through the woods with it. The white bird circled her with joy, the trees sighed with relief, and the wind was at her back. Halfway, she met Halewijn's mother and told her, "Your son is dead; look, his head is in my lap, and my lap is full of blood." The woman twisted and howled with grief. When the princess arrived at her father's castle, she blew the horn, and they celebrated with Halewijn's head on the table. It never said a word after that, or sang a tune. And that's all there is to Alice's tale.'

I knew, by the way they spoke, my mother and Alice were on the maiden's side, and I should have been, too, but I didn't like that ending. I thought of Halewijn's mother howling with grief; if I had been her, I would've rescued my son's head, rubbed it with magick salve and restored him to life. Let him lure maidens to their death with his singing – if they cannot resist a song, let them die for it.

Sir John left for Callan to settle some deals. Alice had coaxed him to put the trip off several times. She had a bad feeling about it, and she was right. When he returned two days later, his daughters were trotting behind him on a white pony. Alice and he argued into the night – she would prefer they were not under her roof. She shouted at him, said he himself had admitted that the girls were living replicas of their late mother, and what new wife would wish that in her house? John reminded her that he was master. They were his only children. It was their home now, too.

'The girls will stay a while,' she told Esme the next morning. 'Adjust the meals accordingly.'

There was a change in Sir John after that trip. He brought men into the house, burgesses or sometimes just stray folk. They stayed up late playing chess, often drinking, but not always. He slept in the hall, wrapped in his cloak like a troubadour, or sometimes he slipped out of the house altogether and went missing for days at a time.

When Lucia came to visit, Alice pretended all was the same as before, but you cannot feign a glint in your eye. Lucia pestered her as to what was wrong, and she soon relented. I was surprised at my mistress.

'He stays downstairs playing chess with his companions; they drink enough mead to flood a monastery. I could sit in my chamber till doomsday and still he won't come up.'

'You should've married a stringy, unlovely man, as sexless as a mushroom. Only a fool or a peasant marries for love.'

Lucia advised she cross into Irishtown and purchase lover's sachets from Margaret Dun. What a humiliation, to buy love spells from her late husband's mistress. I thought Alice would chide Lucia, but she just nodded. What she had for Sir John was a sickness, I decided, but hopefully it would soon pass.

In the kitchen, Esme and her sister were deep in discussion in front of the hearth. They talked of the change in Sir John – 'The Turn', they called it. They didn't notice me leave. I ambled through the plots and orchard down to the river bank. Before long, apple in hand, I caught the eye of the handsome pearl-diver. He showed me a seed pearl in a wet shell; nudged it with his little finger and unexpectedly it rolled into the grass. We searched on our knees but could not find it.

'Tell no one,' he said, 'or I'll be flogged.'

Then he laughed, as he remembered that telling wasn't something I did. I couldn't stop looking at him – his sunburnt face, his smile and his tumbles of hair.

'I find more pearls than anyone else,' he boasted. 'Maybe one day, I'll have one for each of your ears . . . you do have ears, under there?'

He reached up, as if to pull off my head cloth. Piotr Hatton waved over.

'Stay away from the mute!' he shouted.

The mute.

'Hatton's daughter likes me, you know' – the boy squinted as he spoke – 'but I prefer you.'

He ran to the water's edge then, picked up his fishing staff and waded till he was waist-high in the river. I still didn't know his name; just that Sofia Hatton had her eye on him.

16. Petronelle

I was in the kitchen one morning, and Sir John was suddenly beside me. He tugged the hair at my nape till a lock came loose. I longed to slap his hand away but didn't dare. I just kept stirring the whitening paste for his wife's complexion. Sir John stared, his mouth raw-looking.

'I'd love to see your hair undone. I imagine it's very long.' He tugged again. 'It's so dark, isn't it? Yet, your girl is golden-red. Is she really your child, Petronelle?'

'Of course she is, sir.'

I shook a drop of rosewater into the mix.

'Pardon me.'

I carried the bowl past him. My hands trembled, and some spilt. It was unheard of for the master of the house to venture down to the kitchen. There was something in Sir John that didn't care for manners or rules – something in Sir John cared only for the animal in himself.

I went walking by the river, looking out for Líadan. Lately, my daughter was as hard to track as a stray. I stopped to watch a small dog swimming alongside the bank; from its frantic paddling, I guessed it was its first time. A swan appeared from the reeds then and opened its wings. They beat once and the bird rose into the air and speared the animal's skull with its orange beak. The pup sank into the water, and the swan glided back to its nest amongst the reeds. I blessed myself in pity for the creature's short life. I hadn't the heart to continue, so retraced my steps back to the house and slipped into the Altar Room.

I shut the door, wishing it had a lock, and knelt and tried to pray. Was it a sin, I wondered, to pray for a soulless creature? My prayers were short, for I kept being distracted. The candles were burned down, the pew was slightly askew, and the air felt different. Since those sisters had discovered it, my sanctuary was ruined. They preferred the Altar Room to 'the coffin', claiming to hear noises there at night. Well, Cristine made the claims, Beatrice just nodded along. I caught them in here yesterday. They were playing one of their fortune-telling games. A favoured pastime of theirs was to seek the names of their future husbands by looking for auguries in candle smoke or the lines of their palms. I opened my own hand and looked at the lines and creases there. Líthgen read fortunes when I was a child, but seldom that of her own family, unless my sister and I begged. I'd watch her, peering so close to someone's palm that her nose touched their skin, muttering as if she saw the most fascinating thing in the world. That all stopped when Dervla disappeared.

My sister and I were not similar. She was older and very obedient. I was my father's favourite, and she stayed close to our mother. She seemed sometimes like Líthgen's shadow, carding wool or spinning alongside her. As if she had always been a ghost. It was wrong to think that way. I blessed myself. I could not even light a candle, for the twins had wasted the wax on their silly divinations.

'It's much nicer than the coffin, Petronelle – could we not lodge here?' said Cristine when I caught them.

I took the broom and swept them out. They were everywhere. Alice had to brush them off her favourite chair, even off the end of her bed. 'You have no parrots!' they complained, as if pets were as vital as bread. She waved them away with a laugh. 'Vile, vile step-kin,' she muttered.

I almost pitied her stepdaughters; there was no place for

them here. They should return to their late mother's household. They agreed it was a fine estate, but they thought they had better marriage prospects in Hightown. They might have, had there been only one of them. Though many men who passed through the house found them enticing, and wished to bed them, preferably both at the same time, they wanted neither as a wife.

Líadan studied them just as she had Alice, but with a disdain that led to no imitation. The last moon saw my daughter bleed. I'd have to think about things I didn't want to think about. Alice had spoken of marriage, of a new gown. I didn't make another argument against it; that would make Alice only more determined. It was Líadan's own fault that Alice was plotting. She had been drawing attention to herself. I had warned her, but still she sneaked off into town, or dallied by the river, any chance she got. Some river boy had caught her eye.

I had seen her slipping through the orchard, down to where the men worked the shallows. Did she think she was invisible, that no one could see? At least it was only a flirtation. Nothing as serious as marriage. I'd throw myself in the river before my daughter became chattel to some trader.

Maybe Alice was interfering to distract herself. We all knew how besotted she had been, riding into the night to meet that man. Sir John had gone from lover to husband very quickly. I was surprised that Alice was so surprised. She should've known better yet she pined like a girl, fretted that he visited someone else's bed – and perhaps he did. What hunter only hunts once?

Sir John had gone on yet another visit to Callan, while we were left to feed and water his daughters. They had changed this house, he and his girls, and my wish every night before I went to sleep was that I could change it back.

17. Basilia

I was drying my hair by the fire when Lucia entered, and called up the stairs to my mistress. Alice came down, and they took the seats by the hearth. I stayed on the stool and drew my fingers through the damp strands. Alice did not chide me, but Lucia glanced over and frowned. Then she relayed all the news from her household, as if it were of the utmost importance, as if Alice had asked, which she never did. Everything was wonderful in 'chez Hatton', Lucia went on; the only sour thing in the house was her daughter.

'Our Sofia,' she complained, 'is making life atrocious – stomping out of rooms, banging doors, bringing her dark mood everywhere.'

'The curse, perhaps,' said my mistress, glancing over at me.

'Does that little redhead ever speak,' asked Lucia, 'or is she dim?'

'Speaks when she pleases,' Alice fibbed; 'she's perfectly normal.'

'Well, she ought to stay put so, and not mingle with river boys.'

'Arise and tell your husband likewise,' snapped Alice.

There was a pause, and then Lucia peered into her tapestry bag and wondered aloud, as if it were of no consequence, 'What on earth keeps Sir John returning to Callan?'

'Business, of course. Between us, my husband and I own most of the county. You must know that, Dame Hatton, or had you forgotten?'

Lucia didn't stay as long as she had intended. Alice was

fuming afterwards, and ordered me to stay indoors and not to be wandering off.

The following day Sir John returned full of ale. Instead of going upstairs, he stretched himself out in the Altar Room and fell asleep on the floor. He must've still been steaming, for he kept waking and shouting for a woman, calling for a cunt sweet as cinnamon. Disgusted that her favourite room reeked of ale, and on a Friday, too, my mother insisted Esme and Helene carry him upstairs between them. They shouldered an armpit apiece, and Mother walked behind, shoving Sir John upright when he showed signs of toppling backwards. Dame Alice was standing over her desk, holding a parchment flat. She lifted her hands and it sprang closed as the women launched their master on to his bed. When they had him half undressed, she urged them to leave. I stayed on, pottering quietly by the writing desk. She looked over and sighed, but let me stay.

After a while, the late-to-rise twins rushed in, still wearing their sleeping smocks. They tugged at Sir John, trying to rouse him with salts. Dame Alice sent them away, almost shrieking when they lingered. I realized then that the pretty twins unnerved Alice. There was something vile about their pointed faces, pale and powdered, their greased lips.

I watched as Alice lifted her hand mirror and looked at her own face. The door opened suddenly, and Cristine peeked again into the chamber.

'When may we check on our father of whom we are so fond?'

We all looked over at Sir John, who was oblivious.

'Later, my dear,' said Alice.

She flung her mirror at the closing door.

'There are such theatricals expected of a man's second wife – to feign fondness of his children by other women. It's the father I wed, not his bloody daughters. I don't trust those blonde maggots. There's bad blood on the side of the mother.'

After a while, Sir John woke and stumbled from the bed – he was without hose, and his white tunic was unlaced. I kept my hand moving across the page.

'There's talk' – his voice was hoarse from carousing – 'about you.'

'What nonsense now?'

'You were seen riding out at night, galloping to meet with spirit folk.'

'You daft man,' said Alice, 'have you really forgotten who I went to at night?'

He must've remembered, because I heard them kiss. I pressed my quill into the parchment and held it. The spot of ink grew, became a moon. I laid down the pen, rose from my desk and slipped from the room.

18. The Towns of Kilkennie

It was the Feast Day of one of their saints – some minor ancient of whom Ledrede had never heard tell. Cathedral Hill was black with people intent on making their confession. Inside the church, he sat in his chair, as one after another the townspeople knelt before him. The bishop paid careful attention to each face, each voice. What were they saying, what were they leaving out? He felt filthied by their admissions of lust, greed, petty jealousies and sloth, exhausted by complaints from the marriage bed. Though weary, he did not rest: the townspeople thought themselves excellent Christians if they sought penance once a year, and he wouldn't get this opportunity again for some time.

As a penitent knelt in front of his lordship, lifted his feathered hat and proceeded to list his trespasses, at the other end of Kilkennie, in the only house with a chimney, a chamber door slammed shut and the master of the house knelt. Above him, the maid swooned. Her master's tongue was warm and rough as a cat's; she shivered and gasped, the pleasure spreading till she might've been waist-deep in a stream with silver shoals glancing against her naked skin. He rose to his feet, hoisting her legs about his waist and entering her with ease. Each gasp that left her throat spurred him onwards, deeper and faster, till, too soon, it was over. She leant against the wall, still pulsing with desire as he dressed. By the time she had fully caught her breath, he had buckled his belt, kissed her neck and left.

The maid was gathering her clothes when the chamber door began to creak open. She slipped amongst the cold furs in the wardrobe, barely daring to breathe. Someone came into the room.

' 'Tis nothing, I bet.'

'I heard moaning, like someone in pain. Did anyone die in this room?'

'Ach, someone died in every room.'

The chamber door shut then, but the maid was afraid to step out in case they returned. The furs that seemed so sleek at first began to bristle against her skin, and the cool draught at her ankle felt like a small cold hand. She leapt from the closet, wrestled on her gown and shot from the chamber, leaving the door wide open.

'What's wrong with you?' her mistress snapped later that day. 'Moony-eyed, forgetful. You're not yourself.'

No, she was not herself. She was someone else, someone happy. Even amongst fish in the alley – flat-eyed, pungent, waiting to be gutted – her heart was open. She almost grabbed the fishwife and told her, 'I have a love and what he does to me . . . oh, did you know it was possible?' Someone brushed past and she thought of him, imagined him holding her waist, lifting her skirt. *Oh, John.*

Though it was dusk and hard to see, Ledrede was still hearing confession on Cathedral Hill. He ordered more candles to be lit and continued, exhausted but belligerent, asking each person: what heresies have you witnessed? What do you know of Kytler? One after another they repeated the same thing. They had no dealings with heretics, knew nothing of what went on in that household. Was the dame outside the cathedral gates parcelling out bribes? Was each and every one of them in league with, or in debt to, the moneylender?

At last, there was no one left. He sighed and stared towards the ceiling above. The way the beams curved like an upturned boat always gave him succour. The journey might be treacherous, but a ship was strong that sailed in the name of the Lord. His boy appeared with a goblet of wine for the bishop. 'Away, away,' said Ledrede, taking it, 'be gone.'

The bishop loved to savour the rich red, to hold it in his mouth a while before swallowing. He closed his eyes. In the mottled darkness beneath his lids, all those who had confessed before him came back, blessing themselves, some with gloved fingers ridged with rings and pointed buttoned cuffs, others with coarse leathered hands, black-rimmed nails. Humble glances came from under lowered wimples. Some stared down at their clasped hands, chins tucked into rabbit collars, every second one sniffling or clearing their throat. Girls eyeing his amethyst. Guildsmen holding his gaze in over-emphasized honesty.

One after another, their faces came close, their eyes looked into his, but with not enough piety, that was it, not enough piety. These people sought to absolve themselves of everything, everything except contamination with that woman. Today he realized for the first time how completely she had them yoked: by rent, by debt, by habit. They had come to confession in droves, but it was all theatrics, one empty-handed gesture after another. He drained his goblet of wine and was about to stand, when a maiden rushed around the corner.

He glanced at her plump face; her pursed mouth. She was Sofia, she said, the only daughter of Lord Piotr Hatton. A man, the bishop recalled, who had no sense of dignity – a lord who fished for pearls in his braies, and who, by his own account earlier this afternoon, was a martyr to lust in every guise. The girl looked up, wispy ringlets shamelessly springing from under her veil.

'Yes,' she answered, when asked about Kytler's. 'There's much sin in that house. More now than ever, since the new servants.'

'Go on?'

'Alice's new maid and her mute daughter. That girl has been using love charms to steal my sweetheart.'

'And the dame – does she lead the girl in this practice of magick?'

'Oh, yes,' she said, 'though the maids are more cunning, you must remember.'

How dare this foul-mouthed, overfed ignoramus remind the bishop of anything? She had the manners of a lapdog. He longed to make her yelp, but she was the first to come forward. He must treat her well, so others would follow.

'Would you tell of this under oath?' he asked.

There was silence. And then the sly girl picked herself up and skipped swiftly from the cathedral.

LUGHNASA

AUGUST

There once were two cats of Kilkennie.
Each thought that was one cat too many.
So they fought and they hit,
and they scratched and they bit,
till except for their nails,
and the tips of their tails,
instead of two cats, there weren't any.

Old Kilkennie rhyme

19. Petronelle

Most of the household were gathered around the hearth in the kitchen, each with a task in hand. Sir John was still poorly, so, with little else to do, his daughters had joined us. The twins preferred the finery of the hall, but now, with the evenings cooling, they appreciated the warmth of the kitchen. The rare peace was broken when the work boy Ralph rushed in to say that the hives had been destroyed. Dropping my mending, I ran outside, lifting my skirt and rushing down to the orchard. Who could have done such a thing? I recalled the twins' exaggerated gasps at Ralph's announcement. When I got to the hives, I found his words to be true: each skep was smashed to a pulp. Flies, wasps and bluebottles fed from the wrecks. In one, a dark honeycomb remained intact. Light as a feather, and almost black in the centre, a lone bee worked it.

No one asked any questions as I stormed back through the kitchen with the honeycomb in my hand. I went upstairs and lay on my bed and wished, for the first time since I'd got here, for the comfort of another's arms.

I lifted the honeycomb and inhaled. Suddenly I was back in Flemingstown Woods, lying with Otto, licking honey from his mouth, delving my tongue into the dip beneath his bottom lip, liking his salt skin better than any sweetness.

That memory felt like a gift. Lately, I was finding it hard to recall how we were together, as if I were losing him all over again. I remembered the night, years past, when we'd fallen in love. I was a spinster of eighteen. The Bealtaine fire had burned high. Flemingstown's merchants, bakers and swineherds mingled and guzzled with its ladies, maids and harlots. Most were disguised. Beaked vultures sang with fur-clad wolves; leather-faced rats danced with drunken pine martins. Some had their masks perched atop their heads, making themselves two-faced.

My own face was uncovered, my hair garlanded. Musicians played tambourines, flutes and Jew's harps as birds and beasts revelled in the churchyard. A woman in a swan mask plucked violet flowers from her hair and flung them at passing men. As she did, her white-feathered sleeves flared open.

Someone reached out then and tugged my kirtle, and I found myself spinning in a circle. From behind a gargoyle mask, greedy eyes laughed. I slipped free and joined my mother by the sundial. She stood with others, sharing a mether of ale, reminiscing. She chided me, pointed to the revellers. 'You must dance.' A troupe of youths, masked as wolves, broke through the crowd howling and pulling at women's skirts.

'How nice, naked from the waist up,' said a wife to my mother, as everyone scattered in mock terror.

'It's a pity,' answered Líthgen, 'they're not naked from the waist down.'

They fell about with mirth. I didn't join in the laughter. I knew that beneath the muzzles and pelts were boy's faces and bodies, but, as they knocked people to the ground and mauled them, it reminded me of what a real wolf had done to my father. I stepped away from the laughter and was looking about when a youth approached.

What kind of animal he was meant to be, I couldn't guess. He'd the arms of an archer, his belt was thick leather, and his mask was silver. He did not grab me or lift me by the waist – he offered his hand. The stranger lifted his mask then; it was Otto Kytler, back from battle and unmarked, except for the small silver scar on his lip. He wanted to dance; I wanted to kiss his mouth. He said I had changed, and smiled. We danced and danced.

The swan woman thrice elbowed us as she glided past. 'Alice,' Otto whispered, 'is not pleased.' I was surprised to realize that the swan was Alice. I was also surprised she didn't like me dancing with her brother, but found it hard to care about, either. Days after, a lifetime after, he scratched our names inside two ivory rings. He kept the one with my name, and I, his. I wore it every day after that, until I entered Hightown.

Líthgen had said Otto had not made it to battle, that he had met his death in Flemingstown. I believed her: my mother was seldom wrong. Líadan was gifted with the same insight. I wished that I too had it, that I could see what had really happened.

I lay there on my bed, the hollow honeycomb from the destroyed hive in my hands, remembering his strong brown ones and how my skin came alive just by being close to his. The way he rubbed his thumb across my mouth . . .

When I woke, the room was hazy. I stumbled from my bed and rushed to Alice's chamber, just as she herself was entering. She had opened the door, and I saw Sir John lying across the bed, twisting and groaning. As Alice turned towards me, her face lit with anger. She put her arm across the threshold, blocking my view of the room.

'Gone hours just to check a few hives,' she whispered. 'What have you really been up to? Are you off flirting with someone? Is it that Jasper, that fool who painted your plain face on to my sacred altar? Look how you flush. You, of all people. It's ludicrous – it would suit you better to say your beloved prayers.'

She slammed the door in my face. I strode down the stairs and out into the lane, and made my way to St Mary's. So Alice thought I was flirting – it was far from the truth but her contempt at the notion hurt. She played the coquette, encouraged constant jests about a widow's appetites, but if I were to seek love, it would be 'ludicrous'. Say your beloved prayers? Damn her. When Otto entered me, he whispered 'Alleluia' in my ear and I became a prayer.

I arrived at Saint Mary's Church, breathless from the steep steps. Sheets draping the scaffold concealed the mural behind the altar. I sat and prayed, inviting God's glory to wash over me, to wash away the longing I'd had of late. I sat for a while, loosening all thoughts from my mind.

I don't know how long I was there before I heard a rattling cough. I looked behind to see that the portly priest had entered the church. I left my seat and approached him. He listened with a small smile as I put my question. If I wished to dedicate myself to a life of prayer could I become an anchoress? The priest touched my arm. It was wonderful, he said, that my faith was strong, but the women who lived between the walls had to renounce all their possessions. I interrupted, vowing I was more than ready to do that.

'Let me finish,' he said. 'They renounce their property, so as to make a gift of it to the church, a *bountiful* gift.'

As he suggested the path was for women other than I, it dawned on me that he meant wealthy ones. If I were rich, I could become an anchoress. They would take Alice; Ledrede would gladly say her death rites and seal her into a stone cell. But I had not enough riches to be poor. I thanked the priest and left. There was no sense to it all. Even I, a simple maid, knew God didn't need possessions. What wants the saviour with coloured glass and silver, he who created the sun, moon, seas and rivers?

There was no sign of Líadan in the kitchen. She was probably skiving in the Pledge Room again, playing at being Dame Alice, counting gems and the weave in raw silks. Helene came in carrying a basket of washing. She began complaining about the twins.

'Those sisters – I do not like the way they loll in bed, all entwined with each other, laughing at me. It isn't decent. They're not well bred; they're as common as I am. Ladies, my rear end. Ladies indeed. There are strands of hair everywhere. They must be moulting!'

Helene swayed from admiration to loathing when it came to the twins. They toyed with her, at times playing at confidantes, whispering feminine secrets in her ear, other times acting as if she didn't even exist. Alice didn't sway; her mistrust was constant. Since they had moved in, she checked and checked her coffers, counted silver, coverlets, jewels and coins till she recited numbers in her sleep.

A few mornings later, as I opened the shutters in Alice's chamber, Sir John sat up in the bed beside her and announced his sickness wasn't natural, that someone was making him ill on purpose. He looked across at his wife, who stared back. Alice tried to reason with her husband: he had a fever and it needed to break, then he would see sense. Fever or not, Sir John kept his opinion fixed. No longer would he drink the tonics she'd ordered Esme to make. She reached out across to him, but he shook her off.

I left the room, but, whatever happened after, Alice must've cried a lot. I patted hazel water on her swollen eyes later that night, but she would not discuss the matter of her husband's accusation.

It wasn't hard to guess where he had got such a notion. The twins tended him every day. They fluttered and pecked, delivering ointments, sharing furtive whispers amidst sly glances at his wife. They tripped across to Piotr Hatton's house, shoulder to shoulder, their skirts hoisted vulgarly high as they climbed his steps. You could see the back of their shaved shins.

We soon learnt about the suspicions they'd been planting in that household, too. They were repeated by its maids and yard boys, to our maids and yard boys. And by Lucia, too, it seemed, to her seamstress, her cobbler, her girdle-maker. 'Fine strapping knight gets married, then laid low.' 'Again?' 'A coincidence?' 'Well, what else?' 'Poison?'

Some days passed and Alice remained silent. Then one morning, as I laced up her gown, she became suddenly furious. 'He's telling the world,' she said, 'telling the world I'm a poisoner – from a bed I paid for.' I knew then that the crying was over. Sir John seemed to sense the shift, but, instead of backing down, he became more adamant: Alice was poisoning him, and, what's more, she had likely poisoned her husband before him.

If that were not unpleasant enough, there was a thief in the house. The glass bead I'd found at the well went missing from my windowsill. Other items disappeared, too, small things – bone needles, a brass pin, a stub of wax, a cracked phial, a length of mourning ribbon. I suspected Helene was feathering her nest. One part of me wanted to shake out her purse and send her off into the night. The other part understood that a girl fending for herself had to be devious. I had noticed a rash on her face. I wasn't the only one – Esme teased her about bearded gentlemen and Helene teased Esme about bearded gentlewomen. Though she made a jest of everything, Helene seemed different, fragile somehow. There was a raw catch to her voice.

One day neither Helene nor Líadan was anywhere to be found, so Esme sent me up with John's platter. 'No!' he declared. 'Take it away. I'll not eat anything she had a hand in preparing.' As if Alice would lower herself to prepare a meal. His daughters were sitting each side of him, stitching miniature tapestries, eyes cast down; smiles small. I brought the tray back down to the kitchen. The table was in chaos: leeks, onions, carrots and kale had been brought in from the garden, and Esme was shredding and chopping. Helene was polishing silver.

'We're missing a spoon,' Helene said. 'Those twins, I'll bet. They've caused untold trouble. Who do they think they are? They paint their faces like harlots, but they are not. They frequent the tables of wealthy merchants, though they are not. They are no ladies. They trail their tippets in the gravy, sit on their veils and hoist their skirts like peasants.'

'They're far from peasants,' said Esme. 'It is said their mother was Gráinne Ní Dhuibhne. Do not tamper there. Just count the cursed spoons.'

I tried not to smile when I heard the name. If Alice hadn't known about the twins during her love affair with Sir John, I doubt she knew about their mother. Whoever she had been, that she was a Gael must've irked Alice no end. *Gráinne.* Oh, how I would've loved to have seen my mistress's face.

As luck would have it, I spotted a jar of honey on the high shelf. Lifting it down, I carried it and a spoon to the chair by the window. Let the women squabble, let some mad person destroy the hives, there was still honey to be enjoyed. I peeled back the cloth and tasted some. My mouth sang with sweetness. Eating sunshine, that's what Líadan called it when she was a child. Outside, the sun blazed orange, low in the belly of the evening. I could understand why the heathens worshipped it.

20. Basilia

I was in trouble. Dame Alice made me stand in the centre of the hall; she turned and told Sir John to whist. He sat hunched in her chair by the fire – complaining loudly of being feverish. He would be much less so, if he moved back from the flames. My mother watched with her arms folded, while the mistress ranted. Someone had seen me by the river last week; said I was rolling in the grass with one of Piotr's lads. I was no longer a girl, did I understand? I was not a savage, did I understand? I lived in a merchant lady's house and must behave accordingly. Did I understand? I bowed my head, thinking – *Yes, Alice, yes, Alice, I understand, it's a matter of not getting caught, like the dame who stole out by night to lie with her lover.* Said lover spat into the fire and shivered.

When Alice left, my mother came over. She put her arms around me and squeezed tight. 'Mind your heart,' she whispered, 'but don't be too careful with it.'

Later, I was punished further when Alice decided to dress me in one of her gowns. 'A treat,' she said. How was it a treat to be harnessed into layers of cloth?

I stood in my shift as Alice knelt over a massive chest, deciding which costume to burden me with. She chose a green kirtle and, for over it, a red gown with filleted sleeves and skirts. The girdle was made from silver hoops.

'You won't be able to stray far dressed in that,' laughed my mistress. She laid out ivory and gilt combs, gem-topped pins, embroidered ribbons and headbands, and wondered which to use. As it turned out, Dame Alice was completely ham-fisted.

Everything slipped out or looked wrong. The ornaments were thrown back into their box, and a veil was hastily pinned to my head. She stepped backwards across the room to get a good view of her handiwork.

'Now, proceed towards me.'

I shuffled forward, hampered by the overlong skirts.

'Here,' she said, walking towards me, 'like this, with each step, a little kick.'

I noticed for the first time how Alice kicked aside the hem of her gown as she moved. So that was why the ladies swayed the way they did. I tried to copy her and tripped.

A short time later, her son, Will, entered. He was a little younger than I, but much taller. Dame Alice made me sit with them while they reminisced about his father, Alice's beloved first husband, whom she adored, though she seemed to adore them all once they were dead.

Will was quiet, not offering as much news from the house of Le Poer as Alice would have liked. He had been fostered there since he was young, Alice told me. Though he smiled when asked for scandal, Will offered none up. He jigged his leg, as if he would prefer to be on a horse. The scar on his face was deep. I tried not to stare, but after a while it was the only thing I saw, running from his blue eye to his full mouth. He had a cruel mouth, but, for some reason, I liked it. He noticed me gawking and touched his wound.

'It was my first time in battle. I was sent on to the field when it was over, to find each fallen enemy and make sure he wouldn't get up' – he mimed driving a sword downwards – 'but one of them did.'

His mother swiftly turned the conversation to Arnold le Poer, and how many men he had, and how much land now, and who threatened it. Time passed, and they talked. I half listened, half daydreamed. Alice teased him about giving her a grandchild, not letting the line die out.

'What's all this for, all the years of work, mine, my father's – what will happen if there's no one to carry it on?'

'This again.' Will jumped to his feet and left.

When he was gone, I sat a while, sweating under the weight of all the brocade. I was stunned that anyone would treat Alice like that. My mistress broke the silence, angry now with me instead of her son.

'You must speak: it is imperative. If you do not speak, you will never be marriageable. You've been silent long enough. Do you understand?'

I tried to answer but couldn't. My throat was still parched of whatever eases words forth. I saw that grey wolf slipping off, taking my speech with it.

Back in the comfort of my own plain gown, I made my way through the gardens to the river bank. The bank sloped downwards, so when I sat, no one could see me from the house, though the pearl-diver might, if he were looking. I took off the shoes Alice insisted I wear and stretched back, enjoying the heat on my face. The Nore seemed different today – deeper, darker, swollen. It appeared still at first, but when the sun sparkled on its skin, you could see the ripples, see how fast it was really moving. Sofia Hatton passed by. She stared at me, her milky face all haughty. I waved and she turned pink. Some youngsters passed then, wheeling the boy that couldn't walk in a barrow that was lined with hides – a dunghill foundling, raised by the town. I wiggled my feet – green grass, white toes. Clouds hung upside down in the water. The sky was swallowed by the river. A glass throat. The bells rang, my odd thoughts scattered.

I ought to return to the house: Esme wanted me to help

prepare fish – to tweeze out the lethal bones. Her fingers were too stiff to remove them herself any more. 'Be thorough – imagine if one got caught in my mistress's throat?' she always said. She meant that she'd be out of a job, not that poor Alice would choke. I stood, smacked the grass from my skirts and slipped back into my shoes. As I scurried up the bank, the oyster boy appeared and caught my hand. He promised to meet me at dawn in the orchard and told me his name was Morris. As he whispered in my ear, I placed a kiss on his neck.

That night, as I sat in my room, I felt some grit on my heel. I took off my shoe and rubbed it, only to see a pearl fall on to the floor. I had carried it from the river bank.

I met him in the orchard at first light. His hair coiled damp from dew. I walked towards him until we were face to face, opened my mouth to show the pearl on my tongue. I pressed my mouth to his, and, with his tongue, he searched mine for the seed.

Dame Alice summoned me to her chamber the next day. She looked tired and very serious. I was worried that someone had seen Morris and me by the river. Instead of being cross, my mistress became rather pleasant.

'Keep me company. You can look through my black trunk, if you wish.'

Despite myself, I smiled. It had been my wish since I first saw it in her antechamber. She unhooked a key from her belt and opened the chest. It was crammed with items: furs, phials, remedies, mementos and scrolls.

'You're not what you once were, Basilia,' she said. 'Now you're someone who knows her letters, who's learning of the world. You're a woman – too old to do your mother's bidding, or to be brought hither and thither at her bequest.'

Dame Alice knelt like a girl and pointed at black silk

packages tucked in the corner. 'Family relics,' she said. She untied the ribbon from one, held up a narrow ebony box and handed it to me.

'It's a finger casket. It holds the appendage of Sir William, my beloved first.'

I shuddered and dropped it back.

'Don't be silly. It's custom to take such items from the deceased, to bind their fortunes to a household. It's no more macabre than twists of hair, which, of course, I kept, too.' She kissed a small pendant. 'This contains a wisp belonging to my daughter. She died a baby.' Alice tucked the pendant back into the chest. 'I don't keep a relic from everyone. Some people's fortune is best released. Second husband is buried *in toto* and far from my door.'

There was a nest of tiny linen wraps, each tied with red thread and tagged. The writing on the labels was too small to decipher.

'They are meant to aid conception, but it was not to be.'

The linen was spotted with age. Alice leant on my shoulder and hoisted herself up. Rubbing her back, she crossed the room and lifted a parchment from her desk.

I picked up a stitched book, a dream book the size of my palm, full of drawings – fish, a boat, a crossbow . . . each with an inscription. 'A full moon is a good omen.' Could a dream's meaning be whittled down so small? Ever since I could remember, my mother had asked about my dreams. She set great store by their meaning. Lately, they were strong: they woke me, or made me shout out and wake her. 'Have you been dreaming?' my mother would ask. I'd shake my head. They came almost every night, the women. Sometimes even during the day, I'd catch a movement, a glimpse of skirt disappearing around a corner, but, when I followed, there would be nothing, no one there.

There was a foxtail, a rabbit's foot, a set of rosary beads. I realized then that there was nothing of Dame Alice's mother in the chest. There was nothing much of her mother in anything Alice had ever said. I did not even know her name. Maybe she didn't exist? Maybe Alice wasn't pushed from a woman's body at all but just magickally appeared in the crook of her father's arm, her baby fist reaching for his signet ring.

Cristine rushed in without knocking, looking for her 'poor Father', as she called him now.

'Is he still out in the latrine?' she asked Alice.

My mistress didn't wait till she'd left this time. She selected her favourite hog-hair brush and, by way of answer, flung it at her stepdaughter. It missed, but not by much. Cristine threw a hurt look and left the room.

Alice began writing at her desk as if nothing had happened. I wondered whether to stay or leave. I unfolded an old almanac, looked at the symbols inscribed on it – the moon, stars, waves, spirals, the signs of the zodiac. The ink had faded to brown. Someone had sliced a corner off a page, leaving only half an illustration, the curled end of a scaled tail. Was it a serpent, a fish, a mermaid?

Eventually Alice put down her quill and spoke, half to me, half to herself. 'This house, it feels different. I've lived in it most of my life, but, at night, it seems alive, and creaking with secrets. What is happening? Who is keeping Sir John from my bed?'

At that, my mother came in with a tray of food.

'Is it you, Petronelle?'

'Yes, Alice.'

'You,' our mistress mocked, 'who has the habits of a nun – kneeling in my Altar Room, your veils infused with frankincense?'

My mother set peas and trout beside our mistress. 'There are worse habits.'

She didn't know what Alice meant, and didn't care to know, but frowned when she saw me there. I tried to recall where exactly I was meant to be. Alice dismissed my mother, and barely picked at her food. After a while, she left the room without a word. Had she forgotten that I was there? As I finished off her peas, I studied the parchment lying on her desk. It was no letter or account she wrote, but row upon row of wavy lines, like the mark for water.

21. The Bishop's House

Two monks gathered berries while another filled a basket with beech-nuts. They paid no heed to the girl climbing the steps to the bishop's front door. When it opened, she requested to see his lordship. 'It's a matter of urgency,' she added, placing a small foot in the door and a heavy coin in the hand of the serving man. 'I am a knight's daughter.' She was ushered inside, led down a narrow hallway and into a tiled parlour. He pointed to a straight-backed chair, in which she sat obediently. She was to wait. If the bishop decided to see her, it would be at his convenience.

The girl sat in the hard chair for most of the morning. Eventually she stood up, walked around the chair, stared out of the window at a young cleric, who had eaten so many berries that his mouth and fingers were purple. When he saw her look, he stuck out his tongue, which was a similar shade and very big. She stepped back and turned her attention to the orange tiles that covered the wall. They were painted with black circles lined like the spokes of a wheel. When she squinted, they blurred as if moving. She imagined chariots, the High Kings of old, charging into battle. At that, the door opened and his lordship, Bishop Ledrede, stepped into the room. 'Forgive me,' she said, 'your bishop, your lordship . . .'

Ledrede stared at the girl. Under a transparent veil, each braided ram's horn was cupped in a jewelled caul. Her freckled nose attested to cross-breeding: a knight's daughter she might be, but the mare was native. What was it with these men and the native women? Did they not understand their kind would be weakened by such pollution? Gaels were not true Christians; with their pagan love of nature, they were more in awe of the sun than of its creator.

'A travesty has occurred,' said the creature. 'My father is ill. I believe his new wife is at fault.' Her voice rose. 'She neglects me and my sister, favours a servant's daughter over her own husband's . . .'

The tedious girl began to sniffle. A matter of urgency this was not. The bishop would give her penance for wasting his time with her petty complaints. If he had a coin for every stepchild with a grudge, the cathedral would have its new roof.

'My father was never ill before. Her last husband died suddenly.' She paused then and looked up coyly at the bishop. 'What if Alice poisoned him, too?'

Alice. After all this time, the answer to his prayers was kneeling before him. The bishop concealed his interest. He let her bumble on a while before clearing his throat. 'Alice is a common name in this region – to which dame do you refer?'

'Dame Alice Kytler. My poor father – I tried to warn him but he couldn't get his feet under her table quickly enough. She had him bewitched.'

'Bewitched, you say?' The bishop leant closer.

The stepdaughter confided then, in a low voice, how Alice had sprinkled sachets of herbs into her father's food, and kept philtres of love spells by which she held him entranced, even though she was mid-aged and of no allure, indeed as grey now as a badger were it not for artificial means.

'What else did you witness? Did you hear her chant spells? See her make graven images?'

'Once I heard chanting and spied the dame and her maid Petronelle by the fire. The dame was twisting a ring she always wore. It was just them and the dog asleep by their feet. I heard their voices chant faster and faster, and then there was silence. I slipped into the room to find that they'd disappeared. There was no one by the fire, not a creature, nothing! The next day her maid could not stop yawning, and Alice stayed late in bed.'

'Transformed, most like, to travel into the night, and exhausted themselves, the evil creatures.'

'So, your lordship, will you help us?'

'I wouldn't be God's servant if I didn't.'

The girl almost cried with gratitude. She promised to testify if need be; then she left, scurrying with excitement.

The whole town had kept silent, had drawn together to protect Kytler, but now, at long last, he'd got this – real testimony from a proper witness. A knight's daughter – a half-breed, but he couldn't afford to be fussy.

The bishop left his house and walked over to the cathedral. He went down the centre aisle, and over to the spot where Kytler's maid stood every Sunday. There was a carving on the pillar there, a small gargoyle, high over his head. No, not a gargoyle – how had he not realized? It was a forest god – he had seen such things in England. Robin of the Woods. Obscenely sculpted heads with foliage sprouting from each orifice. What did it put him in mind of? Each evil was linked to another like a web spun by a spider – you just needed the right light to see them quiver.

Ah, yes, in the scriptorium here, on so-called holy manuscripts, the bishop had seen heathen tongues curling like vines, tails spiralling from waists instead of legs . . . the work of an old scribe who had mocked him once. The monk couldn't keep from illuminating God's words with pagan creatures, half human, half beast. He looked up at the stone head and shivered. All those times the maid had stood in his congregation, her lips moving as if in prayer. She had worshipped her own heathen god, right in the true Lord's temple, using her mouth not to revere Christ but to mock him.

22. Petronelle

One morning, we heard shouts while in the kitchen. We followed the roars down to the river and saw a crowd of monks there. There was some commotion, fighting and fists raised. Then one of them was carried away by others in a state of great distress. Our household watched as the two remaining monks hoisted their habits thigh-high and waded into the river with the desperation of a mother saving her child, plunging their hands under the water. They were searching for precious manuscripts, we were told. When eventually they found them, it took three more monks to heave the sodden satchels to the bank.

We later heard what had happened from Ralph, who got it from a Franciscan stable boy. Ledrede had decided the works of an elderly scribe were heathen and ordered they be pumiced from the manuscripts. On hearing this, the scribe lost his mind and declared he would rather drown himself and the scripts. He was successful on neither count and now would be hanged for his efforts.

The next day, the pages were dried on trestles in the Franciscans' Lady Garden. The curious were welcome, if they kept their hands clasped behind their backs. I was surprised at the queues. Word had spread that the deadly sins were illustrated in colour. Finally, it was my turn. The pages were very large. Flat stones covered some pictures, but glimpses could be had, if you bent slightly, which we all did. The parchment was river-darkened. On some pages, the ink had rinsed completely away, yet the words remained as deep scores into the skin. I imagined those were times when the scribe had leant heavily. Was he impassioned, were those words important, were they more sacred? Or was he just wishing for his bed?

Two friars were there, standing guard.

'Which scribe has the better hand?' one asked me, mockingly.

I held my tongue. I preferred neither, no matter which hand, narrow and cramped or loose and slant – to me they were just meaningless slashes.

I should never have gone to the hanging. Maybe I thought to aid the old scribe when he looked up one last time, hoping that mine would be the one compassionate face amongst the jeering ones. Afterwards, everyone claimed that he shouted gibberish as the rope was looped around his neck. They said the devil had taken control of his tongue. I saw his angry old face, his mouth that wouldn't stop moving till the last. I stood close. It wasn't gibberish he spoke; it was Irish. 'A life's work,' he had cried. 'A whole life's work.' He never looked up.

I went home and kept my hands busy to rid my mind of his voice. I was in the kitchen with Esme shelling hazelnuts when Líadan slipped in, clutching her wrist. There were scratches on it, four blood-filled lines. Esme stood up and looked at the wound.

'Sofia Hatton?' she asked.

Líadan nodded. I cleared a corner of the table and treated the wound with lavender and honey. Of course Líadan refused to tell me what had happened, or why Sofia Hatton, horrible creature that she was, had scratched her.

'Next time walk away,' said Esme, rubbing Líadan's head.

'What do you mean, next time?' I asked. 'What has Sofia against my daughter?'

Líadan pulled her hand away then and sighed. She left the kitchen, limping a little as she went.

'Well?' I looked at Esme.

'It's a tale older than memory. They like the same boy.'

It seemed silly, childish. Yet a spiteful girl could be dangerous, especially one from a family as powerful as the Hattons. I suddenly felt grateful for Alice's fondness for Líadan. At times like this it worked in my daughter's favour. Scratches would be the least of her worries otherwise. A young lady like Sofia could have Líadan whipped on no more than a whim.

Esme and I worked on in silence. The house had quietened down again – the twins were in the Hattons', and Sir John's friends had ceased to rally round. I recalled those sturdy men in fine clothes, raising toast after toast and Sir John in the centre, loudest and most lively. It was a shame to see one so strong fail. I remembered when he'd reached towards my nape in this very room, the way he'd stared. I recognized something in him that day. Something that used to be in me, an appetite I refused to feed. I would prefer him recovered, and out of this house. Caged beasts do damage.

Helene entered the kitchen, already talking. 'Piotr Hatton has just gone up to Alice, begging for more pearl-diving money. They say those pearls come from Hatton's seed, you know. That he spends it in the river, and . . .' She gestured with her hands.

'Oh, stop, Helene.'

'Well, I won't be putting them around my neck.'

'You won't have the chance to.'

'Piotr's eager to do business before Dame Alice is banished,' said Helene. 'Abracadabra! Vanished!'

'Banished for what?' I asked.

'Magick, of course.'

'Alice doesn't practise magick, and, even if she did, no one was ever banished for such petty craft. Was Margaret Dun banished for selling magickal pouches or healing stones, or Tuttle for divination or palm-reading?'

'You're the only one who believes that, Petronelle. Everyone says the dame will be cast from this town, and her demons will follow, babbling like that witch-monk –'

'Demons? Is this another notion from Sir John's fevered rants?' I asked.

'Cristine told me, and she's not fevered.'

'You shouldn't heed Cristine. It's your mistress who deserves your loyalty. I'll be watching you, do you understand?'

'It might serve you better to watch your daughter.'

She ran out of the room before I could belt her. I returned to shelling nuts.

'Watch your daughter.'

I'd heard those exact words years ago, from the mouth of Alice's ageing nurse, Tabitha. She had been speaking to Líthgen, claiming Alice and I ran too wild. I suppose we did. We met in our makeshift hut not long after that. Alice had news. Tabitha had died. My friend promised, as she squeezed my hand, to ask Jose if I could become her maid. Then I could share her chamber, she said, wear decent clothes. She picked up the fabric of my skirt and let it drop. I would be clean for once, and well fed. I could leave that shambles of a shack.

Heart-stung, I turned away. Unclean, indecent, shamed, I got on to my knees and crawled from the hut. A small thing, but I never forgot the shock. Líthgen had misled me into thinking I had the same worth as anyone else. Alice had shown me that I did not.

23. Basilia

Mother wasn't grateful any more. 'I'll be taking you out of here when September comes,' she kept saying. I was no longer hers to take. I had changed, Alice said so, from the mite who traipsed barefoot to the girl who knew her letters. One morning, my mother pulled the clothes we'd arrived in from under the mattresses. The coarse cloth was grass-stained and frayed. Though I'd worn them only a few months ago, they seemed like they belonged to another girl. She gathered them together, along with almost everything else in the room, into a bag that she stored beneath her bed. Only for my quills and whittled animals in the nook, our chamber might've been a nun's cell. She could pack what she liked – I wouldn't be going.

Later that morning, while Alice was at a meeting of the Greater Twelve, someone rapped on the front door. When I opened it, the wind blustered through the room, and smoke rose from the fire. A portly Franciscan stood on the step. I ushered him in and quickly shut the door. He rubbed rain from his face and said he had come to record 'the knight's complaints'. A short cheerful man calling himself Manchin, he carried a tablet and shouted like I was deaf. A lot of people did that, but I didn't mind this time, for he also smiled, as if to say, 'It's all a lot of nonsense, but what can you do?' When I finally understood it was Sir John he wished to see, I led him up to the chamber and left them to it.

When Alice returned some time later, our visitor was summoned down to the hall. I tucked myself into Helene's alcove, sat in the straw and watched the dame stride in slow circles around the friar. He flushed deeper with each question, till even his bald spot was red.

Cristine had paid a visit to Ledrede, he admitted, claiming her father was being poisoned.

'Who does the bishop think he is, sending an emissary across my threshold to collect false accusations?'

And they were false – Alice wanted Sir John well, anyone could see that. He had cost her a fortune in physician's fees. She had Esme cooking up remedies night and day. Whatever Sir John had said was now written on the tablet, but I could not see it.

'The girl mentioned that none of your other husbands . . . made old bones.'

'Sir William made ancient ones! We were wed for over a decade! She's just a spite-filled stepchild.'

'I assure you, Dame Kytler, that if your stepdaughter is revealed to hold a grudge, her testimony will be considered unreliable, and the dame will be judged –'

'Judged?' Alice sputtered. 'Me? By you?'

She flung open the front door and stared at him. As the monk scuttled past, Alice reached out and tried to grab his tablet, but he clutched it tightly to his chest. So he and Sir John's testimony made their escape.

'Johnny's not on the way out,' Alice shouted after him. 'He's just a poor fool panicking.'

There was never anything poor about Sir John – couldn't Dame Alice see that? I stepped out into the lane and watched the friar scurry off, the rain beating down, darkening his brown robes.

Dame Alice called for my mother, who arrived muttering that she'd been in the Altar Room. She was always there of late, chanting prayer after prayer, as if she alone could save that old monk's soul. I don't know why she cared so much; it wasn't as if he were innocent. He'd flung manuscripts into the Nore. Pages and pages were plucked from the water, like the wet wings of some strange bird.

'Remove all possessions belonging to those wretched twins, Petronelle,' she instructed. 'Throw them into Low Lane, on the dung heaps if you so wish.'

Mother went upstairs to the girls, and such screaming and screeching as came from them. I was about to run up, when my mother appeared, her skirts soaked and filthy.

'They're not girls, they're animals. Beatrice flung a chamberpot at me.'

She marched off, refusing to go next or near the sisters. Alice sent up Esme instead. The cook reappeared almost immediately, carrying baggage in her arms. The twins followed, howling after their clothes, ornaments and powders. Grabbing after the bags, Cristine wept and pleaded. They called for their father, but he did not come. Their possessions were flung out into Low Lane, the sisters followed, and the door slammed behind them.

'Bolt it for the rest of the day,' said Alice. 'The back one, too.'

I followed quietly, as Dame Alice went upstairs. What would she say to a husband who had complained against her, whose daughters she had just booted into the lane? Would more piss-pots fly? I watched her go in and waited. Yet, there was no shouting from the chamber, just murmuring and the odd cough. I pressed myself against the wood, and listened. 'I would never harm you,' Alice whispered, 'believe me.' Then there were no sounds at all. It made no sense. Why would she humble herself to go to him . . . after all that had happened?

That night, after my mother fell asleep, I went down to

the hall. I couldn't tolerate another night of dreaming. I was being woken more and more often by the panicked whispers of women trying to flee the house – something had to be done. I greased the lock with butter, and the heavy bolt slid back without a sound. Anyone who wanted out could get out. Tonight the women would escape. Though I fell asleep quickly, I woke before dawn to a weeping sound. As my mother slept on, I sneaked downstairs. Perhaps Alice had discovered the unlocked door and was chiding Helene, threatening her with the whipping post.

There was no one there. The shutters were closed, the fire staunched with ash, and the pup asleep beside it. I heard a lady's hem sweep across the floor. I turned, but there was nothing to see, just the tapestry, its borders embroidered with golden suns. The dog stretched and stood, ears alert. I felt a presence, as if someone had come close and was about to speak.

The alcove curtain opened and Helene came out, rubbing her eyes. She released the dog into the lane, then knelt by the hearth and began shovelling ash. She had not yet covered her head and her black braids hung loose. A grey cat slinked in and rubbed against her skirts before settling under the window bench. Helene worked on, her shovel grating against the stone slabs. She straightened, lifted her ash bucket and walked back through the kitchen door. As if I weren't there at all. I raised my hand and looked at the lines on it, at the creases on my fingers. The apprentice bell rang. I blew on to my palm, felt breath against my skin. 'I am here, I am real.'

We were eating our pottage. Esme's eyes were swollen; she looked awful. She sighed and yawned, until Helene finally asked her what was wrong.

'I passed a terrible night; I saw something.'

'What?'

'A woman – she wandered about, as if searching for something or someone.'

'A lover?' said Helene.

This was Helene's kind of talk. She had a lively interest both in men and in spirits. They spoke on about other things – banshees, ghost horses and changelings. The talk changed Esme's mood. After a while, she was laughing about a widow who claimed to be pregnant by the ghost of her husband. The next time Esme mentioned her terrible night, the spectre she'd seen was just a figment. She stood and retied her apron.

'Or . . . now that I think on it, she seemed very familiar, that lass – a redhead.'

She winked at me, and in that wink all she'd said turned to jest. She threw it over to me so deftly; I almost felt it land in my lap. But it wasn't me; I'd been in bed asleep, dreaming that awful dream.

24. The Bishop's Quarters

Ledrede arrived to his door to find a messenger dozing on the floor. His irritation dissolved when the boy jumped to attention and held out a letter with a papal seal. He threw the lad a coin and dismissed him. Once inside his chamber, he checked the seal was unbroken, ran his knife under it and settled down to read. When he got to the end of the missive, he could barely contain himself. So many auguries in one week! Christ was showing him the way, as sure as if he stood before him and said, 'Richard, the time has come.' He could finally dislodge Kytler from her position of power.

Here in his hands, all the way from his holiness in Avignon, was a list of magickal offences – *Super illius specula*. 'Upon His Watchtower,' mouthed the bishop, translating – thinking of the ancient tower that shared the hill with his own cathedral.

But he shouldn't . . . he shouldn't have let his mind stray outside his chamber – for all at once he saw the dark chink in the anchoress's cell, the eyes that used to stare, felt her name in his throat, Agnes. *They rise up, rise up if you don't stake them to the ground*. Should he go out now? Could she? No, there was stone, heavy stone, on top of her. At night, at night sometimes the bishop saw . . . No. No. Don't think on it.

A young monk came in with a tray. A new boy. The bishop didn't ask his name. He found the young expectant face irritating. He let him leave without a word, before lifting the cover from the tray – wine, apple pie, berries and custard sauce. He smelt autumn, apples baking – became a small child again.

'*Mother*,' he pleaded, clutching at her skirts, '*reach up, fetch it for me!*' She lifted him by the waist, held him high above her head. He saw then how far away the moon really was, and that even his mother could not reach it.

Ledrede shook his head clear, put a few drops of Aqua Vitae into the goblet and drank back the wine. He already had the stepdaughter's testimony. Her father's, collected by Manchin, was currently being transcribed – albeit with some difficulty, as, in pressing it to his chest, Manchin had caused the wax to become hatched with the weave of his habit.

He spent the afternoon rereading the pope's missive. He almost cried. How fully Pope John XXII, his infallible holiness and God's representative on earth, held exactly the same convictions as he, Richard Ledrede. 'We are in the watchtower,' Pope John wrote, urging his faithful soldiers to hunt down particular miscreants, for 'Many are Christians only in name.'

Ledrede went over the list of magickal offences again. The pope had seen into the heart of Hightown. He described how heretics constructed rings, mirrors, images, philtres, in which, by the art of their dark magick, evil demons were enclosed. From those spirits, they sought and received aid in satisfying their evil desires. The bishop read again and again, thought of the moneylender who always got what she wanted. Who was her demon, who did her bidding? It came to him then: the stone face of the heathen god carved into this very cathedral.

Ledrede read so late that his eyes became dry and sore, and his neck ached. In bed, though exhausted, he could not sleep. He went over a plan, how to get what *he* wanted. His legs were restless; he felt a longing for release and was tormented by an old urge: the longing to bury his face between the legs of a woman, to delve his fingers in there, and, after, his tongue.

25. Petronelle

We were in the hall, Líadan and I, readying to leave for the cathedral. Despite my beseeching her otherwise, Alice insisted we attend the Sunday sermon. We trotted on up High Street, my nimble daughter some steps ahead. She was not as thin as when we had first come, and her gait, that, too, had changed. Sofia Hatton and her maid walked by. I nodded but she didn't notice me; her gaze was fixed on my daughter. Before I knew what she was doing, she ran at Líadan and tugged her veil from her head. She rushed off then, her maid following behind, both laughing. I caught up and helped my daughter to pin her veil into place. She looked at the ground as I tucked her hair back from her face and under the linen. Her wrists were still scarred from Sofia's nails. Something would have to be done about that girl.

The bells tolled as we entered the church grounds. Word of Cristine's accusations had spread quickly. *That's her maid, the one she keeps so close, so close they're almost never apart.* I stood where I always did. If I moved further back from the altar, it would indicate guilt and shame. If I stood nearer, it would indicate guilt and shamelessness. Ledrede was particularly lively. He glared at the congregation and then cleared his throat. A scribe sat on the altar. His arm moved in time to the words from the bishop's mouth: 'The snake has found a home. A sect has gathered in the house of Kytler.'

What he claimed next beggared belief; it brought gasps from the congregation. *'Did he say fornication?' 'With devils?' 'Shush.'*

'Dame Alice Kytler lies with a demon incubus, and all in

her house are accomplices; heretical sorceress, *haeretici sortilegae*!' he hissed.

The congregation listened without a whisper or nudge.

'Kytler's husband is emaciated from her magickal powders and lotions. She has taken a lover from the underworld, a demon known as Robin, and, with his assistance, cast heinous spells. Her brave stepdaughter told me all about her house of witches, the sect she fills with her own kind, who dabble using rings, mirrors and philtres.'

The bishop pointed towards the twins, who were perched in the Hattons' pew. They bowed their heads in a modest gesture of pleasure.

'Come forth all who are privy to her sorceries. For she will plummet to Hell, and anyone who does not speak will join her.'

He lifted a scroll and began to recite a curse. 'Those who do not bear witness shall be cursed, struck from the book of the living, let them not be written down with the just.'

'Yes, yes,' gasped a voice behind me.

The bishop left the pulpit, and stepped to the edge of the altar. 'Let their eyes not see, let their backs be bent. Pour upon them, oh Lord, your anger, let the fury of your rage embrace them.'

He looked up from the scroll. 'Let their souls plummet to Hell with the devil and his ministers. Let all this happen.' He raised his hands into the air. 'Let all this happen. Amen!'

There was fear in the silence that followed. The congregation began to leave the church. Did everyone believe him, believe that women like that existed, and we – my mistress and daughter – were one with them? It wasn't true, but, even as I thought that, I felt the guilt of a liar. I would've believed this awful house of evil existed were it not the one that I ate and slept in.

A space formed around Líadan and me as we made our

way through the churchyard. I touched my daughter's shoulder, but she quickened her pace, lifted her gown and skipped down the steps. The people were quiet: there were no rebukes, nor was there any mocking. They were waiting till Alice's maids were out of earshot. Did they fear us? Someone grabbed my arm – a stab of pain jolted through my shoulder. It was a solemn lady I'd seen once or twice in Alice's.

'We know, my husband and I, we know these rumours are spurred by envy. Tell the dame she still has friends.'

She returned to her husband, who waited by the tower. My daughter walked ahead, arms folded, head bowed. Was she ashamed? Had she believed the bishop's words?

As we neared High Street, I saw Sofia Hatton duck down an alleyway. I bid Líadan to head on home and followed the Hatton girl. She was taking slow steps, one hand steadying herself against the wall, the other lifting her cloak. She looked like a dainty child. I almost returned my scissors to my purse. A boy rushed towards her, from the other end of the alley. His expression of lust transformed into fright at the sight of me. He greeted her brusquely and kept going. Confused, she turned around and saw me, too.

'Sofia,' I called.

She reluctantly came up. I grabbed her wrist.

'You broke my daughter's skin.'

She tried to wriggle free, but I was stronger. Her nails were long, cut narrow like the nib of a quill. I lodged the blade of the scissors under each and snipped. She cried with wretched frustration, and was still crying as I walked away. It was good that I'd caught her with one of her father's workers: she would not dare speak of our encounter lest I speak of theirs. It was a pity it was the same boy Líadan had shown such fondness for.

*

In the house, Lucia Hatton, of all people, had arrived before me. She sat by the fire with Alice, embellishing the bishop's claims. I would've preferred to be the one to tell my mistress. Why else had I endured the sermon? However, Alice said I was not required and waved me away. I tarried by the stair-well and listened a while from the shadows. No matter that it was unlikely to happen, I worried that Sofia would burst in and tell her mother what I had done. Lucia seemed to relish the details, some of which were new to my ears.

'And you've weakened your husband, sapped all his strength using sorcery learnt from your demon lover, with whom you fornicate at midnight wearing nothing but jewels and your wimple.'

'Who would believe such things? Alice answered. 'A dame fornicating with a demon. Is that even possible? Surely such a lady would get scorched!'

They both feigned laughter.

'We'll have a feast,' Alice said, 'and show the bishop, regardless of his words, that he does not reign.'

'Yes, a feast.'

'And all my allies will come?' she said slowly.

'We will.'

'And you'll each swear an oath, to defend against all attacks the dame's innocence?'

Lucia cleared her throat.

'It's strange, isn't it,' Alice went on, 'that no one warned us against this onslaught of lunacy? I heard that Cristine and Beatrice now dwell under your roof –'

'They called in the rain . . . I had little choice –'

With a wave of her hand, Alice halted Lucia's excuse. 'And yet you didn't know what they planned to do?'

'We didn't, I can assure you.'

'You'll send them from your house now of course . . .'

Lucia had to return then, to 'her brood', as she called them. I watched as Alice left the hall, her velvet skirts trailing, the golden rope of her belt swinging. I imagined giving voice to my thoughts. *They say you're a witch, Alice – are you? Can you cast charms to stir love in the hearts of men, can you make magick happen?*

After dinner, at which she ate little and everyone was silent, our mistress licked her lips and announced it was futile to observe the day of rest, considering she was under such threat from the Church. We were all to attend to our chores instead. She added quietly that Líadan and I were to assist her in selecting the relics and sacred objects needed for the swearing of oaths at the feast. When the time came, she explained, after the guests had eaten and drunk their full, each would be invited to swear an oath in front of Sir Arnold, their seneschal; with one hand on a holy relic and one on their heart, they would promise to support Dame Alice against each and every one of the bishop's claims. A quandary surely, as swearing loyalty to Alice would draw down the wrath of the bishop. I could hear his words as we followed Alice down to the cellar. *Let their souls plummet to Hell.*

Alice unlocked the heavy door to the Pledge Room and went down the steps. She picked her way through the jumble of furniture towards a wall hung with pelts. Líadan followed, equally sure of her way around the objects in the room. I moved more slowly, not having been in the room before. I did not expect the Pledge Room to be such a mess, nor to meet such an array of stuffed animals, all of which seemed to be looking in my direction. Alice pushed some furs aside and stepped into the darkness. We waited, wax dribbling down our candles, till her pale hand darted out from the furs and a crooked finger bid us to follow.

Behind the pelts, more steps led down to an oak door

secured with a heavy padlock. Alice bent, lifted a stone slab from the last step and retrieved a key. She knocked clay from it and unlocked the door to reveal a narrow room. Barely her height and width, with earthen walls and ceiling, it was full of cloth bags. One had spilt and coins lay about it. Alice smiled to herself: she was proud of her hoard. Lodged in amongst the bags was a box. Alice instructed us to lift it between us and carry it up to the Pledge Room. We did so with difficulty. As we hauled the box up the steep steps, Alice locked the door behind us.

I was glad to be back in the Pledge Room, for, stuffy as it was, I could at least breathe. I had lived in this house for months without once being inside that room, let alone the chamber hidden by the wall of furs.

As if reading my thoughts, Alice turned. 'Speak of the hoard to anyone,' she said, 'and I'll cut out your tongue.'

I noticed her words were not directed at Líadan and wondered where all her trust had gone. Back in the cellar, where the light was a little better, Alice quenched the candles and locked the Pledge Room door. As we carried the box up the cellar stairs, I saw my knuckles were spattered with wax burns. It was quiet when we entered the kitchen. The way Esme and Helene leant close to each other at the table told me that the silence had just fallen.

We carried the coffer upstairs to her bedroom. There, Alice carefully lifted each item from the box and laid it on the table by the window. All were wrapped in silks and linen. She looked, and thought for a while – seeming to know what was inside, without having to open them. She selected three. It was only then, as she unwound the cloths, that we saw what she had chosen: a saviour on a wooden cross, a serene-faced ivory virgin and, finally – the most valuable, according to Alice – an amethyst pendant. She held it in her palm.

'The chamber in the pendant's heart holds a thorn from Christ's head,' she said.

Líadan gasped. I looked at Alice, but she didn't seem to be teasing. Did she really believe that a thorn from Christ's crown could end up in Hightown, that she could buy anything in this world that she wanted, no matter how precious? Líadan was touching the pendant with the tip of her finger – she looked like she was making a wish.

That evening, while collecting windfall for Esme's chutney, I remembered my oak hive. With the grief of losing the skeps, I had forgotten about the swarm that had settled in the oak last May. When I got to the tree, I saw the hive was still thriving. I eased my hand in amongst the bees and lifted out some combs. They were laden with honey. I placed them gently in my basket and carried them back to the house.

Daylight was fading and there was the satisfied air of work well done. Esme was delighted with the wild honey and apples. Her chutney jars were dried and set in a row to be filled. She put the honey under a cloth, and warned that no one should touch it before the feast. The rushes were lit; the silver knives and spoons were laid out for polishing. We were to prepare as if royalty were coming. This supper must remind everyone where the power truly rested in Hightown. We sat together in peace for most of the evening.

'Alice was caught in bed with him, you know,' said Helene.

'With who?' Esme asked.

'The demon from whom she learnt the dark arts . . . his seed gives her power.'

The maid seemed thrilled by such awful notions. I don't know why – none of us would remain untarnished by such accusations. Did she not know that as the lowest she would be the first on the pillory?

'The only dark arts are those lies,' I warned her, 'so don't spread them – you're damaging Alice's reputation.'

'What about your own reputation? It's said,' whispered Helene, 'that this fornication happens in the presence of her maid.'

'You'll polish silver till the sun comes up for that.'

I marched upstairs, my good humour ruined. Sorcery, fornication, bedding demons? Alice needed no demons; her power came from herself. I opened our chamber door. Líadan lay there, eyes squeezed shut, feigning sleep. I took off my kirtle and put it on the hook. There was a dead butterfly on the sill, a red one. Wings folded, its body was dark and furred. Then its wings trembled open and fluttered briefly before closing like a fan, becoming still again – to all appearances dead again.

I lay in bed, listening to the orchard whisper. Lies were hard to stem: they excited people more than the truth. Many falsehoods already abounded about Alice. She couldn't even count – her wealth was due to wiles of a more carnal kind. Or her good health was thanks to ancient remedies procured from a Persian alchemist. But what the bishop said this morning, it was not like anything I'd heard before, foul accusations pouring hot from his mouth. I could almost see them, a river of poison travelling from Irishtown, rushing over the bridge and crashing through the gates and into the lanes, passageways and crannies of Hightown – pushing through gaps in shutters and doors to rustle the straw pillows of the poor, the velvet drapes of the rich, whispering – *Witch, witch, witch.*

26. Basilia

A few merchants were sleepily setting out stalls as I passed. I had risen early. Morris was to meet me this morning. It wasn't yet time. It wasn't even light but I couldn't sleep. At Watergate, the gate was locked. I strolled along the banks of the Breagach for a while. My skirts darkened with dew as they dragged through the grass, but I kept going, for I liked the swooshing sound.

I worried that he might not come. What the bishop had said wasn't true, but Morris mightn't know that. Then I thought: what if what the bishop said was true? What if Alice chanted charms, casts spells, invoked protection? How was she any different to him reciting his ancient curse, surrounded by candles, shrouded in incense? What made one prayer holy and another not? I thought of my mistress, of her pale hair, her heavy jewels, her ink-tipped fingers. A sorceress, he had said. I thought about her black chest full of medicines, talismans and relics, of her good fortune, her hoard of coins, her case of tally sticks, her high ornamental bed stacked with feathered mattresses. And, yes, there was something magickal about my mistress, and I was glad. Glad there were rubies, silver, velvet and ermine in this mud-shriven world, however they arrived.

I stopped and looked into the river, and my watery twin looked back from the mud and reeds. The bishop said an underworld lover courted Alice. Where did he come from? Did he arise from the Nore, spear in hand, soaked from the green depths? Whether there was or wasn't a Robin, he showed himself to me just then. The river sparkled as he broke through its skin, his head as sleek as a seal's, his body glistening and his mouth crammed with pearls. Then, in a blink of an eye, he was gone.

I rushed homewards, not wanting to forget what I'd seen. It was getting bright. There were many more people about than earlier. Some were gathered in the market square, clustering together by the whipping post. Every one turned and watched as I passed. A child stood alone, apart from others who were skipping. Her face was blank, and her dress had been slashed by the whip. As I wondered what her crime had been, my hand was grabbed and I found myself encircled. The children skipped and chanted, slyly glancing up at me. 'What'll you give to be free? What'll you . . .' I unlocked two hands by jerking them apart and rushed away. When I looked back, the children were holding their wrists. Their cries turned to shrieks as they pointed towards me. I strode more quickly towards Low Lane.

Suddenly my hair was yanked back and my coif was torn from my head. I thought my neck would snap. I glimpsed the fierce face of the woman who had grabbed me and felt her breath against my ear. 'Little witch.' There must've been two, maybe three women, but all I could see was the blue sky as my hair was pulled from all angles and I was dangled between them like a hated doll. Enough! a man's voice called. Released, I fell to my knees. My coif was on the ground, muddied and flattened. Tangled clumps of my hair were all about me. I felt the shadow of a crowd gather but didn't turn to look. I picked up every shred of hair, stuffed the tufts into my purse and placed my coif on my head. I walked slowly towards the house, refusing to run, to show fear.

By chance, the hall was empty and I made it to my chamber without seeing anyone. As I opened the door, I heard crooning coming from nearby. I stopped. At first, I thought a song was being lilted, but then I realized what it was. Fornication, the bishop called it, blessing his mouth afterwards, as if he himself had been begotten by prayer alone. I heard it again, little gasps this time and a man's groans. Sir John was bedding someone and it wasn't Alice. I shut the door. I cleaned my face with witch-hazel and pinned a clean veil on my aching head. Soon my hands weren't shaking any more.

I waited a long time in the orchard. He never came. The boy must've believed all the bishop had said. Many had shunned us after the sermon, but I thought he would be different. He had seemed different. I returned to the house to find everyone preparing for the feast. The rest of my morning was spent damning the bishop, plucking and gutting hens, hauling buckets from the well and trying not to cry. Helene was almost dancing about the kitchen as she worked. As she began to sing, I recognized something in her voice. It was she I had overheard earlier – she who had lain with the master. How could she do such a thing to our mistress?

Later, when I saw her sneak from the house, I followed. She took the river path and back lanes towards Irishtown. The keeper was brisk; there was no flirting this time as she passed through. I was let by, too, without any comment, good or bad. Though the keeper refused to greet us, he didn't dare to stop or insult us, either, for we were no longer just maids, we were now maids from the house of a sorceress. I thought of the women who'd almost pulled me apart between them. I remembered my vision of my mistress, the way she had cowered in fear, about to be hurt beyond repair.

Helene entered Velvet Lane, a narrow path that wound like a ribbon round the cathedral grounds. Following, I found myself on a trail, a stone wall on one side and wooden fencing on the other. I felt uneasy, like an animal being lured into a trap. Helene stopped suddenly and lifted a plank from the fence and slid through. I waited a while before doing the same, coming out on to a wooded slope of birch trees. When I cleared the trees, I realized we were on the outside of Irishtown's walls. It gave me a strange feeling to be outside: I'd grown used to all the watchtowers and gates keeping us safe, keeping the bad things out, and us within. Now, we were the bad things.

Two tiny cottages were set against the wall. Margaret Dun sat in the doorway of one. She looked younger than she had at Sir Roger's wake. Helene approached her and I hunkered down behind a hedge. It was unsettlingly quiet; there were no other people, no dogs, swine or children. After Helene spoke a while, Margaret reached into a basket at her feet. Her hand closed over an object and she passed it to Helene, who tucked it into her girdle and left. I tried to stand without cracking a twig or rustling a leaf, but Margaret called out anyway.

'Come forward.'

I came out of hiding. She signalled I should sit with her, so I did. The door was ajar. Inside, there were trinkets and oddments everywhere. Gloves, beads, threads were pinned to the walls. I recognized a drinking horn belonging to Sir Roger, Milo's sheepskin waistcoat, items belonging to Helene, and Esme, even Alice. Something from everyone in our household, except my mother. She had no dreams or longing but one, to be free of this town.

'Basilia? From Roger's household?'

I nodded.

'What do you seek?' She raised each finger one by one, as she listed: 'Luck, healing, wealth, protection?'

I touched the last finger she held up.

'For yourself?'

I shook my head.

'Someone else. Use something of theirs – a strand of hair, a nail, or spit, or cloth. Bind it to a poppet made in their likeness. Keep it safe, but never ever bury it.'

I laid a gift on her lap, a scented rosewood bracelet. She held it under her nose and smiled. She reached into her basket. 'A relic for you.'

It was a wrap of red cloth, tied with black thread.

As I rushed back into Velvet Lane, Helene leapt upon me and twisted my arm.

'Aha, I knew you were following!'

She grappled the relic from my fist and waved it over my head. I jumped to retrieve it. She flung it to the ground and stamped it into the mud.

'I wouldn't worry about losing that,' she laughed, tapping my head as I searched. 'Margaret's known for her endless supply of rare relics.'

As Helene ran off, I realized why she had visited Margaret. I recalled her worn cuffs, her hands splattered with blue dye as she snatched my relic. A thought had come when her skin touched off mine. *Helene wants a baby.* It made no sense. Alice would tear her limb from limb if she bore Sir John's child. Did Helene think it would bind her master to her, that he would keep and protect them? I recalled her slim wrist as it slipped from my grip, felt again her cool skin. Helene would never have a child, Sir John's or anyone else's, but she would live a long life.

While the rest of the household listened to Alice's instructions about the feast, I slipped up to her chamber and gathered hair from her ivory comb, and ripped a fraying hem from an old silken chemise. I had just tucked them under my belt when my mistress charged in. It was lucky I was standing near the writing desk.

'No more lessons, if that's what you're pining for.'

She went to her own desk, and, after some rooting about, pulled out a hinged box with a slant lid. In it lay rough squares of parchment, patterned with rows of evenly slanted dents, the sanded-down sentences of another's hand. It also held a pumice stone, some quills, a blade, a bar of ink. I could work on, Alice told me, in my own time. She seemed sad about that. She lifted the flask of brandy from her table and swished it about. It uncorked with a pop, and she lifted it straight to her mouth. She took a few gulps, wiped her mouth and smiled. 'I'll need this – Lucia has just arrived. It'll stop me killing her. Come, cheer me on.'

Lucia and Alice sat by the fire. Dame Hatton pretended to embroider cloth, but glanced up so much at Alice that she kept stabbing her finger. Alice made no conversation, just sipped her spiced wine. When she saw no gossip was forthcoming, Lucia folded away her bloodied embroidery, muttering something about wanting Esme's advice about strudel. I helped her down the steps into the kitchen, where, asking no such advice, she left by the back door. We watched as she waddled through the orchard with her serving boy two steps behind, holding up the train of her dress.

'That's how she came in, across the gardens,' Esme said, 'afraid of being seen in this house.'

'At least she came,' said Helene. 'No one else has, not since the sermon.'

She was right: no one else came – the trail of merchants had stopped.

Mistress Alice, brightly clothed and jewelled, sat alone in the darkening hall. I stood by the stairs and watched. She leant back in her chair and shut her eyes. I closed my own, and made not a sound. The fire sizzled; she'd flung her dregs into the flames. My skin prickled, and I shivered, as if someone somewhere had just stepped on my grave. I heard the door, felt cold rush in. The door shut, smoke filled the room. I opened my eyes. My mother stood before the hearth, her skirts billowing. She rubbed her arms.

'It's chillier here than outside.'

'Shall I *conjure* some warmth?'

'Oh, stop. The things that man said –'

'Lies, you know that.'

'Yes, I know.'

'Dangerous lies. I've hired a guard for the door; he'll be here by first light.'

'And what will you do about him upstairs?'

'What can I do? He's my husband.'

'He's a danger, too.'

'Nonsense, he can barely walk.'

'What on earth is wrong with him?'

'I don't know. Don't you think if I knew . . .'

Alice turned away and stared into the fire. My mother crossed the hall and stood in front of the tapestry. She pressed her palm against the weave. The way she closed her eyes and slowed her breath reminded me of the woman's stone of Flemingstown Arch and how she had touched that.

That night I dreamt the twins were back in Kytler's, and sitting at Alice's table. We were having a banquet. Everyone was enjoying themselves; even when the talk came round to the poisonings, the accusations, it was all said in jest. 'You know what happens to little girls who tell lies?' asked Alice. 'Yes,' smiled Cristine, 'their tongues go black.' 'No,' said Alice, 'their heads come off.' And chop, Beatrice slumped on the table, and her head rolled to the floor. Alice wiped her bloody blade and we all laughed and laughed, and Cristine fainted, so she, too, was slumped on the table, but she had a head.

MEÁN FÓMHAIR

SEPTEMBER

Three darknesses into which women should not go:
the darkness of mist, the darkness of night, the
darkness of a wood.

The Triads of Ireland, ninth century

27. Hightown

The door to the moneylender's house opened and she stepped out. Dressed in her riding cloak, the dame strode down Low Lane. She was going hawking with Sir Arnold, but first she would examine her altar mural. Every person she met along the way turned their back, but the dame hardly noticed. She was thinking of the future. Her image would remain in the church for centuries to come, ensuring the Kytlers and their patronage would be long remembered in this town. Her father would've been so proud.

Inside Saint Mary's, the artist was nowhere to be found. The dame examined the mural alone. No longer a sketch, it was now painted. The virgin's hair was lighter but Jasper hadn't changed her features. He must've redrawn the face after she'd wiped it away. It was beautiful but Alice hadn't donated her money to have someone else's image adorn the altar. She would summon Jasper and have him rework the fresco, even if she had to watch over him. Alice stared at the woman on the wall. She was almost life-like, every detail finely rendered – a vein in the neck, the deep groove over her lip, the long eyelashes . . .

Alice suddenly realized that she'd been mistaken – it was not Petronelle's likeness at all. She stared at the heavy lids, the soft expression, the small mole above the corner of her mouth and saw who it really was – Dervla, Petronelle's sister. Such a serious girl, and so quiet that when she had disappeared it hadn't seemed that untoward somehow. If the artist had spoken the truth, and this was the face of Sister

Agnes . . . then Dervla had become an anchoress. Had she chosen that living death or had it been punishment for some misdeed? Imagine – living between the walls of the cathedral and no one knowing who she was, not even her own sister. Petronelle would have been so happy to have found her. And now it was too late.

'You stupid, stupid girl,' whispered Alice to the virgin, deciding then and there to tell no one. But she wouldn't have the face repainted after all. It was fitting, really, that Dervla should be there, watching from the altar, no one knowing it was her. Dame Kytler was good at keeping secrets.

Back down the lane, beyond the guarded door and up in the moneylender's chamber, her maid of all work unlaced her kirtle and climbed into her high canopied bed. The master placed his palm between the maid's breasts. The leather pouch, the remedy to ward off a baby, wasn't there. 'Where is it?' he asked, but she began to move her hips, and he lost the will to repeat the question.

As was his habit, he fell asleep afterwards. As was hers, the maid lay watching him for a long time before slipping from the bed and tiptoeing around the chamber. She shook a flask of scent, tugged the stopper free and brought it to her nose, the cork soaked with ambergris, vanilla and musk. She opened the armoire and slipped her hands between the folds of stacked fabrics – cold raw silks, bright velvets, dark woollens, white linens.

She lifted her mistress's polished mirror from the dressing table and saw her own face so clearly that she wanted to look away. Was that really her – that dark-eyed wench, mouth flushed from kisses? She lowered the mirror to her navel. How odd it looked, a navel in an oval held in mid-air. Would Alice miss this mirror – she had three others after all? A small theft; a well-earned gift? She lowered it further and saw blood had smeared on to her thighs as she'd stolen about the room. She wadded a kerchief between her legs and put back on her clothes.

The maid wanted to grow the master's child inside her. If she did, Sir John would keep her safe, maybe even secure a hut with her own bed, her own chair. He made promises when he took her. He would keep those promises – why not? Look at the way Petronelle was taken in. Esme didn't agree – but the maid believed that Basilia had been sired by old Jose Kytler. She had seen a miniature of Alice's father – he had the same narrow face, the same golden-red hair, as Basilia. Why else was Alice so fond of the girl? Why else would Alice take as servants two outsiders who just arrived at her door one night? They must be blood; blood takes care of each other.

Sir John was spreadeagled across the tossed bed as if he had just dropped from heaven. She gazed at the soft pulse in his neck, the down on his chest, and longed to lie beside him. She couldn't – she might fall asleep and get caught. If Alice discovered she was slipping in between her fine white sheets, handling her mirror, her raw silks, her scent, she would have her whipped, cast out, or worse.

The sound of hoofs came from outside. She peered through the gap in the shutters. Alice and Arnold were riding in, circling each other, playing some game. Home from hawking, Alice flushed, wearing a brown gown over her green kirtle, her white linen veil unkempt, her hawking gloves muddied. What were they hatching between them, Alice and Sir Arnold? There was no time to wonder further. She checked the pillows and sheets, and gathered up her long black hairs.

28. Basilia

Cristine cornered me at the shambles and begged to be smuggled in to Kytler's. 'Oh, Basilia, I must tend to my father,' she said, dangling coral beads. As if I would betray my mistress for a trinket. I might as well have, for she got in anyway. I saw Helene in the hall not long after, flushed and swinging the same corals. She winked at me and skipped down into the kitchen. Cristine was probably already upstairs tending the patient.

My mother didn't believe Sir John was sick – said it was all theatrics. Someone was creeping downstairs at night, gorging and leaving the kitchen in disarray, and she thought it was him. Still, the master's health waned and his complaints grew. He said his blankets weighed heavy at night and his feet were tormented with pins and needles. He had a new-found affection for Helene, and didn't hide it. 'Where's my little maid?' he'd asked all morning. Irritated by this, Alice charged me with changing his bedclothes and gave Helene other tasks.

I carried a wicker of fresh linen upstairs and was about to knock, when voices came from inside the chamber. I put down my basket and listened.

'How's Beatrice?' Sir John sounded weak.

'Same as ever,' Cristine answered. 'Wants to go home, misses her horse, worries about you.'

'The horse first,' he said.

'Always.'

'I'm worsening, Crissie.'

'Don't worry . . .'

Her voice went to a whisper. I couldn't make out what was said till they began their goodbyes. I tiptoed quickly to the coffin and slipped inside. I left the door open a crack and watched Cristine leave the room. I nearly died when instead of passing she stopped just by the door. I shouldn't have felt such dread – she was the trespasser, not I. Yet I did. We stood there, silent, each holding our breath, an arm's reach from each other. She gripped the banister, then moved swiftly out of sight. She had been making sure no one was about, so she could escape unseen from her stepmother's house.

I picked up the linen basket and went in to Sir John. He lounged half naked in Alice's chair, fiddling with her quills and tally sticks while I gathered the damp sheets. There was a strange coppery smell off the linen. Cristine had left a platter of gifts: wine, half-eaten bread and stuffed figs lay on the bedside table. Sir John had a lively tongue for one so ill.

'The monk, the one who came – he said a witch leaves an effigy in the bed when she flies off at night; it lays absolutely still, the very image of the woman herself. Well, I watched Alice last night and there wasn't a movement, not a flicker. I'm sure it was a replica of my wife beside me, not her at all . . .'

Irritated by my silence, he snapped a tally in half. 'Why are you here?' he asked. 'Where's my little maid?'

He told me no more stories, and when the bed was made, climbed in grumbling. I had just pulled the coverlet over my master when the chamber door swung open so forcefully it hit the wall. The priest from Saint Mary's entered, roaring his greeting. He must have been as deaf as a bell-ringer. While they were distracted, I swiped the wine, tucked it in my basket and hid in the anteroom to listen.

'Oh, Father,' Sir John said, 'give me the last rites.'

'But, sir, you're not dying.'

'I am. She's poisoning me, like she did the others. Oh, I daren't eat a thing she serves. Look under the bed. I hid every morsel in the pot!'

'Let me look at you.'

'Hear my confession, Father, for I am not long for this world. I know where I'm going if I have not the rites, I see it in my dreams, the dark floors of Hell, many hundreds of floors all burning eternally, and the damned running scorched and screaming from one to the next, but never escaping. I've seen the devil and his tongue hangs long as a dog's and he's waiting for me, just waiting. Hear my confession, save me from the flames of Hell, I've suffered enough in this life . . . I knew not what I was doing when I wed Alice Kytler.'

'You both looked happy enough on the day.'

'She got what she wanted: my wealth.'

'Surely her wealth surpassed yours?'

'Whose side are you on, Father? My daughters saw Alice prepare a mixture, take from her sleeve a sachet of powders and secretly drop it into my broth. Every day she does this, and every day I grow weaker – look at my arms, look at the flesh!'

'What is it exactly that she feeds you?' He picked up a crust from the table.

'I won't let a morsel from her kitchen pass my lips, not for days! The little maid brings food, or my daughter.'

'You accuse her of poisoning, yet you don't even eat her food. Where is this maid? I wish to speak with her.'

'It's been days since she visited – who knows what the witch has done with her.'

'That's dangerous talk, sir. Alice is a respectable woman.'

'Do you owe her money, too, Father?'

'That's beside the point.'

'Don't you see? Doesn't anyone see what she's doing? All lead me to think I'm mad when I'm dying. Oh, not to be believed is a terrible thing.'

The door banged shut.

'Come back, Father! She flies; I've seen her fly at night with her women. They take off through yonder window, fly over the moon, meet with the devil. She has powers! She'll have all of Hightown copulating with Satan's servants!'

Sir John shouted so loud the whole house must've heard. Then he let out a great heaving sob. Oh, how he wept, the poor strange man. As if he were in a play and God was in the audience.

I slipped from the house and made for Irishtown by the back lanes, keeping off High Street. I didn't want to have my hair pulled again. Steam was coming from the comb-maker's when I arrived. I wondered too late if he would shun me after what the bishop had said. I stalled by his door, clutching John's wine. He came out and took it, and drank it back. He didn't care what accusations anyone threw at anyone else, he said, as he wiped his mouth.

Fiachra talked like a man who had fended off an accusation or two in his time. He bid me to come in and I did. Bones simmered in a cauldron over the fire. He poured the wine into a mug and said it was sumptuous, and very strong. I could select a few whitened bones and a small knife in exchange and carve something for myself. I took my time. Only the best bones, only the whitest, smallest, unscarred bones would do. I would make a poppet to protect my mistress.

My purse was full of bones when Margaret Dun entered. Soon she and the comb-maker were arguing. He was carving an ornate handle for the deacon's staff and she teased him for taking the churchman's coin when he claimed to despise all the clergy.

'What can I do? This town was built to service the cathedral.'

'Our settlement was here long before that thing.'

'The clergy might be scoundrels but that thing, as you call it, is a place of faith,' answered Fiachra.

'Fortifying the highest ground, pushing us out – that's not faith, that's warfare.'

'Pushing who out? Your lot are still around . . . more's the pity.'

'Ah, but those of us who stay must burrow deep to stay safe.'

He growled at her. They were enjoying themselves so much they hardly noticed my leaving. I stepped out of the hut just as a line of monks was going by. Eyes cast down, each snapped a whip over his shoulder, singing a low, mournful, scourging song, lamenting their own sins and those of the town.

I forgot myself and returned by High Street instead of the back lanes. People turned away. Some spat, even the beggar boys I'd often fed leftovers to from our doorway. The first time people had turned away from us, it had hurt. Now the pain was something I nursed, something I might miss if they were to turn and greet me as one of their own. A group of girls followed in my wake, taunting, as I made my way down Low Lane.

'Alice gets her wealth through mating with demons. They say Alice has accomplices, accomplices!'

One edged closer and whispered: 'That's you and your mother.' She stepped on my skirt, making it rip. 'You dumb little witch.'

I turned and swung my fist at the girl. Her jaw clicked and

she fell. I lifted my skirt and ran for it. The rest of them chased me right to the door. The guard shouted them away and let me in. It was only then I recognized the surly smith I'd seen my first week here. Ulf.

Ulf must've told my mother what had happened. It wasn't long before she came for me. She kept knocking on the door of the Pledge Room till I let her in. She stood over me, hands on her hips. 'Use your voice this once, Líadan, and answer me this – why did you wallop that girl?'

I opened my peacock fan and hid my face. My mother knelt, used a more soothing voice. 'It was about Alice, wasn't it?'

I lowered my fan and nodded.

'That rumour will run through the town and out the gates when another one comes along. Do you understand? The trouble you bring on yourself will not be worth it.'

Did she mean I must listen to people's lies and do nothing? It wasn't only Alice people were calling a witch – didn't she know that?

'I know you look up to Alice, I know our mistress is an important woman, an admirable one – but she's not always a good one.'

Why must my mother spoil everything with what she considered her Truths, why couldn't she keep them to herself? Alice was a good woman, without her we'd be begging or dead. I closed my eyes, and eventually, after some sighing, my mother left me alone with the treasures in the Pledge Room. I thought of her amber beads, wrapped in velvet, going dull in the dark – and longed to polish them till their crackled centres shone.

That night my mother did not come to bed at her usual time. Finding it hard to sleep, I stood at the top of the stairs and listened to the voices that rose up from the hall. Sir Arnold had come. He and Alice were discussing the Hattons. I sat on the step and listened.

'Piotr and Lucia claim to be as surprised as anyone at what Cristine did. Do you believe them, Alice?'

'I chose to believe. I need as many on my side as possible.'

'They harbour two girls who've betrayed you.'

'Sure the man in the bed upstairs has betrayed me – claims I've had relations with a servant of Satan!'

'That doesn't sound like you, Alice; a servant of Satan wouldn't do, it would have to be the man himself.'

How they laughed. I did not like it. Why would they laugh? I went back to bed.

I drifted between waking and sleeping, the taper burning low and the rim curling in. The house filled with voices, a laughing that dampened to an endless whispering, which felt worse somehow, more dreadful. I heard Alice. 'We must use a better poison: this one's not working – it's just driving the bugger insane. A few more pills, grind them down, good girl. Tell him it's a treat, mix it with honey, let him lap it off your bosom, every grain, with his big doggy tongue.' Laughter. 'Someone is listening, shush . . .' There was silence, and I tried not to breathe. There were footsteps on the stairs. Then, a noise just outside my door. It was about to open. If I saw her face, if I saw Alice, something terrible would happen. I must not see her face.

I woke up breathless and drenched. I was standing on my bed. They weren't true, the things they made me think about Alice. They weren't true. My mother was there, mopping my brow. 'Are the dreams back?' she asked. There was a white light around my mother; her face was so kind. '*Be careful*,' a voice whispered. '*You must be careful*.'

29. Petronelle

The day of the feast finally arrived. I looked forward to it all being over: once the oaths of loyalty were signed, the bishop would retreat. The town would've shown whose side it was on. And my daughter could sleep, or walk the town without being attacked. Tapestries were unrolled, shaken out and hung on every inch of the walls. Shields bearing the Kytler, Outlawe and De Valle coat of arms were propped along the shelf over the hearth. I doubted anyone needed reminding of Alice's connections – if she called in her debts, every merchant on High Street would be ruined overnight.

Swords had been fitted to the wall, hammered into the mortar that morning. In jest, Alice had tried to lift a blade. It dropped straight to the ground and sank into the earth.

'What weight,' she said, rubbing her back. Sir Arnold had pulled it out. 'Like Arthur,' he said, laughing.

'If Arthur were a grey beard!' said Alice.

'Dame, this beard is black, mostly . . .'

The Hattons arrived first, followed by Sir Arnold, his nephew Stephen and young Sir William. 'Oh, Will, Will,' said Alice, as if she had not seen him in years. Her face fell when only four of the Greater Twelve showed theirs. They arrived together, ruddy with Dutch courage. When the lords and ladies had taken their places, I took mine to the right of my mistress, who, heading the table, faced Sir Arnold at the other end.

There were trenchers of treats laid out – figs wrapped in almond pastry, honeycombs, liver and hazelnut pâtés. The thick honeycomb on my plate was white with honey; I broke into it with my thumb and savoured its sweetness. Lucia Hatton elbowed me, and honey trickled down my wrist, inside my sleeve, darkening the fabric. She pointed at Alice and whispered, 'All the decoration in the world can't hide the decay.'

The candlelit chandelier cast deep hollows under Alice's eyes, and the rubies at her neck appeared glassy, grotesque. Lucia had never criticized my mistress in that manner before, not in my presence. I thought of the relics in Alice's chamber, the oaths of loyalty these people would soon be required to swear. As Sir Arnold proposed his toast, a blade glimmered from the wall behind his head.

'Didn't you hear me, Petronelle?' Lucia muttered. 'I said all the decoration in the world –'

'I heard, madam,' I answered.

'Never mind decorations, my sweet,' Piotr interrupted, cupping his wife's bosom, 'misshapen shells hide the best pearls.'

Lucia smacked him away, pink-faced and squealing. Greased in musk ambergris, she reminded me of a scented pig. As Lady Hatton laughed, a nearby merchant turned to his neighbour and asked, 'Where did the demon sard Alice?'

Piotr rose up and approached my mistress. He bowed and presented her with a short string of freshwater pearls. Thanking him, she dropped them by her platter. He had expected more by way of thanks.

'Do you know what work it took, to find each pearl on that necklace?' said Piotr. 'The hundreds of mussels opened? To keep searching, we'll require –'

'Yes, yes, yes, now sit,' Alice said. 'We'll talk tomorrow.'

My mistress looked at the empty places around her table. She was taking note of those who had not shown up. Helene and Esme bustled in and out with platters of steaming pies, blood puddings and sausages. Beggar children pressed their faces up against the green glass till their noses were flat. Sir Arnold was served first and got the choicest portions. The knight drank from an ornate silver mether engraved with his initials. Several conversations petered off into silence at the same time. We heard the rain fall on the roof. Everyone was thinking of the bishop's accusations. A ginger merchant kept peering about him as if wondering how the demon might have got in. Was it through the chimney? The window? Sir Arnold grabbed Helene's waist as she passed, pulling her close. He stood and cleared his throat. 'Hear ye, hear ye! The dark arts have taken root, and need to be cut with a sharp blade, and Ledrede, the wizened little foreigner, is the very man to do it!'

Alice played with the gold in her ear. The scourge on her house had been mentioned.

'Hightown is rife with talk of curses, covens and sacrifices to demons,' he cried. 'A nest of sorceresses, led by our very own Dame Kytler, have summoned the devil to Hightown. And, lo and behold, obedient as the rest of us are to the dame, said demon answered her call. Hell may manage best it can, for its master is busy having sport in Hightown!'

As Alice began to laugh, everyone else did, too.

'Hush! He may be listening as I speak! Are you under the table, sir? Do you hide in the kitchen? I raise my cup to thee, my fellow conspirators! Dining as we are, in a veritable nest of vipers.' He winked at Helene, who was snug at his side.

We raised our goblets. Even Piotr Hatton forgot his pearls and cheered.

'Respected lady, friends, devoted servants . . . dare I say, you disguise your hoofs and horns well? Show me your toes, your fingers, your tongues. Show me' – he looked into Helene's eyes and kissed her – 'your witch marks.'

Amidst whistles and claps, Arnold bowed and took his seat. The harpist began a lilting tune. Helene filled my goblet with red wine from France till it bubbled to the rim. She moved away with ease, like a dancer. I smiled at Alice, and she smiled back.

Esme came up from the kitchen and lowered a platter in front of Alice, who nodded her approval. A young swan, neck curled and beak resting on her wing, lay on the gleaming silver. Surrounding the cygnet were medallions of meat soaked in black sauce.

'We cannot eat a raw beast,' cried Lucia.

'My dear,' said Alice, 'the meat was roasted and the swan reclothed.'

'My goodness, the talent of your cook. It looks alive still.'

We had never eaten swan before. Alice was showing her guests that she was as good as royal, heeded no churchman's law, and neither should they.

I recalled the swan rising over the pup to defend its young. And here was a cygnet, maybe from the same nest, skinned and redressed; wings as intact as when they once spanned water. I smeared a piece of meat in sauce and swallowed. I didn't taste a morsel. Why am I here, I thought, eating what I don't want to eat?

Sir John entered the hall and approached the table. There were pouches under his eyes; his face had thinned further. Despite the shock of his appearance and the damage his daughter's accusations had wrought, all feigned delight that he was well enough to join us. He was, after all, master of the house. Sir Arnold made as if to give up his chair.

'No,' Sir John said, 'there's no need.'

He stood over Alice, and her neck flushed. She pushed back her chair, rose and sat beside me on the bench.

'It's a pleasure to see you so well, Husband.'

'Oh, the pleasure is all mine, Wife.'

Alice set a goblet of wine in front of him; her rings glittering under the candlelight. John clapped his hands. A boy appeared then, a thin whip, hardly dressed. Our master handed the cup to the child, who looked about to cry but obediently drank a mouthful. Sir John watched him, and we watched John, who then handed the child a slice of meat. The boy chewed it quickly and wiped his mouth. The master dismissed him with a wave, and he sat by the wall, his arms wrapped around his bony knees. After a time, when nothing untoward happened to the child, our master began to eat, displaying a hearty appetite for one who looked so ghastly.

'Sir,' Alice said, waggling her knife, 'you've no need for a taster. Were your wife intent on murder, which she is not, she would not waste good food on the deed.'

'Forever thrifty, my sweet Flemish dame.'

Alice gestured and the harpist began a livelier tune. 'Moll of the Meadow'. Guests picked over poached pears and almonds. More pitchers were brought out. Helene lingered beside Sir John after filling his cup. Without looking up, he grasped her wrist and brought it to his lips. A minstrel entered and skipped to the fire. He lit one of his torches and juggled them so one lit the other. Guests settled back to watch the spectacle. All concerns forgotten, they found the room had become warm and magickal.

The door swung open and the monk Bede barged in with two stocky Franciscans in his wake. Drenched from rain, their faces were sleek, and their robes clung to their stomachs. Bede strode over to Alice and took a rolled parchment from his sleeve. Sir John kept stuffing his mouth with swan and gulping wine, glancing every so often at the taster boy.

'Dame Kytler,' Bede proclaimed, 'you are summoned by his lordship, Richard Ledrede, Bishop of Ossory, to an inquest in his presence and the presence of all the clergy of Kilkennie to answer to the charge of heresy and sorcery.'

He placed the parchment in front of Alice. She touched and touched the red beads at her throat. They were like speckles of blood on crushed silk. I wanted to stop her hand, stop it going back and forth. When Will and Arnold moved as if to lift the swords from the wall, Alice spoke.

'How very gracious of you, to deliver a message on such a wet night. Get thee away now, Bede' – she waved her hand – 'and take thy plump songbirds along home.'

The friars absconded. The guests left one by one, murmuring breathless niceties to Alice, who sat there, dazed. Sir John jumped up, lifted a ewer and a chicken thigh from the table and trooped into the kitchen after Helene. Stephen le Poer followed after him. Their leaving seemed to wake Alice. She waved the scroll in the air and addressed Sir Arnold quite sharply. 'What do you make of this?'

'His summons has no authority in Hightown. It hasn't been sanctioned by our corporation.'

'But the bishop has pressed his own law on us since the day he arrived. The man is relentless. How dare he summon me on the basis of some phantasy?'

Alice broke the seal of the scroll with her eating knife. Her hands trembled as she opened it. When she spoke, I hardly recognized her voice. 'My Lord God, he threatens excommunication if I'm found guilty. And, of course he will find me guilty.'

'The louse just wants to seize your property; it's a trick as old as Job.'

'What about Hell? It's older than Job – would you have me spend eternity there?'

She started to weep. Arnold put his arms around her. Instead of swatting him away, she laid her head on his shoulder a while.

'You'll not be excommunicated,' he said softly. 'I'll see to that. Archbishop Bicknor has no time for Ledrede. He'll make a move soon; he's promised.'

Alice lifted her head and looked at him. Her voice, when she spoke, was equally gentle. 'Well, while we're waiting for word from Dublin, Seneschal, deliver these charges against the bishop: defamation and threat of excommunication without conviction.'

My mistress looked shaken; it had all come real. She instructed me to retire. I blessed myself and left as Alice and Arnold began to word her counter-complaint.

The following morning, the hall stank of ale and wine, but the earth was swept. The front door was opened on to the lane and a triangle of sun brightened the floor. Helene was scattering fresh herbs on the rush mats.

'Sir John is dozing in the kitchen like an old mutt,' she said.

'What on earth is he doing there? Send him upstairs.'

'I tried.'

'Esme,' we both said.

'Yes, Esme will be able,' I said. 'Go fetch her from her sister's.'

I studied my mother's tapestry. If Alice thought as little of it as she claimed, why hadn't she removed it? I studied the scenes again. It had faded over the years. The reds and browns remained strong, but some of the blues had paled to grey. The hunter still aimed his bow. In another panel, a creature lay in a birdcage. In the next, the hunter was on the ground, wounded. A woman stood in the distance, her gown crimson, hands joined inside a muff. If they told a story, it was one that eluded me. Helene stepped close.

'Why are you always gawking at that monstrosity?'

Helene didn't know the weaver was my mother, but had the female talent for finding the soft part of a person and taking aim.

'Go fetch Esme – do as you were bid.'

Alice rang her bell and I went upstairs to check with her. She was sitting up in bed, half awake. The relics were gone. Had word got to the bishop about Alice's plan to secure loyalty? If so, he had acted swiftly. Bede had arrived before any oaths could be sworn. It was quite fortuitous, both for him and for our guests. How quickly Lucia and Piotr had left. Were they as surprised as they pretended? Was anyone there really surprised? I laid out her loose blue shift.

'A man's clothes are so easy to get in and out of,' she said, as she picked it up.

I'd never heard her sound so sad. She was thinking of before, no doubt, the nights she wore her late husband's clothes and rode out by night to meet her lover. How much had changed between her and Sir John in that short time. I took her jug downstairs to fill with warm water for her ablutions.

The guard, Ulf, was eating in the kitchen. He was thickset and olive-skinned, with little to say for himself. The beggar children called him 'The Giant' and rallied round, teasing, trying to make him give chase. 'Roman face, Flemish name,' Esme said when she saw him. 'Irish body, child's brain,' Helene had added, laughing. His sword rested against the table. As I filled the jug from the water barrel, he pushed a square of thick paper across the table.

'This was nailed to the front door this morning. Will you give it to your mistress?'

On the paper, was written one word – a large, snake-like letter and some smaller ones. I brought it up to Alice and handed it over.

'Look at your stupid face. You want to know what it says, don't you? *Sortilego* is what it says. You like the sound of it? *Sortilego* is what I am now, a witch.'

She unhooked her scissors from her chatelaine. I left her trying to cut the parchment in two. Let her vent her ire on the source of it, not on a humble servant.

Low Lane filled and faces pressed against our dull windowpanes, goblins against the green glass. Ulf ushered them away or tried to. We closed the shutters and bolted the door. Alice sent Ralph for Arnold, but he had called a meeting of the Greater Twelve. She sent him for Lucia, but she was indisposed. Sir John had moved from their marriage chamber into Jose's old room. He threatened to fetch the locksmith and have a new key made. He kept calling Kytler's 'his house', and demanded that Alice leave and 'try her poisons elsewhere'. He forbade her to enter Jose's chamber. There was nothing of value inside, nothing Alice needed, yet I saw her pace outside the door, as if considering breaking through. She was heart-sore.

A lifetime ago, Alice wished to keep Otto and me apart. She spoke cruel words, renounced our friendship. Would she behave differently today, I wondered? Would she be kinder? She was very young back then, possessive and proud. It occurred to me that, besides being young, Alice was still both of those things.

30. The Court of the Seneschal

On the day of the inquest, the bishop stormed into Sir Arnold's court with his vestment skirts swinging, carrying a chalice. He had waited in his own court for the moneylender, but Kytler had not shown her face. He took a host from the chalice and addressed Sir Arnold. 'For love of Christ, whom I hold in my hands, arrest that pestiferous woman so the Church can judge her.'

'I know not of whom you speak.'

'Dame Alice Kytler. She, who sits with the leaders of the land in public assemblies, the said lady, is a sorceress, heretic and magician.'

'Listen to this ignorant lowborn tramp,' answered Sir Arnold, 'with that lump of dough in his hands!'

The crowd pushed forward, all wanting to see. The bishop took the highest stand, not realizing perhaps that it was the bench where criminals were tried. Bede, and some others from the bishop's chapter, elbowed through the crowd to stand behind him.

'You must observe the writings of the Holy See against heretics,' cried the bishop. '*Super illius specula* . . .'

'Oh, take your writings to church and preach your sermons there. Heretics have never been found in Ireland. It's known as the Island of Saints.' Sir Arnold turned to the people. 'This Englishman says we're all heretics, on the grounds of some papal constitution we've never heard of. Defamation of this country affects every one of us, so we must all unite against this man.'

There was a great cheering in support of Sir Arnold.

'It does not defame the country – was not Judas found amongst the disciples? As here, in the midst of the decent is found one diabolical den, more foul than ever found in the kingdoms. I do not fear your power, Lord Arnold. I'm willing to suffer for the Church of God –'

'Suffer all you like,' Sir Arnold interrupted, striding through the people and leaving the hall.

Most of the burgesses followed him, leaving the bishop preaching to an emptying court.

The bishop imagined the magickal contagion spreading through the town: women sharing their chants, charms and invocations, meeting at night to draw down evil, stealing souls from the Church and gifting them to Lucifer. If this sect were not stopped, Kilkennie would become a seething nest of devil worshippers.

As the last burgess stood, the bishop realized exactly what was needed. He announced, there and then, to a lone merchant that Kilkennie was under an interdict.

'On what authority?' Bede dared to whisper.

'Under my authority,' answered the bishop. 'On the authority of *Super illius specula*. Am I the only watchman awake during this terrible time for Christians?'

The bishop rushed from the court and held a meeting of all his clergy in the nave of the cathedral. Each one agreed with his stance; the only opposition came from the archdeacon. He implied laypeople, such as Alice and her servants, had not the wherewithal for such sorcery as described by the bishop.

'This is not Avignon with a court full of astrologers and alchemists; these people are not learned.'

He said that neither the dame nor any in her household could conduct the spells His Holiness Pope John cited – could not bind a demon, being unable to decipher the complicated Latin formulae.

'Women gain knowledge in a different manner, you innocent virgin,' the bishop told him. 'It is lucky for this city that I, not you, am the watchman.'

'*Quis custodiet ipsos custodes?* "Who watches the watchmen?"' asked the archdeacon.

The bishop did not trouble him with an answer. He instructed his clergy to make declarations. They left and made speeches in the market square, in front of the Tholsel, in Low Lane, outside the castle, and each said the same thing.

'The merchant burgesses and knights of this town who refuse to arrest their moneylender have insulted Christ. A great revenge must be taken. There will be an interdict – no clergy will perform any duty. There will be no sacraments, no marriages, no baptisms, no penance, no last rites – and no burials. May the souls of your old, ill and new-born plummet into the fires of Hell.'

In the days that came, the townspeople flocked to the bishop like desperate pilgrims. He received gifts and pleas to rescind the interdict, at least to bless the dead, let them be buried. There were already bodies in the cellars of the Black Friars – two infants and an elderly nun. But Ledrede would not budge. It was a suitable penalty for a people who chose to protect a wealthy sorceress against the Holy Mother Church.

31. Petronelle

Alice sent for some spiced wine and stuffed breads. I placed the tray on her bedside table, alongside the loosely rolled summons.

'To put our town under an interdict, just because I refused to attend his hearing!'

I sat on the blanket box by the wall. If she wanted my ears, I might as well rest my feet.

'The bishop has no right to authorize an interdict. Take this away – how can I eat?'

I went to remove her tray, lifting the scroll. Alice snatched the summons and rolled it tightly. Her hands were shaking. I sat alongside her.

'Are you frightened, Alice?'

'I've nothing to be frightened of. It'll be Ledrede who ends up under lock and key, not I. The man is nothing but a commoner; you've heard him speak.'

'Yes, I have, many times. You know Alice, when he said, "The women of the house of Kytler," he looked directly at me. He knows my face, I worry –'

'Oh, he hardly knows you exist. You are not, if you forgive me, the most memorable of women.'

Resentment rose in me, as I watched her tug thread after thread from the embroidered sleeve of her robe.

'I should tell you this,' I said. 'I'm readying to leave, to –'

'No.'

'We must.'

'You can't. Maybe I'll put a spell on you.'

'That's in poor taste, Alice.'

'What would you know about taste?'

I thought of Helene smuggling food into Sir John's chamber, and how he had become sicker and sicker. I might as well say it.

'What if Sir John *is* being poisoned?'

She looked at me coldly. And then, as if we had been speaking of it all along, she announced that I must learn to dye cloth. She ran her finger over the dark streaks in the weave of her cuff.

'Helene dyes unevenly.'

'It's not my task to dye clothes,' I said.

'It's not your task to decide your task.'

'Who, then, will assist you?'

'Basilia's quite civilized now; she'll tend to my wardrobe.'

I could hardly baulk against my own daughter being shown favour. And, after all, it would only be for a short time.

We rose the next morning to find the shutters had been forced and the windows smashed during the night. I was sweeping the glass into a pile when a lady pushed past Ulf. She wore a filthy blue gown and clutched a bundle to her chest. She was familiar but I could not place her. Ulf caught her before she could climb to our mistress's chamber. Dark stains oozed from the small bundle. She kept calling out to Alice: 'Surrender to the bishop, so I can bury my baby.'

When Ulf lifted her off her feet, she stopped weeping and went limp. He carried her out into the lane. After a time, he came back in, slammed the door and bolted it. He bent over, heaving. At first I thought the stench of the dead child had him retching, but soon saw that he was crying. Alice must've heard the commotion, but she didn't show her face. I went out to the yard and drank in the cold, clean air. I remembered who the lady was then; she had been to the house before. Sabina. She had come to see Alice because her priest husband had cast her and his children from their home. I had held her child then. I recalled its face, the soft warmth of its body in my arms. A soul condemned to eternal Hell by the bishop's interdict – one so blameless, yet all the prayers in the world would not save it. I fetched frankincense from the Altar Room and scattered pine needles into the fire to freshen the air.

I heard oaths from the kitchen. Esme couldn't find any butter, so I went up the lane to buy some. The way was slick with mud; it had rained all night. When I entered Butter Slip, the milkmaid elbowed her sister, whose eyes were raw from weeping. The milkmaid longed to ignore me, but she needed custom, whatever she felt. Perhaps a trinket of hers was tucked up in Alice's Pledge Room, something the pretty maid longed to hold again. She patted butter into my crock and attempted a quick nod. It mightn't be safe to snub Kytler's maid, not yet. I climbed the slip and stepped on to High Street. I looked back and saw the milkmaid frantically blessing her wares.

I stepped back as a herd raced by: boys were chasing the swine and waving blades and sticks. There was some attraction at the Tholsel; children crowded the great door. Some were skipping backwards and then leaping forwards. When I got closer, I realized they were throwing stones. I pushed nearer. There was a head on a spike by the great door. His eyes were half closed, as if he were deep in thought. *An bhfuilimid i bhfad ó Chill Chainnigh?* It was the young Gael.

I left the Tholsel and turned into Saint Mary's Alley, where I stopped to steady myself. These steep lanes, they take my breath. That is all, I thought; that's the reason I hold my heart.

The Gael should've kept away. I remembered how fiercely Donagh warned us as we left the mountain: 'Steer clear of those towns; seek out your own kind.' I missed him, missed them all. I had folded my memories up when we arrived, tucked them like a relic, close to my heart. Líadan and I had been lucky; we had followed the same path as the Gael, yet here we were, housed and alive. Lord knew where we would have been, had Alice not taken us in.

In Low Lane, I saw Helene leaving the Hattons' with a flagon of wine and a parcel. When I entered Kytler's kitchen, there was no one there but Esme with a freshly bandaged wrist. She must've scorched herself again. I handed her the butter, which she dumped on the table. It was already scattered with crumbs, almonds, rinds, cardamom, figs and apple cores. She had made circlettes and was now spooning jam on to each. There was a pig roasting over the hearth.

'Did you see Helene?' I asked her.

'Rushed through like a wind. Don't you go doing the same – stay a while. I'm starved for company and so worried, my breathing is not good. Listen . . .' She took some deep wheezing breaths. 'What if I die? I'll have no last rites. I haven't had penance in six years. I'll go to Hell.'

'You won't, Esme, your cooking's not that bad.'

She smiled.

'Now you find humour – when the town is in such despair. Does terror suit you, Petronelle?'

'My name, my real name, is Bébinn.'

'What does it mean?'

'Oh, I've long forgotten.'

'There's much worth forgetting in life, believe me, I know that.'

Esme began talking about Kytler's in Jose's day, and how much better things were then. I tried to listen, but it was hard to shake the Gael from my mind. The cook wiped the board clean, sprinkled it with flour and began rolling out pastry. According to her, life here was far better before *she* took over.

'See, Alice got a taste for business early; that was the problem. Jose taught her the way you would a son.'

Someone's son drew his last breath today. What, I wonder, was the last thing he saw? Was there anything to give him comfort? I blessed myself. Esme misunderstood my gesture.

'I know; disgraceful but Jose indulged that girl. In his last few months of life, it got worse; he had begun to dote. Alice took to lying at the foot of his bed whenever merchants came for loans. They thought it was adorable, she looked so harmless; pretty in her violet gown with her little smile and braids of yellow piled beneath a pearled veil . . . such a tiny person.'

'Harmless?' I laughed.

'I know! Of course, in no time at all, you can guess who was ruling the roost. "*Parle oui, mon père*" or "*Parle non, mon père*", she'd whisper into her father's ear. He'd do exactly what she said.'

'You don't care for her, Esme?' I asked.

'I love the bones of the wretch.'

I considered telling Esme about the young Gael, but she'd only get upset.

I spotted the boy then. Sir John's taster was looking in the window. I went outside. He was holding his stomach. Judging by his hair, the boy had slept on leaves. He was so thin; I guessed his years to be four. His black eyes were set deep in his wan face.

'What's your name?'

'Jack.'

He accepted a cup of buttermilk and a chunk of black

bread, and ran off. I returned inside and set about preparing a tray of circlettes and mead to bring up to Alice. Esme had already begun to make pies, slicing slivers of meat off the pig and throwing them in. She pressed her thumb along the edge of each crescent, talking all the time, letting the flames go low.

'That fire might need more fuel,' I said. 'The hog's on the big side.'

'Seized in the cemetery, caught rooting at the merchant dead. A fine beast, isn't it?'

'Enough to feed a small country.'

'Not me. Let the rich eat the swine that nibbles their ancestors; I'll stick to my broth.'

'The little fellow could help you clear up,' I said, thinking the child might like some sops.

'What fellow?'

I went out to the garden, but saw no sign of the child.

I brought Alice up her tray. She was sitting at her desk, her hair loose and tangled, her mouth tense. There were papers in front of her but her attention was elsewhere. She never mentioned the lady in blue's visit, or her cries to have her baby buried, but I could see it had upset her. She instructed me to clean out the coffin room, wash the walls, boil the sheets and get rid of all trace of the twins. She wanted to free up the room, to have young Will home – just while the house was under threat.

I fetched a basin of warm water and lye. Helene had swept the room, but the walls were blackened from the tapers the girls had burned night and day. I could hardly breathe with the stench of fat. I propped open the door with a stool and began rinsing down the wall when Helene slipped past carrying an empty basket. If Sir John was being fed, why was he getting thinner, losing his hair, his nails? Was the source of his illness contained in Cristine's gifts of food? It couldn't be; the twins adored their father.

The tasks Alice had set me for the day were well beneath a lady's companion. My next was to dye cloth. I walked slowly down the cellar steps. My skin began to prickle, and not just with the heat. It was a place I didn't like, cut into the earth beneath the house; it had the feeling of a large tomb. I looked at the Pledge Room door, and wondered at the fact that my daughter had a key to it and I didn't. Helene smiled to herself when she saw me, but didn't mock. The light was poor, coming from narrow grids high on the wall, some rush lights and the brazier. There was a fire set beneath two large vats.

'Salt to fix the colour, stir with the ladle, make sure the dye takes evenly.'

'I know. I've dyed before, flax, yarn . . .'

She gave me a floor-length apron of sack cloth. Before I knew it, I was stirring the water with a stick, squelching the silk.

'Gentle, don't lean so heavy,' said Helene. 'I can see you've not dyed precious cloth before.'

After some time and an aching back, we lifted out the cloth, dumped it in cool water and wrung it out. When I unravelled the folds, I saw the embroidered nightingales had come up darker than the silk itself.

'Give it another dunk. Use the stick. No need to soak your hands like that – look at your skin!'

My hands were tinted darkest at the cuticles, next to which my nail crescents gleamed grey.

Later, in the kitchen, I tried to scrub my hands clean but my skin kept the blue tinge. I turned up my palms: my life, love and heart lines looked as if they were drawn with a quill.

They seemed strange, as if they belonged to someone else. I thought of the lady, her dead baby and her desperate pleas. If only I had been able to help her. I knew some of what she must've felt. After I had stopped hoping Otto would reappear – just one day walk towards me again, after I had given up raging against the fact of his death – I had longed for his remains, for a grave to tend. I had none of those things; instead I had a ring, the beads. Each bead held a memory – his smile, the silver scar on his lip, the feel of his arms about my waist. The salt of his skin when I kissed it; his eyes behind that mask as we danced.

Next morning, I brought Líadan to our mistress's chamber and showed her how to prepare Alice for her day, laying out all the correct waters, powders, combs and pins. Her hair had got so fine, it didn't need many pins. A hundred couldn't keep mine tethered.

'I told you to stop moving my perfume,' she snapped, picking up the glass flask, 'and there is less than before – have you been using it, Petronelle?'

I shook my head.

'Don't look so repulsed. Would it sicken you to smell sweet, instead of like a priest?'

Alice sat by her mirror and paid me no more attention. I glanced back as I left the room. Was there satisfaction in my daughter's eyes as she lifted Alice's hair? Were they one of a kind?

I went downstairs and began to sweep the hall. My daughter was still my daughter, I thought, and soon this house and its darkness would be behind us. Sir John appeared then, fully dressed for a change, in a black tunic and hose. He had gone to some effort; he wore all of his rings, and his pointed poulaines shone. He leant a while on the door jamb, and then stepped out into the lane.

I peeked after and saw the twins had joined him and were linking him by the arm and guiding him towards the Hattons'. He was dark between their scarlet gowns; together, they were shaped like the butterfly on my sill. As I watched them, I sensed someone watching me in turn. The taster boy was crouched in the alcove. He still clutched the cup I'd given him. A grey cat was curled beside him, purring heavily. I knelt and looked in his eyes – there was something . . .

'Do I know you?'

He didn't answer. I leant forward and touched his face: it was like ice.

'Move closer to the hearth and wait.'

I went up to Alice's chamber. She was stuck halfway in her favourite brocade, with one arm caught and one arm free. Líadan was wielding a small scissors and snipping at some lacing. I quickly told my mistress about the boy and asked if he could stay. He could help in the stable or in the kitchen garden.

'John's taster, you mean?'

'He's but four or five years old.'

'Put him out.'

Maybe it was for the best; perhaps a mother searched for him. Downstairs, I told the boy he couldn't stay and unbolted the door. He did my bidding without a word, just walked out into the lane, even pushing the door closed after himself.

Later, near sunset, I checked the lane. The boy was sitting on the bottom step of Market Slip. No one had come for him. I crooked my finger and he rose stiffly and came over. When I picked him up, he weighed nothing. He didn't try to wriggle free like most wild children would. This one was used to being handled. I carried him upstairs and placed him on my bed, piled the furs up around him. I'd be infested with fleas by morning, but what harm. He shook with cold – his fingers were swollen with chilblains.

I warned Líadan of his presence, in case she came upon him later and got a fright. I made up a milky pottage of bread, honey and raisins, and brought it up. The boy ate slowly, looking at each spoonful before swallowing. When he was finished, he sank back down on to the bed. I put my finger to my lips to warn him to be quiet. He gave a small nod, and his lids closed slowly over his brown eyes as he began to drift off.

I could find a place for him. There was plenty of room in the stable. I thought on this as I mended my mistress's hose by the kitchen hearth. When I went up later, the child was gone. I felt the blanket – it was cool. Líadan was bent over her wax tablet. I looked more closely: she was etching butterflies. They were arranged in a delicate circle, wingtips touching. It was so lovely; it almost took me away from my question.

'Was the boy here when you came up?'

She shook her head. I looked all over the house for the child. I took my candle and ventured into Low Lane. There was no one there except a harlot waiting in the shadows for trade, her yellow hood covering her face. The next morning, I checked every nook and cranny, even the well. I dreamt of his small cold hands – they were reaching out for me. He had completely disappeared, but yet I didn't feel that child had gone anywhere.

32. Basilia

The town had been oddly silent without its church bells ringing. I made my way towards the comb-maker's. No one came near or taunted me, but I remained wary and kept my head bowed. It had been easy to slip away; my mother was searching for the taster boy. I had recognized him. He was the boy that had been turned over to the town despite the town not wanting him at all. My mother was fretting about him, a child she knew nothing about. The monks passed, heads down in prayer, as if there were no one else in the world but them.

I arrived at the comb-maker's to find his door shut. I listened, but heard no sawing, no hacking or sanding. The trees about the place were full of crows. He might be anywhere, I told myself – gathering bones, hunting. As I was about to leave, Margaret Dun ambled towards me. She was pale, her face all tight and sad.

'I found him twisted and cold. There was something unnatural about it, I'll tell you that for nothing. He waits on a slab in the Black Friars Abbey; there are more corpses than monks there now.'

She looked down at me, then patted my shoulder. 'Go say farewell.'

When she had gone, I shoved open the door to Fiachra's hut. There was no heat or steam; the fire had gone to ash beneath the cauldron. I would've liked a keepsake, something he had toiled over – maybe one of his combs to run through my hair. Thieves had been. There was nothing left but shards and dust. The clay wine jug from Sir John's chamber lay on the pallet he slept on. When I turned it upside down, not a drop fell out. The last time I saw him, Fiachra had given me bones and a carving tool in exchange for it. I wish I'd spoken to him then, said something – nothing special, just something everyday, like thank you.

I had never been to the abbey. It was just outside the town walls. The friars there wore black robes and were said to be few. I approached Blackferen Gate. It stood open, and people were coming and going freely. A priest pushed a handcart in which a woman lay wrapped in blankets. I walked close behind him, hoping to be mistaken for his daughter if the keeper chose to check. No one even noticed me. Once through the arch, we followed the winding path to the abbey with a clutch of other people. There was a side door. There were many there, some reciting the rosary.

'We cannot take many more,' said a large friar.

'Take Sabina, please, so she can rest alongside our son.'

The friar sighed and nodded. As the priest lifted the woman, her long rust hair draped over his arm. I saw that her mouth was mauve, and her neck rope-burned. He carried her through the door, too much in grief to notice me. As we went down the steps, the incense became thicker, and the air colder. At the bottom we found ourselves shivering in a large, dim cellar, off which one domed cavern led to another, even darker one. There were no windows, just torches on the thick pillars. On slabs against the walls lay bodies wound in sheets, bodies that should have rested beneath the earth. I imagined the interdict going on for ever, and all the dead of Kilkennie piling up. The priest and the friar were gone from sight, moving deeper into the vaults.

I looked from one body to the other – at first they all seemed the same. After a while, I understood that some were too small, or too heavy, to be Fiachra, and that some winding sheets were brighter, less stained than others. I found him then, not on a slab but on the floor. I recognized him by his length, and then by his hand. It had fallen, or been tugged, free of the winding sheet. I looked at his callused fingers, the white line where his ring had been. Even here, there were thieves. I touched his chest and felt the shape of his wolf charm and wished him a safe journey to the afterlife.

When I got back home, I stopped outside the Altar Room. I felt drawn to join my mother for a while. She spent all her spare time praying. She must've heard me, because the door opened.

'Come in, come in.'

Once inside, she handed me a cup. 'The boy drank from this earlier. Close your eyes; hold it.'

I held the cup and shut my eyes. It came quickly. The boy, curled in a nest of yellow leaves, his thumb between his lips, his colour draining as he slept. Reeds swayed nearby, and a millwheel turned.

'Do you see anything?'

I shook my head. I don't know why, only that I had become afraid. What if I searched and found the boy exactly as I'd seen him? If that vision was true, would my other vision come true, too? Was my beloved mistress going to find herself trapped, terrified and about to die? No. I decided the dreams and visions were the notions of a child, a girl – not the woman I was now.

I ran from the Altar Room and up to our chamber and dragged my crate out from under my bed. Besides the writing box Alice had given me, it held little of interest – I kept my real treasures under the loose board beneath it. I wriggled under the bed, pushed down on one end of the floorboard, and the other flipped up. In the crevice lay the few items I'd rescued.

Wrapped in felt was the ivory ring. What good did it do my mother, under her mattress and long forgotten? I slipped it on to my finger and wondered what my father had looked like. She told me so little; he was a good archer, had died in battle and had loved her. *Otto*. Sometimes I imagined he was a knight; if so he might've had a family name. If he had, she never told me it. I picked up my glinting silver scissors, one blade man, one blade woman. Alice had dropped them. I reached in, deeper again, and lifted out the amber beads. One of them still hung around my mother's neck. Folded tight beneath them lay the closed wing of my peacock fan. There were other, smaller things: quill feathers, a block of dark purple ink, red thread. I carefully added Fiachra's wolf tooth to my hoard.

DEIREADH FÓMHAIR

OCTOBER

This business about these witches troubled all the
state of Ireland, the more for that the ladie was
supported by certeine of the nobilitie.

Holinshed's Chronicles of Ireland

33. Petronelle

With almost every chore done, I sat on the stool and rested by the hearth. The fire crackled around the branches. After a while I closed my eyes, enjoying the heat on the side of my face. I was carried right into Flemingstown by the wood smoke, heard leaves rustling, smelt Scotch pine. *An owl flew past, its soundless wings close to my head.* My trance was broken by a clattering. I opened my eyes to see Alice draw up a chair. She looked tired, her ram's horns were lopsided, and her sleeves weren't properly buttoned. She had endured a distressing afternoon. People were calling to the house again, but not to offer loyalty. They were begging her to surrender to the bishop so he would lift the interdict. She drank from her mug of mead, then poked the fire. Cinders spun towards her face, but she didn't sit back.

'What's troubling you?' She surprised me by noticing.

'Do you recall a boy, the taster? There was something about that child. I keep seeing him in my mind's eye – the blanket around his shoulders, the fluffy hair on his crown, his small fingers around the cup. I worry –'

'Stop worrying. He's just some stranger that passed through.'

'But he didn't pass through, Alice, that's my feeling. He's still here somewhere.'

Alice studied me for an age.

'It's a notion, maybe,' I added.

'Another notion of yours – like John being poisoned.'

She was angry. She thought I was suggesting wrongdoing on her part.

'So where is he, if he's here?'

'I don't know.'

'You can't know, can you?' she sighed. 'He gave you the slip – boys like that are vermin – beggars, thieves and spies.'

My mistress dismissed me then, said she needed to be alone. I left, cold again after only a few steps away from the fire.

I remembered the way Alice leant over and handed John a goblet, her ring glittering in the candlelight. The boy drank from it. I remembered the way he shivered uncontrollably in my bed, and then was gone. She had worn Jose's locket ring, the one which opened on a tiny hinge. It had a small compartment. 'It holds a lock of precious hair,' she told me once, but never showed me. I fetched my old cloak from upstairs, unfolded it from under the bed. It was not as fine as the one Alice had given me, but, being heavier and lined with beaver, it was warmer. Where was that small boy gone? What had my daughter seen when she held the cup? Where was I to turn to find out? I found myself walking up the hill towards the cathedral. No one returned my greeting as I strolled into the graveyard. Instead they stared off into the distance. Some crossed themselves. The blackbirds sang as I knelt at the grave of Agnes the anchoress. People didn't stop coming because she was dead. Her stone shone with morning damp. A nun was drawn on to it. I put my hands flat over the engraved ones, palm to palm.

'What happened to the boy?'

The stone was cold. Yet I felt the weight of a long-pressed silence pushing back.

That even-time, a very old burgess came to the door. It was a long time before anyone let him in, thinking he was just another trouble-maker. He spoke gently; his long grey hair floated outwards when he removed his felt cap. His mantle was threadworn, his manner impeccable. It turned out he was looking for Jose. My mistress informed him that Jose was long dead. The man asked for a bed, for old times' sake. He said that he and Jose were boys together in Ypres, and he had visited this house before, some years ago.

'You used to call me daddy-long-legs, do you remember?'

Alice remembered, but refused him shelter. Anyone could be a spy from the bishop, she claimed. He challenged her then, asked to speak with the master.

'I'm in charge here, sir; I was my father's sole heir.'

'If the rumours were true,' he said in a low voice as he left, 'you made yourself so.'

'Bitter old men,' Alice sighed. 'The world is full of them.'

I went down to the kitchen to prepare her supper. Many men would've passed over their daughters in preference to any male relation, no matter how distant – but Jose hadn't. That she was a woman, was that what the burgess couldn't stomach? Jose had made Alice his successor whether the old burgess liked it or not.

Esme had left the breadcrumbs and herbs on the board. She never mentioned my lowered station but did small things to ease my load. I laid the lambs' hearts out, wiped the blood away and fetched a small sharp knife. *You made yourself so.* I sliced each heart with a blade; broke the thin skin between the cavities with my thumb, stuffed them one by one with breadcrumbs, butter, parsley and thyme. I threaded a bone needle and stitched each heart shut. I set them on a tray, a dozen hearts with sutured mouths. *You made yourself so.* Something was wrong. Something was very wrong, but I didn't know what.

34. The Households of Low Lane

Outside, it rained in torrents. In Hattons', the fire was still being fed. They stayed up past their usual time, for there was much to discuss. 'Poor Alice' was how the evening began, but not how it ended, for Lucia and Cristine were women who liked to have sport with their tongues.

There was ale, port and singing. Some of the pearl-divers bedding down in the kitchen awoke and joined them. One was the boy they teased about the mute. Lucia stood at the top of the room, her husband's hat on her head, and declared she would instruct them in the dark art of courting a demon lover. On cue, Beatrice appeared in a long thin chemise, her hair loose. Lucia would deliver the instructions and Beatrice would play them out. Her role was solo, silent.

'You must close the shutters, build up the fire. Act as if a lover is coming, for of course a lover is coming, but he may have a tail or horns, he may have nails that leave marks, he may have an evil look, one that will make you quiver with lust.'

'Oh, stop, what next?' said Cristine.

'Candles next. Church wax. From monastery bees, the purest of the winged insects. Prepare the finest of vitals – salted butter, bread, meat, preferably lamb. Cover all the platters with cloth; the cloth must be linen and clean. The doors must all be shut, for he does not enter in the normal way.'

'Neither do I!' called Piotr.

'You must not fawn, for he'll show contempt. Your maid, if she is present, must be discreet.'

'And stripped to the waist,' added Piotr.

'He'll come as the shadows grow longer, but only if you invoke him. I cannot tell you the words tonight, for if I repeat them here, he may come, and we're not ready.'

'For our maid is not yet stripped!'

All were drinking from a huge mether that was being passed about. Each flushed faced was fixated on Beatrice, who stood in front of the fire, her strong limbs a delight through her thin chemise.

'You must not wash, for the demon likes the scent of a woman's skin; you must not use perfume in your hair; you must have your head uncovered and your braids loosened. He does not like combs, or veils, or rings. You must be as bare as when you came into the world. As the candles go low, you must say those certain words, that incantation I cannot share. You must drink a libation and close your eyes. You may hear his hoofs on the roof, or you may hear creaking – do not open your eyes, do not break the spell. The first sign will be a smell of animal, or earth, for he has travelled from the underworld; his hands when he touches you will be rough. You and he will become a beast with two heads. And henceforth he will be bound to you, and do your every bidding.'

'I would have him churn butter,' said the maid.

'I would have him mend my hose,' added Cristine.

'I would have him lie with my husband while I slept on,' laughed Lucia as she took a bow, and jumped on said husband's lap.

Beneath the same beating rain, further up the lane, in the best room of the stone house with green windows, a man leant on his elbow and looked at the maid standing in the doorway.

'Where have you been all this time?' he asked from his bed.

'I came yesterday.'

'You haven't come, not for days.'

Helene slipped in beside him and comforted him with whispers. There were tufts on his pillow, thick golden locks. With every day that passed, he looked less like the man who had married Dame Kytler. Why on earth did he marry that creature? Cristine claimed the dame had bewitched him with a charm. Petronelle said the charm had a simple recipe: Alice's wealth and Sir John's avarice. But what if Cristine was right? The maid thought of how she bled as she was about to filch Alice's mirror, the way she was ill every time she'd lain with Alice's husband.

'The night I have spent, little maid,' said Sir John. 'My whole body is in pain, and see, see my nails, they are falling out.'

There was just a raw bed where the nail of his little finger had been. Repulsion crawled in her belly, and she swallowed. Could it really be . . . was the mistress a witch? She herself had often teased Petronelle about Alice's demon lover but only for sport. The woman had a simpleton's loyalty to Dame Kytler, and it was fun to watch her pale with anger.

'You'll be better soon,' she said, pressing her mouth against his collarbone.

'Only if Alice is contained and kept from me. I opened my eyes this morning to find she'd slipped into my bed and her face was right next to mine.'

The maid felt a surge of jealousy that the mistress had lain exactly where she was stretched out. John continued with his story.

'"What's the matter?" Alice asked, all innocence, when well she knew what the matter was, since it was she who had been chasing me in my dreams, trying to disembowel me.'

The maid reached under the covers and tried to coax her

master to life; she did not want to hear any more. He pushed her hand away.

'Don't you love me?' she asked.

'Love?' he laughed.

What did he mean? The way he used to look at her, kiss her, touch her. That was love – it had to be. Had Alice found them out and cast a spell? Had her mistress done something to make Sir John forget his love? Some could do that: cast spells to start or stop love. What if she, Helene, could also make things happen? In her mind's eye, she saw herself as mistress of Alice's house, and him under her, bucking.

35. Petronelle

It was dawn as I rode towards the town gates. I carried a package for Líthgen under my cloak. Amongst the food was a nice piece of pork for Milo. I was glad he had chosen to stay with my mother, company was no harm when you were as old as she was. As I neared the gates, I noticed archers climbing along the town walls. The keeper, when I finally got his attention, said I couldn't leave. No one was leaving Hightown that day. He was trying to put on a chainmail tunic, but it was proving too heavy. He dropped it and told me that the tribes had burned Castlecomer and were on their way to take Kilkennie. The bridge was up, and the gates were closed. I rode back through High Street, and the crier rang his bell and shouted: 'All men to the gates! All men to the gates!'

Entering Kytler's yard, I saw townsmen patrolling the river bank, knives at hip, bows in hand, crushing mussel shells underfoot. I left the mare in the stables, only to find the back door locked. I had to bang and call out my name before it was unbolted. Ulf nodded recognition and let me in. It was with much resentment that I thanked him for allowing me entry into a house which up until some weeks ago he was a stranger to.

There was great fear and excitement inside. No one said which tribe threatened – it could've been Ó Braonáins, Ó Tuathails or Ó Cearbhaills. Despite the differences between the Gaelic tribes, to the dwellers of Hightown they were one and the same. The whole household crushed against each other getting upstairs. Arnold's army was leaving town to defend us, with only Stephen and a few laymen left in Kilkennie. Everyone wanted to watch them leave and the only good view was from Jose's chamber. From it could be seen the drawbridge, the gate tower and the road out of town. Alice banged on the door, and, after a little wheedling from Helene, Sir John opened it and let us all in, even the mistress. He seemed alert, but could not, he complained as he crawled back into his bed, move very far. 'Keep the witch from me,' he said, glaring over his blanket at his wife.

Líadan, silent as ever, climbed on to a chest and sat fiddling with some doll. Alice opened the shutters wide and leant so far out I feared she would topple. Esme, Helene and I stood close and looked over her shoulder.

'Look at Arnold's men, how they gallop,' she said, pointing at the shapes moving off into the distance. 'By sunset, there'll be a dozen native heads staked on John's Bridge.'

'How can you speak so?' I whispered into her ear. 'You know my mother's Irish.'

'She may well be, but you're not,' she snapped. 'Your very name proves that.'

'My name is Bébinn.'

'There's no such person, never was.'

The words felt like a slap. No such person. I glanced over at my daughter. Had she heard? Her face was flushed but she kept her eyes fixed on her doll, smoothing out its small black skirt. I didn't understand Alice's blood thirst. She wore Irish cloaks, hired harpists, granted shelter to Líadan and me. I thought of Líthgen out there somewhere, of our people on the mountainside, the ones the burgesses called mongrel.

'What if they cross the river and burn us in our beds?' asked Helene.

'Those thieving barbarians won't get in spitting distance of the Nore,' said Alice.

'Thieving?' said Esme. 'You forget, lady, whose country this is.'

'How dare you speak to me like that? Leave here, go on, get out!' Alice was furious.

'I'll go and stay gone – yours is not the only kitchen in Kilkennie.'

'Oh, Esme,' Alice surprised us all by cooing, 'you can't, you must never. Stay with us.'

'You know Lucia Hatton is after me, and you would rather die than have me cook for her household. That's the only reason you speak so.'

'I know no such thing' – Alice stroked the cook's arm – 'just that you're a treasure, if a little brusque.'

As we left the room, Sir John was smirking. He seemed pleased by the quarrel.

That night, as Líadan slept, I sat by the bedroom window thinking on what Alice had said. *There's no such person, never was.* I looked out at the deep shadow made by the bridge, the black water moving beneath. I thought of all the watchmen, all the locked gates. The night was full of eyes and blades. As suddenly as an animal feeling its harness, I bolted. I don't recall unlocking the door or going out into the night, but I must have, because I soon found myself crossing the marketplace.

The moon hung like a worn slip of silver over the ancient tower. I rushed in the direction of the town walls. It was so dark that I kept veering off into brambles and scratching my hands. The wall was somewhere near, but would I ever find it? My hands eventually met cold stone, sharp in places, smooth in others. I tucked my skirts into my girdle and began to climb. My sleeves snagged on the jagged edges, my foot slipped on moss, vines snapped when I gripped them. I stood there. What if I did manage to get over the wall? What would happen, with nearly a hundred archers ready for any movement within shot of the walls? And what would Líadan think when she woke and found her mother gone? I came to my senses then and journeyed back towards Kytler's.

In Low Lane, Ulf held a lantern close to my face. 'I may fetch the mistress. You shouldn't be out at this hour.'

'Do and she'll know you left the door unguarded earlier.'

'A man has to relieve himself.'

'If you were gone long enough for someone to get out of the house, someone could've easily got in. If I were you, I wouldn't wake your mistress.'

He let me enter. The sound of the bolt grating as he locked the door behind me made me feel ill. Next morning, when I woke, it might've been a bad dream, but for the scratches on my arms and my bramble-torn sleeves.

We had just cleared the trestle after dining, when Ralph ran into the hall.

'Sir Arnold has forced the tribes to retreat and the Irish have fled south! The crier called word.'

'Dress me, Petronelle, I want to ride out,' said Alice.

'I thought Líadan was dressing you?'

'I don't have the time it takes her.'

I followed Alice to her chamber and helped her into a hunting gown. She glanced at the cuts on my wrist and frowned. I tugged my cuffs further down. After scooping her hair into a knot, I pinned her veil and held out her short riding cloak. I asked where my amber necklace was kept, but she didn't answer my question, just kept telling me to hurry, hurry, hurry.

'No one is allowed out of town,' I reminded her, 'and you can't go alone.'

'I'm different, you know that. And Ulf will come.'

She rode out of the stable with Ulf by her side. We gained entry to Sir John's room, and Líadan, Esme, Helene and I watched the bridge from the window, to see if our mistress got past the keeper. Sir John was snoring lightly in his bed, his skin grey, the bones of his face prominent. He had aged years since his wedding day. The distant bridge went down, and two riders galloped from the town.

Leaving Helene lighting tapers, Esme, Líadan and I went downstairs. How had it happened that the lowest maid held the key to the master's chamber? Why was Alice tolerating such changes? In the time before, she would've had Sir John and his daughters thrown in gaol for their accusations. Yet she made no move to fight him. It was as if she wanted that man under her roof, no matter what. If anyone was under a love spell, it was she, not her husband.

As I followed Líadan, I noticed she made a drily musical sound with each step. It reminded me of bone weights on a loom. At the bottom of the stairs, I bid her to wait up and knelt to lift her skirt. Small ornaments were stitched to the underside of the cloth: mussel shells made smooth, a carved bone heart, some beads – one of which was my stolen bird head. So Helene was not feathering her nest after all. My daughter was the light-fingered one. I should've known – from the time Lía could move, if she saw something she liked, she'd just pick it up.

'Why stitch trinkets to your skirt?'

She stepped away and put her hands on her waist. Then she threw her arms in the air and spun in circles, her skirts widening and chiming like Salome at the Midsummer fair. It was a lovely sound, gentle, hopeful. How could I be vexed at such a small silliness, when people were going to battle? I put my arms about her and held her close. There was an ease between us then, the first in some time.

We all set about our chores while we waited for word. It was late in the day when we heard the screaming. I ran to find Alice doubled over in the hall. She was swearing oaths; her face ran with tears and snot, and she rocked back and forth. I tried to put my arms around her, but she told me to get the hell away. Esme helped her up to her room, and I paced. What was happening? Were the tribes on their way, would Hightown burn?

I went down to the kitchen to keep my hands busy, and to get away from Alice's wailing. Shortly after, Ulf came in, a little out of breath.

'What on earth happened?'

He sat at the table and reached for the small jug. He drank from its mouth, and buttermilk ran down his chin.

'A while outside town, just beyond the crossroads, there were bodies on the ground. "They got them," Alice cried, "ride on." She cantered ahead, so I followed. Suddenly she veered around and galloped past me. I saw then what she had seen. They'd taken their livery, so we would not know them at first. It wasn't Gaels who lay slain – they were Arnold's men. The bodies were scattered but the heads were piled into a cairn. One was staked on a sword, apart from the others. It was Sir Arnold.'

'Oh, mercy . . .'

He looked up at me.

'They might come – they might kill us all.'

'How many heads?'

Ulf jabbed his finger across, and then down, as if the sorry heap were between us. 'Twelve.'

'There were over a hundred men with Sir Arnold. There's hope yet.'

The man helped himself from the pewter of ale.

'We must be careful of Alice,' I added, more to myself than him; 'her grief will be enormous.'

I went to the Altar Room and prayed for Sir Arnold's blessed release. I felt saddened for him and his people, but his life had been full, and, for the most part, he seemed a good man, a loyal one. His soul would find its way home. As for us, I would ask Alice to return my amber beads, and my daughter and I would leave. I felt it strongly then, Líthgen's presence. A memory returned: my mother coming out of the woods, carrying something. She beckoned towards me, wanted me to come. 'Soon, Mother,' I whispered, 'soon.'

Alice wanted everything, everything dyed black. As I prepared one of her cloaks for the vat, I noticed how the woad had stained my scratches. They were like blue scrawbs.

Helene looked at me oddly. 'What happened to your hands?'

'I fell when tending the hives.'

'What tending is done in October?'

'Watching, Helene – watching can be useful, you know.'

I meant just to confuse her, but she blushed and did not ask any more questions. There was a certain satisfaction in being ruined, to have my longing to escape etched on my skin. What must it be like to be a common woman of the roads, a woman scorned by everyone, yet answerable to no master, no mistress? Was it as bad as we'd been led to believe?

Hightown now had no seneschal and Alice has lost her protector. We waited days but none of Arnold's men returned. His remains were carted to Waterford, where no interdict prevented their burial. Word came that Castlecomer stood unharmed by fire or raiders – that it had never been attacked in the first place.

Arnold had both allies and enemies amongst the chieftains, but none claimed credit for his death. Alice readily believed that the Gaels had slain Arnold, but the songs, when they came, told a different story: that it had been a trick and that it was Ledrede's men who had lain in wait. The rest of Arnold's troop turned up in Athy town, a day's ride away – their bodies floating in the reeds, their heads staked on the bridge. I thought of Ralph – how he had delivered the false account of victory, the one that meant Alice was the first to find Arnold. As it happened, the boy never crossed our threshold again. His work in Kytler's was done.

36. Paradise

Around a fire pit in Flemingstown Woods, Líthgen told the boy something she had never told anyone.

'It was a lifetime ago – a winter of starvation, floods, disease. Old or child, you became savage to survive. My husband was slaughtered while out hunting. The men heard no call for help, just stumbled upon him lying in a hollow, his throat and eyes open. They told me it must've just happened. That their arrival had startled his attacker. And whoever they were, they had run off unsated. The men made a stretcher and carried him home. I told my daughter a wolf killed her father. No need for her to know the desperate things starving people were driven to.

'Numb with grief, I walked the clay paths between these trees, the shadows of their branches like a quivering ladder beneath my feet. I was a dazed ghost, hardly knowing which world I trod. I had seen my husband laid out, his furs about him, his waxen fingers gripping his dagger. I had sung him away. Yet I woke each morning expecting him to reach out and pull me close.

'For days on end, I'd set out from our bed and walk the woods, often baring my neck to the glint of the winter sun, with the hope that someone would slice it, too. Once, not far from here, while standing like that, I heard the scrape of a spade entering soil. I followed the sound through the bushes and came across a girl shovelling earth. I stood in the shade, and watched Alice Kytler bury her brother.

'She gathered leaves and debris, and spread it over the

mound, a small smile on her face, as if she were sprinkling petals on a bridal bed. She walked off between the trees then, and disappeared. I waited, watching the leaves tumble in the breeze till the grave was bare dark earth again.

'I waited, and Alice came back. I knew she would. To check no ribbon, no lock of hair, no fallen bead, was left, to check that she had really done it. And I was there, waiting at the foot of Otto's grave. I startled her, she said; she came to be alone a while. Her brother had just ridden to battle; she worried for him, for all the men. "He's beneath this soil," I answered. "You put him there." She was only young, but already knew how little my word was worth.

'"Your daughter did it; they had a lovers' quarrel. She used poison, you know. The type your people use. Wolf's bane. I can swear to it. Perhaps you prepared it? Or, perhaps" – she took a deep breath – "he has gone to battle, is just now catching up with the men?"

'It would be nothing, an afternoon's work, to string up myself and my daughter, to end us both – outsiders, Gaels, no more than animals under the law they swore by. "How dark the woods have become," I said. "It is time for home."'

'What a story,' said Milo.

He rose to his feet and plunged his blade into Líthgen's chest.

If only she had not spoken of it, if only she had kept her silence a while longer. He had grown fond of her, liked her company, her ways. His mistress had wanted her killed months ago, but Milo had waited, because Milo was curious. He wanted to know exactly why Dame Kytler wanted the old woman dead. And now that he knew why, he could demand a much higher price.

37. Basilia

I was the only one allowed into Alice's chamber after Sir Arnold's death. My mistress spent days alone, not caring for anything or anyone. Each morning was spent lying across the end of her bed, while she cried into her pillows. One evening, she began to talk: her voice was different, ragged and hoarse. Arnold was a love of hers once, she confessed. I stretched out my arms and legs and stared at the ceiling as she spoke. The first time Arnold was made seneschal, he carried the town seal right to this chamber. He had inked the seal and laid it on the smooth skin between her cunt and belly. Alice remembered exactly how it had looked: the thin black lines of the circle; and, inside the circle, the arched gates; and, beyond the arched gates, the castle turrets.

You've done this before, she told him. Never on such fine vellum, he whispered, trying to kiss her navel. No, she had laughed, I want the seal to remain unblemished. You can think of me when you go to battle tomorrow. Remember that under all my clothes, your seal is on my skin. If I had known that, Arnold said, I would've sard you soundly first. Alice looked at me and laughed – a dull sad sound that turned into more sobs.

Back on my own bed, I bound yarrow about the poppet and rubbed her heart. She would not fall apart, I vowed, not Alice. And she did not. After another night of crying, she called me to her early. When I entered the room, her face was raw but I saw her mouth was set. She wanted to be dressed in her finest; she planned to meet with the Greater Twelve.

That was the start of Alice's crusade: Arnold's successor, and the next seneschal of Kilkennie, would be her son, Will.

Though it kept her from the house for days at a time, her scheming came to nothing. Stephen le Poer won the vote for seneschal. Alice was furious. She blamed Will. Stephen had sired children, both in and out of the marriage chamber. 'My son,' she said, 'has yet to prove himself with a whore, let alone a wife.'

The day after the voting, my mistress summoned Will, trussed me up in one of her gowns and left me waiting for him in her chamber. He had given his word to his mother, but it was so late it looked like he might not arrive at all. I stood by the window and watched the river for the pearl-diver, but he wasn't fishing with the others. I had hoped he'd catch a glimpse of me, be persuaded by my ladylike appearance that I was no sorceress.

I watched the water rush, brown and dark, and suddenly, in my mind's eye, I saw a nest of reeds littered with tiny white feathers. It was lodged on the river bank, and nearby red apples were rotting in the grass. Beneath the leaves and feathers lay a small child: the taster boy, Jack. The poor boy was close. I would find him, I decided, and bring him to my mother.

38. Petronelle

That morning, Líadan had awoken screaming from a nightmare she couldn't or, more likely, wouldn't share – for if she could scream, surely she could speak. Downstairs, sluggish from broken sleep, I had noticed Líthgen's tapestry was unravelling. Here and there, bright yellow threads were snipped, as if someone had taken a blade to it. The golden bars of the birdcage hung loose. I looked closer. It was not a bird inside but a girl. It was not a cage but a hut. Just like the one Alice and I had built together once. I had lain in it, waiting for Otto on the day he must've died. Thinking he was off to battle, I had wanted to say goodbye. My mother had begun weaving this tapestry around that time. I longed to see her, but I couldn't. I would make do with mending her work.

The golden thread was not with the others. Of course, it was too valuable. It must be somewhere safe. I needed to choose the right time to approach Alice about it. She so hated Líthgen it might please her to let the tapestry disintegrate. In the evening I found her in the Altar Room, kneeling in prayer. She was patting her tears. Stephen le Poer would be here soon, she told me, and she would have to serve her best wine to the conniving backbiter. Why, she asked, had he not insisted on riding out with Sir Arnold, as a real knight would've done? If he had, he might've died, too, and her Will would've been elected. That Stephen was seneschal of all Kilkennie instead of her son – oh, it was dreadful.

She started to cry. 'And now my son announces he's in love!'

Will, she went on, wouldn't agree to marry. He was a fool for some silly manservant. And, worse, he was insisting he had no interest in moneylending and never would. Alice had demanded he come to the house that very evening.

'I'll have a daughter-in-law, if it kills me.'

I listened for a while, wondering how long she would go on for. When she finally paused and began to dry her face, I explained about the tapestry and requested her permission to mend it using her gold yarn. Alice looked at me as if I were mad.

'Since when did you need permission?'

Since I fell out of favour, and my daughter became your lady's maid, I could've said, but I didn't want to delay. I could almost feel the tapestry coming undone.

'Try the ivory chest in my anteroom,' she said, 'the one with nightingales.'

She unhooked a loop of keys from her belt and sat up on to the pew with a long sigh.

I found the yarn in the white chest along with all the other threads, beads, sequins, cuffs and collars. I had the skein of gold thread in my hand when I noticed the other trunk, old and black, ribbed with brass bands and covered in tiny symbols. It might hold my amber beads. It was a chest that Alice guarded closely, where she kept her most personal mementos. I began to test the keys. The smallest one opened the lock.

Inside smelt of rosemary, tinctures and a dry sweet rot. It was brim-full with phials, jars, leather pouches, an engraved horn, minute relics wrapped in white linen and tied in black thread. I knelt and unwrapped one and found a fragment of bone. Beneath were small manuscripts full of suns and moons – miniature almanacs. A sheaf of parchment, scrolled tightly, was sealed with wax. A box held candles, dried yarrow, black ribbons, a gilt-handled dagger. Another contained phials of shimmering powder – my mistress's Spanish Fly. At the bottom of the chest lay a small parcel, the black fabric faded to violet in places. Inside was an ivory ring. A larger version of the one I kept beneath my mattress. I lifted it up. It was inscribed, as I knew it would be, with one of the few written words I knew: *Bébinn.*

Otto wore it always.

I thought of what the old Flemish burgess said, after Alice announced she was sole heir. *You made yourself so.* I realized then exactly what he had meant. I knew it in my gut when I first heard those words. I just couldn't bear to truly understand. I sat back on my heels, slipped the ring on to my finger. My heart beat so fast, I was afraid I might collapse. I never saw Otto ride out of Flemingstown. My mother said he never left at all, that he was already dead. 'He left at dawn,' Alice had said. Why had she lied? The ring on my finger had last been on his. I stroked the smooth cream bone. I don't know how long I sat there like that.

When I came to my senses, the room was the same, though everything had changed. The life Alice had here, everything she owned, everything she built – was because of Otto's death. If he had lived, he would've been the owner of all Jose Kytler possessed, not Alice. She had the ring he was wearing when last I saw him. Did she have a hand in his death? Did she take him from me, from his daughter?

Yes, I realized, she did. Alice had made herself Jose's sole heir.

The knowledge pressed into my chest, till all I could do was to try to breathe each breath. I found myself kneeling on all fours like a woman labouring.

Laughter came from downstairs, rare visitors. Stephen le Poer and one of his women. They were laughing about the accusations. 'Ale? Have some stew, some mutton? A drop of deadly nightshade? Some hemlock?' mocked Alice. The woman guffawed back. 'Yes, yes, Alice! Fill my cup, fill it up.' They laughed down there, as her husband lay dying. Poisoned, I had little doubt now, by Alice. I would go down and tell the new seneschal what I knew.

In my mind's eye, I could see it happen: their laughter stopping, her expression changing as I told what she had done to her brother, what she was doing now to Sir John. It would bring an end to her reign, an end she deserved.

I saw myself standing there in the hall, telling the truth, and I saw, too, that what I wished to happen, what should happen, would not. My word was worth nothing. I was a maid; she was a burgess. She would reveal that I was Irish, claim that I was mad. They might even laugh.

The phial of Spanish Fly lay on the floor beside me. It wasn't to blame, though – our master was not bleeding. Something else sickened Sir John, some strong root perhaps. I rummaged through the chest but found nothing fatal amongst the remedies and relics, just the keepsakes, charms and powders that any woman might own. I picked up the phial, turned it about. A thought dawned – what would Sir John know of potions or herbs? And with his fear of Alice, wouldn't he believe someone that others wouldn't? He would take me at my word. I stumbled like a drunk towards his chamber.

Sir John pulled himself up and sat leaning back against his pillows. I was panting a little and my voice shook as I held up the phial.

'I opened a chest of Alice's and found this poison, and other evil objects – I can show you.'

He rose slowly from the bed and followed, shaky on his legs as a drunk. Once there in the anteroom, he recoiled from the open chest.

'This is proof,' he said, 'that she is what they say; only a sorceress could possess such items. It is right, only right, you gave up your mistress. Maybe you, too, can be forgiven your sins and the part you have played.'

Part I played? I played no part. I should've left then; I should've taken my daughter and left, even if I had to pull her through the streets of Kilkennie by her hair. But I didn't. I just stood there. Because I wanted Alice Kytler punished.

'We must bring word of this to the bishop. No one but he will dare stand against your mistress.'

With that, at least, I agreed.

'I must do one thing,' I said, 'and then we'll go.'

I left John to dress himself and went to find my daughter.

I didn't have to look far; Líadan was down the corridor in Alice's chamber. Her head was veiled; she wore her mistress's gown and sat at her desk. I told her quickly that Alice had been poisoning Sir John; that she must pack, for we would leave tonight. The rest, I would tell later, when I had more time. Líadan looked at me and released a long sigh. Here she was, my skin, bones and blood, sutured into a merchant lady's life, with ink on her fingers, showing only disdain for her mother. I would tell her the full truth. She wouldn't want to spend another night in this place once she knew. Just as I opened my mouth, Alice and Will entered the chamber.

I turned and saw Alice as if for the first time, saw the bloodless creature that she was. The rustling of her skirts made my stomach turn. Something, my expression perhaps, made her spin around and leave the room. I followed at her heel. Once in the corridor, she kept walking. I grabbed her elbow and pulled her backwards.

'How could you?' I whispered.

'How could I what?' Alice stepped close, close enough to kiss me.

I held up Otto's ring. She shrugged as if it were nothing, meant nothing.

'You seem unwell,' she said.

'I know the truth, I know it, and so soon will she.'

I pointed towards the door behind which my daughter sat: a living imitation of the woman who had disposed of her father. Alice's face remained a mask: even her eyes told nothing. It was her hands that gave her away. She kept a tight grip on her wrist, because another word from me, and she would've reached out and slapped my face. I felt afraid. That was the least of what she would do, if she knew my plan. If I didn't go now, I mightn't live long enough to carry it out.

39. Basilia

After my mother and Alice rushed out, Will and I were left alone. He was glad he'd lost the vote. He'd never wanted to be seneschal, he confessed; he'd prefer to travel, but, before he left on his adventures, he was going to avenge Sir Arnold's death by storming the bishop's house, kidnapping him and burning down the cathedral. Then everyone could be buried and there wouldn't be so many rats and such a stink about Hightown. Will jumped around, going through the different moves he could make with his dagger. He talked as if it were all happening in a distant land. He was very young to be a man.

'Look at you frown. You needn't worry; I'm not going to kiss you. I came only to please Mother.'

That wasn't what worried me. I was sad that my mother, of all people, believed the accusations against our mistress. The way she had looked at me, studying my clothing with scorn. She was accusing Alice, just like the twins, just like the bishop. Had nobody noticed that Helene was never out of Sir John's room, running back and forth from Hattons', smuggling parcels from his daughters? Whatever was wrong with Sir John, it was not my mistress's fault. I wouldn't do as Mother asked; I would not pack. She had brought me here, and here I would remain. Someone had to protect my mistress. Alice was not a poisoner, no matter what the bishop called her.

After Will left, I removed my outer surcoat and tried to untie the laces at the back of the gown but couldn't reach. I felt trapped. Why would anyone wear clothes they couldn't remove? I went to Alice's desk. If I could snip one lace, the rest might pull free. Her drawer was unlocked and slightly ajar. The summons was in there – I saw the edge of the scroll. I opened it out, but it was all in Latin. I couldn't read a word. I realized how very simple my lessons had been – I was no more 'learned' than a pup. I recognized some words on the page – Petronelle de Midia. I looked over the rest and read 'Alice Kytler'. I couldn't understand anything else.

Everyone believed that Alice alone had been charged with sorcery. If my mother knew this, she would be so frightened; she would've already fled. I understood then why my mistress did not tell – she could not bear us to leave. I put the scroll away. There was a decanter on Alice's desk. I tipped the bottle and swallowed a mouthful. It burned my throat, and everything it touched on its way down. I drank a quart more and then used Alice's knife to cut my laces free. I put on my own gown and fixed my girdle belt around my waist, checking that my poppet was tucked safe and snug in my purse.

Feeling queasy, I climbed on to Alice's bed and rested against her pillows. I didn't know how she could sleep so propped up. The room seemed to shift about me and then it stopped. My mother's name was on that summons. She should know to be careful. Where had she said she was going? Had she said? I lay back, making plans to set everything to right.

40. Petronelle

I was relieved to find Sir John dressed and waiting outside the door. He was leaning against the wall, chatting to Ulf as if it were any ordinary day. He winked at me and took my arm. He moved slowly – it took a long time to escort him up Low Lane. I kept looking back, worried Alice was going to appear. We finally got to the bishop's house, to be told he was over in the cathedral.

Friar Bede stood at Saint Canice's porch, his hands tucked into the sleeves of his frayed robe while John told him how I, Kytler's maid, had found poison in one of the dame's chests. He handed him the philtre of Spanish Fly.

'There was this, and much more,' said Sir John.

'Now we'll rid, rid, this town of Kytler,' said Bede. 'We'll destroy that house, wrench her –'

'The house is mine,' Sir John said, before limping off at a faster rate than I thought him capable of.

'Sir,' I called after him, but he didn't turn.

The twins appeared then and assisted their father. Each took an elbow, and they strode away together. I tried to follow them, but the monk caught my arm and steered me into the cathedral.

'Don't worry; I've heard you are devout,' he said.

He ushered me up the aisle and around the corner to where the bishop sat on his cushioned throne. His grey hair was swept back from his forehead. His eyebrows seemed to sweep, too, away from eyes that were deep-set, watery. Bede announced my presence.

'The maid Petronelle, your grace, from the house of Kytler, come to confess to the sorcery and poisoning there.' He handed the bishop the philtre.

'Begin, my child,' said Ledrede.

The way he said 'my child' felt like a knife grazing my skin. And what did Bede mean? I had spoken of no sorcery. Oh, why did I run to Sir John and say what I said? Why did I not just take my daughter and leave this place?

'Begin,' he insisted.

'I was wrong, mistaken. I don't know what came over me.'

'The Blessed Mother, Holy Virgin, came over you. She is here now, urging you to continue on the path you were on when you first spoke, when you first told of the great wickedness of that viper, which you revealed like a true Christian. Our Lady is looking after you; can you feel her, child, feel her close to you?'

From the tall glass windows of the cathedral I did indeed feel light and heat travelling over my shoulders, up my neck and over my head, till my crown tingled. If I did not speak, no one would. Alice would go unpunished and another man would die. I didn't claim Spanish Fly had sickened Sir John, for I didn't believe it had. I simply told the bishop about the philtre, and how I found it in my mistress's possession.

When I had finished speaking, the bishop raised his hand. Bede reappeared by his side and without a word led me to a small room at the back of the cathedral. For some reason, I thought he was going to give me food and drink. He didn't follow but bolted the door behind me. There was a window high up in the wall, stained in blue and red. It was round and let some light in; and then less, and less. I stood as if I were a statue, I did not move, and I did not stop watching the painted glass. If I did nothing, barely breathed and kept perfectly still, maybe nothing else would happen, nothing bad.

I led my thoughts nowhere but on to the red glass, and then the blue, as they both darkened. I closed my eyes and breathed in the dry air and listened to the crows outside, and to the slap of leather against tile, coming closer and closer, and then to the metal bolt drawing back and the door opening and the same monk saying, 'You may leave – it is done.'

I ran through the dusk, and as I passed through Irishtown gates, the watchman cried out as if I were a phantom. I made my way up the town, hearing only my breath, my feet on the ground. When I got there, Kytler's was guarded by armed monks. Relieved they hadn't seen me, I moved near the wall, where the shadows were darkest. Where was Ulf? What had happened? Torches appeared at the far end of the lane and moved closer. 'Le Poer,' muttered one of the monks. They all lifted their daggers and surged towards the townsmen. I didn't wait to see what happened, but slipped forward and pushed at Kytler's door.

There was no one in the hall, but the fire blazed. The pup whimpered from the alcove. The board and benches had been overturned. Everywhere there were wooden crosses, tacked to the walls, the beams, the nooks. The tapestry lay in two halves, as if sliced by a sword. I thought of the thread that had led to the chest and to the ring. I ran upstairs and checked every room, then down to the kitchen, down further into the cellar. There was no one home, they had taken everyone – they had taken my daughter.

I went through the kitchen and out the back. I crossed the stable yard and the orchard, running towards the black square that was the Hattons' house. Yells came from Low Lane, as the monks and the townsmen disputed who had the most right to guard Kytler's. I tried the Hattons' back door, beat it hard, but none there answered. When I went to the window, the shutter slammed. I heard Lucia's cluck, her lap-dog's yap, and then there was silence. I noticed that the quarrelling in the lane had stopped. There was a strange quietness, as if there'd been a hue and cry and everyone had left.

On arriving on to High Street, I saw the crowd. They filled the road all the way down to the Tholsel. As I neared, some turned to look. They stared as if I were someone unknown.

'What's happening?' I touched an ale wife's arm.

'Kytler's sect were seized and taken to the Castle Gaol.'

I moved swiftly away. The bishop's voice carried from outside the Tholsel; he was on a plinth. The crowd quietened when he spoke. His message spread from one person to another. Alice Kytler and her sorceresses were imprisoned, so now, at last, the interdict could be lifted. Cries of joy, and caps were flung up in thanks. Heaven's gates were open again to the people of Kilkennie; all they had to do now was testify!

I walked against the crowd, shivering with cold. The whole household had been taken because of me, because of what I had said. The bishop took my words, and added to them the ones he wanted to hear. Even had she done it, there was no sorcery to tipping poison into a wine cup. But there was poison in that house, I was sure of that. I thought of the taster boy. That child had drunk Sir John's wine, eaten from his plate – and now no trace of him could be found. He might be dead. Gaol was the best place for my mistress, however she had worked her evil. When I reached Stephen le Poer's house, their servant Catherine answered. She shooed me away before I'd uttered a word. Everyone was busy, she said, no one could be disturbed.

'Sir William's mother has been imprisoned.'

She relented and opened the door. Will and his manservant were pacing the hall, arms around each other's shoulders, hats askew. One might've been holding up the other, but it wasn't apparent which. The servant called Will over. The men veered in our direction. Their lips and teeth were wine stained.

'Tell the master what you just said.'

'Sir William,' I said, bowing, 'your mother has been gaoled by the bishop.'

Will laid his head on his serving man's shoulder, half smothering a guffaw.

'Mother in a cell – how peculiar. I'd like to see her expression. I'd wager it's quite sour!'

'My daughter was taken, too.'

'Basilia?'

Sir Stephen entered then with some of the Greater Twelve. There was a fresh cut under his eye. He took one look at me.

'Yes, yes,' he said, 'I know – the bastard arrested Alice.'

'Were my uncle still alive, he would not have dared.'

I stepped aside with the servant, and we stood with our backs to the wall. We remained silent. Stephen shook a smirking Will by the arm.

'He's telling the crowd he'll burn Alice for witchcraft.'

'Unheard of,' said Will.

My throat went dry; could there be truth in that? No, no one would allow it. The men sat around the table discussing the situation. Stephen and his men had secured Kytler's but Ledrede had gained an advantage: the interdict had turned the town against Alice. There were many who would now take the bishop's side in this. Stephen didn't seem overly sorry that Alice had been arrested. It was all about Ledrede. If he were seen to overrule them in this matter . . . well, they would have as much authority *as that wench over there*. They all glanced over at me.

I wanted to grab Stephen and beg him to free my daughter.

They needed to see the bishop's papers, Stephen decided; the arrests probably weren't legal. His men nodded in agreement.

'A bribe will change the bishop's mind,' one said, 'quicker than any negotiation.'

Will, who had quickly sobered, decided to go straight to the gaol. Sir Stephen left shortly after him. When they'd gone, the other men discussed how Stephen was faring as seneschal. He compared poorly with Arnold, but was made from finer cloth than Will. They speculated on Alice, if she really was a magician; it was only what had long been suspected. The men imagined what a witch would be like in bed. 'Greedy,' one said, and they all laughed. Catherine glanced at me and nodded towards the back door.

'The bishop will excommunicate anyone who shelters a –'

'I'm going,' I said.

I had barely stepped from the house when I was seized. Fingers snagged and scratched at my person, my wimple was torn, and my hair tugged till I feared my head would come off. *Sorceress*, they said, *sorceress, heretic, witch.*

41. The Bishop's Court

The court was crowded. The people of the town were, finally, eager to talk and braced the cold in droves. A boy was testifying. Known as Morris from Wales, he had seen the mute transform spittle into pearls and let them spill from her mouth. She did this to enchant him, but the boy was not so easily seduced. A young scribe at the bishop's left-hand side was there to record proceedings.

'A mouth that turns fruit to gold, what powerful alchemy, what witchcraft,' said the bishop. 'Make note of that.'

Margaret Dun, a commoner, stepped forward. Whatever about Alice, she said it was lunacy to claim Petronelle de Midia had relations with a demon. Said demon stood as much chance of getting under those skirts as the king of England himself, which was no chance at all – not that it was skirts the king of England was after. There was laughter amongst those listening, but the bishop was not amused. 'Get thee from here,' he said, and ordered the tramp to be put in stocks.

Beatrice and Cristine, stepdaughters of the dame, were next before the bishop. Since they had the same appearance and spoke almost in one voice, Cristine being loquacious and her sister being timid, the bishop instructed that their testimony be recorded as that of one person. He instructed them to repeat for the court what one of them, Cristine, had told him in private.

The twins spoke of how their father, Sir John of Callan, wasted as if poisoned. How they heard Dame Alice chanting his name, then muttering a curse and spitting into the fire.

They had both seen poisonous powders prepared in her kitchen – her cook wore gloves to prepare them. An unknown fellow interrupted the proceedings, exclaiming that said sisters were harlots. The twins denied the accusation, proclaiming the dame must've cast a spell to make any man shout such falsehoods. The bishop noted aloud that the sisters did indeed wear copious jewels, immodest gowns and rouge their mouths.

He thought a while on it before countering that, whatever the sisters were, harlots or no, they had eyes and saw poisonous powders in Kytler's household. They were also witnesses to injuries done to Sir John by witchcraft. The sisters further testified that their father had become so ill he had lost his hair and nails. At this, they wept and declared, 'Dame Alice has killed our father.' Sir John interrupted to remind the court and his daughters that he was not as yet dead.

The bishop expressed his concern that the twins had not reported this sorcery from the outset. In fact, had they not resided in Kytler's and enjoyed the dame's hospitality until recent times? The sisters claimed that they had been frightened and weakened by the evil they witnessed in the house. The women there, they claimed, were very cruel to them. In their own words, 'Your lordship, you cannot put an ordinary maiden in with a nest of vipers, and not see her get bitten.' The bishop understood this to mean they had been inducted into the sect, and stated so for the record. The twins vehemently denied such a fact, and there was much decrying of innocence and holding up of the heavy crosses that had lain on their plump chests. The bishop decided the sisters should be detained in Kilkennie Castle Gaol. The twins' unholy screaming on hearing this confirmed the bishop's suspicions. They were taken from the court, their father hobbling behind them on crutches.

*

Ledrede detested screeching; it did terrible things to him. That anchoress had screamed non-stop when she first arrived. A thought came then, a childish one: that on meeting her maker, the anchoress told tales; told what he had done. *Ledrede in his nightshirt, crouching outside the cell window, and on seeing the woman . . .* No. Ledrede chastised himself. That he, with his fine mind, should entertain such a notion! A sinner like her would never see the face of God. She was somewhere else entirely. Getting her there had been far from easy. He had transferred the old nun who fed and watered her to the Leper House. Townspeople were kept away, told she was abstaining for a special petition. One young man had proved a pest, tapping at the stone cell, calling her name. He could tap all he wanted. Ledrede had blocked both apertures himself – first the one in the altar wall, then the one in the outer wall. It was a fitting end for a nun famed for her veneration of fasting. *Being dead to this world and being dead – is there really such a difference?* That's what he had asked her. The scratch she'd made in the centre of his palm still festered.

42. Basilia

I had fallen asleep in my mistress's chamber and dreamt the dream I'd been dreaming all summer. It began as always with soft rustlings, footsteps on the stairs, but then it grew louder, and pewter clattered; frantic whispers were replaced by sharp screams. I woke to find Friar Manchin, devout of mouth, sure of thumb, pressing my arms, my shoulders, my breast bone. 'Have you a heart at all?' he mocked, before dragging me from the bed and down the stairs.

Alice was in the hall, being held by a slight but muscled bald man. I ran over to her. Helene and Esme were huddled together; the monk beside them waved a dagger every time they moved. Bede was there, too; he watched as his men smashed the trestle board and lifted the swords from the wall. Ulf was bent over, his hands clamped over a wound on his thigh. There were faces at the window, people gawping in.

'We have a warrant for your arrests, sealed by Sir Arnold,' said Bede.

'You have no such thing. Arnold is dead.'

'He saw sense before the end.'

'Never, it is forged. The bishop did this.'

'More heresy from the witch!' said Bede.

Two men began hauling Alice's black chest down the stairs, banging it on each step.

'That is my property, give that back! It is not yours to take!'

'Its contents will condemn you,' said Bede. 'Come, we are taking you to the gaol.'

'I'll not move.'

'Then you will be trussed, and carried like a hog.' The bald man patted the thick rope around his hips.

'No, no,' Alice said. 'I'll come willingly. I will walk. We all will.'

We were led down through High Street to the Castle Gaol. People followed on each side. The boy Milo appeared and ran towards Alice, tugging and tugging at her cloak. 'I want what's owed to me,' he said. 'I want what's owed.' One of the men pulled him away, laughingly saying that he had come far too late. The people jeered as we passed, pointing at Helene's torn gown. Alice moved slowly with her head high, staring at something no one else could see. Did she always walk like that? Was Helene's expression always so shameless? Did Esme always hobble so? It didn't matter what we did, or what we were, when our every movement declared us strange.

At the Castle Gaol, we were met by a white-haired constable. 'Such distinguished guests,' he said to Alice, who merely nodded.

The door shut behind us and the crowd quietened. A voice rose, clear and haunting. Margaret Dun was keening. We were led down a narrow passage, and steep steps that I thought would never end. When they did, I was pushed into a cell and Alice was ordered to join me. It was small and dank, a square space with a tiny window. The gaoler shut the gate and locked it.

'Your maid has just been arrested,' he said to Alice. 'Soon your whole household will be behind bars.'

Poor Mother, all alone. At least the rest of us were together. Outside, the keening carried on, a torn voice that rose and fell, as if Margaret were stumbling from high ground to low in blind despair. Such grief for us, it was terrifying. Just then,

Cristine and Beatrice strode past our cell, walking so near each other that their cloaks mingled as one. A gaoler marched close behind them. So the sisters, too, had been arrested, after all the accusations they themselves had thrown.

My mistress put her arm through mine, but did not speak. I patted my pouch; it held only a smooth stone and my poppet, nothing to aid our escape. Snow began to fall outside; it filled the window with a blue-white light. The song kept on. I closed my eyes and imagined my mother as if she were here, reaching through the bars. 'Líadan,' she said, grasping my hand. All those times she spoke my name and I refused to answer. Again came the sorrowful verse, and with it the piercing cold, and Alice turned to invite me under her cloak.

43. Petronelle

They threw me to the ground. The air tasted of clay, like that from a pit, a grave. I heard a gate shut, then further away another, then, fainter still, another. I looked up. Helene was crouching in the corner of the cell. Though tear-stained, the maid's face was unmarked.

'Where were you, when they came for us?' she asked.

'What have they done with my daughter?'

The wretch didn't answer, just turned away and folded herself tighter. I checked my girdle: my purse was gone, but my knife remained. I knelt alongside the maid and pressed the blade against her flushed cheek. The dull steel brightened. The vain thing whimpered.

'Where is my daughter?'

'With Alice, in another cell.'

I went to the gate and called out. A gaoler came, a wiry bald man. When I asked to be put with Líadan, he thrust a stick through the bars and sent me flying into the corner. 'It's not an inn,' he snarled.

Retching with pain, I stayed there. Helene held her silence, but watched my every move. As time passed, the light from the high window became weaker and weaker. A shadow fell. I looked upwards and glimpsed leather boots: a watchman was on patrol. We must have been put in the lowest cells, the dungeon. I heard hoofs clop across the cobbles. Voices came from outside – a question, a quick laugh. I couldn't hear what the rider said to the watchman, but it was the bishop who had spoken, I was sure of that. I looked to

Helene, but she just glared, eyes narrow with accusation. *Where were you, when they came for us?*

'It's All Hallows' Eve, you know,' she said, as our cell darkened. 'The night the dead return to earth.'

'If that were true, there wouldn't be room to move.'

I was glad when she rested her head on her arms and closed her eyes. After some time, her breathing slowed and she slumped sideways. How could she sleep in a place like this? I couldn't, not while my daughter was out there, in some other cell. A terrible grief rose in my chest. We were trapped in the stone burrows of the Castle Gaol, accused of dark arts, together yet apart.

As the night passed, I began to shiver. It became colder and colder. I looked over at Helene, but could not bring myself to huddle close for warmth. Sometime before dawn, I heard a strange sound – something swinging back and forth. A dull clink-clank, clink-clank, clink . . . and then it ceased, like the tongue of a bell stopped by a hand. The silence hung like an unanswered question.

SAMHAIN

———

NOVEMBER

A certain pyx was found containing ointment with
which a beam of wood called a cowltre was anointed.
When it had been so anointed Alice and her
followers were able to be carried wherever in the
world they wished to go without let or hindrance.

Annales Hiberniae

44. Basilia

My head rested on someone's chest, someone who was limping. His tunic reeked of onions and smoke, his neck was stubbled. He groaned with each step. A figure with a torch led us – he looked like Sir Stephen, had his height, his swagger. We travelled swiftly through a dark passageway. I glimpsed shadows behind us, a small group shuffling forward. I made out Alice's shape amongst them. There were many small figures – children? Was that my mother, coming after? I wriggled to be set free. The man looked down: his heavy-lidded eyes were kind, but he shook his head and tightened his grip. I recognized him then: Ulf. My ear rested against his heart – it beat fast; the hollow beneath his Adam's apple was beaded with sweat. At the back of my skull, a sharp pain came and went. I tried to recall what had happened, but I couldn't.

After, we passed through an arched gate. Our route became straight and the way sloped steeply upwards. I began to suspect that we were under High Street; that up there, above our heads, traders, barrow boys and wives were treading the streets, setting up their wares. We turned off into a passageway that narrowed towards a studded black door. Stephen, for that's who it was, unlocked it. We entered and saw steps, no more than a ladder. They led to a wooden trap-door above. At last, Ulf dropped me to my feet. My legs were numb.

Alice entered aided by Stephen. I pushed past her into the passage. There was no one there. Ulf pulled me inside and shut the door. There was only Alice, Ulf and I, and Stephen, who was already at the top of the steps, pushing frantically at the trapdoor. When it eased open, my mistress sighed with relief. Was it possible the door might've been sealed against her?

Where were the others I had seen? Where was my mother? I turned to Alice.

'Your mother is safe; she will join us soon.'

'Hurry,' Stephen urged, looking down. 'They'll have discovered you gone by now. The bishop wants you executed.'

'The people would never let that happen.'

'They let this happen, didn't they?'

Alice began to climb the ladder. She made slow progress. Ulf climbed up, and I began to follow. I finally reached the top step, and the giant caught my wrists and hauled me upwards.

I recognized the barrels, bladders of wine, the wall of furs, the trestle table covered in ornaments, jugs and candlesticks. I was standing in Alice's Pledge Room. We were in Kytler's once again, but we were not alone: the constable of Kilkennie Castle Gaol was warming his hands over a brazier that had been set up. I was frightened till I realized that no one else was. Another man, wearing Le Poer livery, stood by the wall. It was colder here than below, despite the brazier.

I ventured towards the door, but Stephen pulled me back. 'Stay away from the cellar door. Quiet as a mouse, you understand?'

I nodded. That I could do.

'Is my husband up there?' asked Alice.

'I've spent the night rescuing you,' said Stephen. 'I wouldn't know.'

Alice put a heavy cloak with a furred cowl over my shoulders and gave me a tumbler of spiced wine. Then she loosened the strings on her purse and joined the constable. She counted coins into his hand. She hesitated then. A strange surge of spite rose within me, against the flounced cuffs at Alice's thin wrists, the tight grip she had on her money, the rings that bulged beneath her grey gloves.

Realizing I was squeezing my purse, I released my grip. It would not do to damage the poppet. I should've made one for my mother. Her name was on that summons. Why had I not made something to protect her, too? Soon she'd come through the trapdoor. I would hug her then, I would speak, say anything she wanted me to. I would find Jack for her. The constable listened at the cellar door before pulling back the bolt and climbing up the steps. The candle flames wavered as he left.

45. Petronelle

By daybreak, the window was a square of trembling white. Snow. Helene unfolded, stood up on her toes, stretched her arms and rubbed her eyes. There was some commotion down the corridor. She pushed her head between the bars of the gate, trying to peer out. Her cap fell off. With her black mane part plaited and part wild, she took on the appearance of someone wanton, someone easily guilty of the accusations thrown at us. I was about to reprimand her, when the gaoler rushed past, red-faced.

'Kytler and the girl are gone!'

We heard horses in the courtyard outside, hounds barked and horns were blown. The hue and cry had been raised. *The witches have flown, make haste.* I knelt on the floor and opened my arms in prayer for my daughter. The bishop's men would be merciless. 'Blessed Virgin, help her, help her run far, then further.'

'Sorcery!' Helene cried. 'They used sorcery to aid their escape!'

'The only magick at work was Kytler's silver.'

'Tell me' – she stepped in front of me – 'why didn't you go, too? Why didn't you fly?' She flapped her arms. 'Or do you love it here? Do you love being wretched? Does it bring you glory?'

'I can no more leave than you can.'

'Aha! But you can. Alice could, your daughter could. You, you chose to stay. You're pleased by humiliation, you always were, praying, sanctimonious Petronelle, with your plain gowns and your plain face, and your hands . . . look at them, still stained! You want people to see you've been dying cloth, knowing they'll say – oh, shame, the dame makes a lackey of her lady's maid!'

To be so misunderstood, and by a girl I once pitied. If there was any witch it was her, her eyes shining, her mouth swollen. I knew what she would do, how she would save herself if she had to. Helene sat cross-legged then, spinning the rat-tails of her hair, casting frequent glances in my direction.

I was thirsty but didn't dare call for the gaoler again. He came soon enough anyway, pointing his stick at me.

'You're to be moved after all.'

He chose a large key from his ring and sprang the heavy lock; the gate drew an arc through the earth as it opened. Helene began to croon, her voice low and hoarse – *Winter's day, and rough is the weather.* I stepped into the corridor and watched as the gaoler relocked the cell. There were boils on his neck. He turned and, prodding me with his stick, drove me down a long passageway. We stopped at a gated chink in the wall, and he pushed me. The cell was so narrow I could stretch out and touch the wall on each side. The gaoler hooked the key-ring on to his girdle, and winked. I watched him saunter off. He had some brawn, but was narrow. Why had I let myself be driven like a biddable animal? I could've grabbed his keys, knocked him to the ground, but where to then? I remembered the rough hands that had lifted me into the air. How my hair was pulled from every direction and nails dug into my wrists, my neck. There was nowhere to go. They would tear me apart like a hawk does its prey.

46. Hightown

The crowd outside the gaol was getting larger, swelling with nobles and annalists from all the kingdoms of Ireland. All waiting for a glimpse of the notorious witch, Dame Alice Kytler. Then they heard – Kytler had vanished. How could that be true? Why, they had seen her pass along this very road and enter the prison. The crowd, who had taunted her servants, merely stared at the dame. Her velvet hood was edged with fitchet; the creamy yellow fur was packed about her face as if it were porcelain. It was hard to believe such a woman had led a sect, made sacrifices to demons, bewitched husbands, poisoned them even. She took her maid's daughter with her. How on earth had they escaped? Did her demon lover rescue them both?

They remembered the girl, a mute. She had stumbled behind the dame in a daze, looking over her shoulder, as if expecting someone to follow. Her mother, most like. *Petronelle.*

Petronelle had avoided capture at first, but they soon found the wretch at the back of the seneschal's house. The townsmen tied her wrists. The women tore off her veil, pulled her hair loose and sliced her purse. She had kicked and kicked as they carried her to the gaol. Later, the children searched the ground for ribbons or coins – but all they found were pins, so many pins.

47. Petronelle

Melted snow ran in rivulets from the window-ledge above my head. Driven by thirst, I pressed my tongue into a crevice, let my mouth fill and swallowed. Grabbing the jutting stone, I sought purchase with my foot, tried to hoist myself towards the window, but kept slipping. The wall was slick as marble. Suddenly they were there, at the window, their voices dripping into the cell. 'Shame, shame on you,' they said. 'Turn, turn, show your face,' they urged. Some recited the Pater Noster or evoked the saints – by Kieran, by Patrick, and by Brigid, they condemned me. I curled tight. Some threw snow, some pelted stones. The guard's boots replaced their hands, and I was left in peace.

I soon heard a gate clash, voices rise and fall, a silky rustling. Bishop Ledrede appeared with a clutch of monks behind him. The hem of his embroidered robe was sluiced in muck. When last we'd met, I'd knelt at the foot of his throne and he had seemed as solid and powerful as a statue. Standing outside my cell, he was shorter than I, and swamped by his ornate robes. I thought of a servant trying on costumes while his master was away. It was a mistake not to be afraid, I reminded myself; this man had taken my liberty.

He blessed himself and began to recite . . . *Ave Maria, gratia plena, Dominus tecum. Benedicta tu in mulieribus, et benedictus fructus ventris tui* . . . It would become his habit not to speak until he had recited a Hail Mary. I didn't know it then, but it was his means of protecting himself, from me – the woman he kept caged, whose skin he would break. He cleared his throat and took a step forward, gripping the bars. I stared at his white knuckles, the large ring with a purple stone, the fingers as ink-stained as my mistress's.

'Where are Kytler and the girl? How did they conjure their escape?'

Conjure. If I knew how to conjure, would I be here?

'I don't know where they are. Please have mercy on my daughter.'

'Those who cast their lot in with Satan must suffer the consequences. There'll be no mercy.'

'Your lordship, she's an innocent girl –'

The bishop pounded his crozier.

'Innocent? A practitioner of evil alchemy cannot be innocent. She and your mistress transformed and escaped this gaol.'

There were easier ways to gain release: for a woman like Alice, everything could be bought. The bishop must know that, yet he ranted on, insisting there was magick to it. He claimed that I, too, possessed the power to change.

'Confess,' he insisted, 'to your magickal crimes.'

'I've nothing to confess.'

'The rest of your household had plenty, ignorant heretics that they are. You, though, you're more cunning, aren't you? I see it would not be wise to let you journey to court. You'll be interrogated here, in the gaol.'

What had they confessed to, what had they said? The bishop left and all followed except one: a monk who began to tie a sign to the gate. His hands were big, his fingers thick and chilblained. He worked in haste and avoided my gaze.

The sign curled up after he'd left – a length of parchment crammed with lines. Whatever it declared, it was not the truth. 'Let me see the mouth moving whence these words have come.' My voice echoed over my head, and I looked up: there were fathoms between me and the roof.

As the sun set, the bars in the window cast their shadows into my cell. They stretched across the ground, across my body. My feet became misshapen – I could almost see them split, see them cleave into hoofs as the shadows cut me in two. I retreated into the corner, my own person suddenly seeming strange, uncanny.

I realized then that my gown was ripped and the thin linen of my smock showed through. I reached up – my veil was gone. All the time I'd been judging Helene wretched, I'd been as bad, worse. My sleeves hung open from the elbow, most of the buttons torn off. No one had taken my knife, but they would. I undid the buckle of my girdle belt, hoisted my gown and smock upwards. I fastened the belt and knife about my waist and tugged the clothes down over them. I loosened the side lacing on my gown, not caring that my smock showed through the gaps. The slack shape of my dress would hardly be noticed, not when I was in such a state. The bishop's gaze, I noticed, never fell far below my face, though he had glanced once or twice at my throat as he recited his Ave.

When it was dark, a figure approached my cell. A different gaoler, he had a long beard, stocky shoulders. He knelt and without a word began to push something under the gate. A parcel of some sort. I crept forward and grabbed his wrist; he could've pulled away, but he didn't.

'Please,' I whispered, 'release me, like you did the others.'

'I didn't aid those women. I'm locked in, too, at least till morning, when the constable opens the outer door.'

He nudged the package forward. It was warm: a stone from his fire wrapped in rags. 'Thank you,' I said, but he had already gone.

The wind whistled through the window and soft blasts of snow floated down. It dusted the floor, my shoulders and arms. If the gaoler did not release Líadan and Alice, how had they escaped? Stupid with tiredness, I knelt there, crystals melting on my gown. I held the warm stone close, my fingers aching as they thawed. The snow blew in, over and over. I might die a woman of ice, frozen in prayer. Would they call me witch then? Yes, they would call me witch no matter what.

After some time, I heard the gaoler snore, smelt the spice of wood smoke from his fire. What was the noise I had heard last night? Was it a gate opening? Was it the wind? Maybe it was nothing? Yet, at sometime during the night, my daughter and Alice had escaped. I had presumed a simple bribe, the night gaoler turning the key, guiding them through the passage, releasing them into Hightown, but I was wrong. What if the words of the bishop were the truth of what happened? What if all I ever believed was wrong, and all I was accused of, was right? I imagined my mistress and my daughter in their cell that night – Alice with her hands clasped, praying. My girl leaning close, her lips in silent movement.

As if by unspoken agreement, they begin to softly chant, chant words that are strange yet familiar, as if all the tongues of Hightown – Welsh, Irish, English and French – are mixed together into a gentle gibberish. My girl pulls down her hood, unties her plaits and releases her hair. Alice does the same with hers. Their hair flows down, covering their bodies, darkening their shape. The vision ripples as if water flows through it. Shards of colour, the blue of Alice's cloak, the red of my daughter's hair, the black of their skirts, rush towards and away from each other. Then it stills, rinses clear, and the cell is dark and empty.

That couldn't be what happened, could it? It couldn't. I was being driven mad by fear, cold and hunger. I wanted this night over, for light to come, yet I dreaded dawn and the people returning to the window. Those same people had carried me to this place; their hands had reached out and torn my clothes. They thought me diabolical, yet wanted to touch me.

Had I been, unwittingly, diabolical? I was not always good. I remembered preparing Alice for her marriage with scented oils, satin ribbons; then, sated from the feast, lolling in my chair, entranced by the best harpist in all the kingdoms. As Kjarval's tune strummed my blood, I forgot about those outside our door, people suffering as I once had, starving as they waited three long days for our leavings. And, worse, much worse than any of that, I had held a knife to my own daughter's neck. Maybe this, my punishment, had always been coming.

Dawn came and a guard's boots appeared for a time outside the window. Women bickered nearby. I recognized Cristine, Beatrice and Esme. I heard Helene, too. The voices came from the end of the corridor. They fought, tried to make sense, to apportion blame. Often I heard my name.

The noise ceased. I looked up at the high window. No guard. No taunting faces. Snow was still falling. I squinted till the bars looked like distant trees. I thought of the woods of my childhood and suddenly longed to return to them. Skirts rustled, someone let out a soft sob. Then, one by one, they moved like ghosts past my cell – Helene, Cristine, Beatrice and Esme. Each had a large yellow cross, roughly cut and stitched to her front; each looked at the ground.

They were gone. A gate clanged, a heavy door ground shut. They were gone. I was now the only one of the accused left in Kilkennie Castle Gaol. I leant against the bars. I was imperfect, flawed, but not this thing they kept calling me, not that.

*

The gaoler opened the gate, and Ledrede stepped inside – checking first that it wouldn't swing closed. What did he think might happen, if he and I were shut in together?

'It's a saving, you know,' he said, 'this halting of your sinful life.'

He studied me. I didn't know what to say.

'You're dark, for a Fleming.'

A Fleming. I thought of my father, his golden hair caked in blood, his lids stitched shut. I didn't answer. What could I say? Yes, I am dark for a Fleming, and you are evil for a man of God. As Ledrede unrolled his parchment, a boy scribe entered with his head lowered. His shaved skull gleamed with sweat despite the cold.

'Dame Kytler and your daughter – where are they?'

'If only I knew.'

'But you do! You must.'

'I don't.'

'Note that the creature does not cry or show any remorse, and is bold in her denial.'

The boy inscribed his tablet. I remembered my daughter, sitting by Alice's best-lit window, frowning as she learnt to write her letters. I realized suddenly that Alice had left me behind on purpose, to stop me telling Líadan who had killed her father.

'Who aided Kytler's escape?'

'I do not know.'

'You do – it was her incubus.'

'I never heard of such a being.'

'You sat beneath the demon's likeness every Sunday.' Ledrede came close, bent his head near mine and whispered, 'You adored him in the cathedral by day, and watched him writhe over your mistress by night. You prepared the way; took said Robin's snake in your mouth to ready him for your mistress.'

The scribe's arm stopped moving and he stared at me. I was startled to realize it was Ralph, his black hair shaven off. To think that raw boy had tricked us all.

'Answer!'

'None of that is true. I don't know such a man.'

'Man, she calls him! A demon, it was, who had carnal knowledge of your mistress, and well you know it, for who else wiped his seed from the sheets?' He turned to the boy. 'They do that, did you know? Steal seed.'

I blessed myself.

'She makes the sign of the cross at the mention of her demon lover. What kind of a woman are you?'

'An ordinary woman who knows nothing of what you speak.'

'You're no ordinary woman, you're a monster.'

'This is sinful, and against God, the things you say –'

'Against God?' He crouched, held his parchment next to my face. His ring was a big milky amethyst. 'This is God's work. Everything I say has been sanctioned by the Holy Father, Pope John, sanctioned in turn by Our Lord, God in Heaven. Look . . .' He dug his gem into my nape, pushed my face against the curling page. 'This,' he said, 'is Latin, the only clean weapon against inclement women.'

The manuscript was scratched with letters. I saw the pores of the skin, bristles where it hadn't been smoothened clean. He snatched it away.

I kept my head bent as he left. The padlock clanged against the bars. What the bishop said about Alice, fornicating with a devil, to think such a thing. And for him, a holy man, to speak freely on such matters. An incubus . . . how does a demon travel from the depths of Hell and step into our world? Does he come with luggage and horses, does he roar at the town gate to be let in, the way they say Ledrede did?

I wrapped my arms about my knees and gazed at the window. Snow continued to fall outside. I stared till the black bars became trees, like the trees a girl in a brown cloak once slipped between – leaves crunch beneath her feet as she walks into the forest. I watch her. It has not yet happened, all that will happen – a rounding stomach, banishment, a sackcloth soaked red, a new-born child's mewl. The girl hesitates. 'Onwards,' I whispered, 'it must be, all of it.'

48. Market Square, Hightown

The moneylender's chest of magick was set by the bishop's feet. Three monks stood behind him, their torches already lit. They would burn the evil coffer when they were done with the public examination. First, he would lead a prayer to protect against the evil that lay within the chest.

Ledrede raised his crozier to command silence from the crowd. Sage was burned, candles lit, and the Lord invoked. No soul was safe while Kytler was still at large. They began a rosary. The bishop said the words, but his mind travelled elsewhere. Kytler's escape had him confounded. He had questioned the creature Petronelle. She denied all knowledge, but, when she looked up, her eyes glinted, and the devil shone from them. He was certain Fournier had never come across the likes of her. She knew where her mistress was – she must.

The bishop had examined the sorceress's cell but there was nothing of the women left, not a glove, not a scent. The window was out of reach, the bars too close even for a child to pass through. On a stone jutting from the wall, he found a bright hair. He wound it to a coil and tucked it away. Back in his rooms, he had pressed the strand into a piece of warm wax. 'What is the answer, how did you flee?' he whispered.

This escape of theirs – it had shown the whole town that the bishop spoke the truth: that their magick was powerful and that they and their sect must be stamped out. Bede touched the bishop's shoulder, bringing him back to the present – the prayers had come to an end and all were looking at him. Did she lurk amongst these people? He searched their eyes, for her pale ones. Was she here in disguise, gloating from the depths of the crowd? The bishop felt ill, dizzy. Those eyes – were they the moneylender's? No, nonsense.

'This is evidence of witchcraft of the highest order.'

With much ceremony, the chest was opened. The jars, relics and potions seemed small, harmless even. Bede crouched beside the chest. He wore gloves and picked up items with his fingertips. He lifted each object and named it, while his scribe recorded a list. Bede spoke faster than the bishop wished. It was more dignified to take one's time.

'A ra . . . rabbit's foot,' said Bede, 'a fox's tail . . .'

There was silence from the crowd, then a shuffling of feet. The bishop sensed some disappointment. These people did not recognize such implements as demonic. Then again, common people were superstitious; perhaps many of them possessed such items. He must translate. The bishop stepped forward and snatched the foxtail from Bede. He'd show them how evil could reside in the most mundane of items.

'A devil's girdle, to be strapped around the naked waist and used for transformation.'

There was something a little irreverent in the expressions of the women. What went on inside their heads and who had authority over it? He had heard of a woman using the arms of the Holy Cross to . . . a depraved image flew into his head. He blessed himself to exorcize it. Which of the wretches had flung such a sinful picture at him? Was it Kytler, was she here? No, no. She was not; she was probably pressed fast to her horse, galloping from Ossory.

The bishop wiped the sweat from his lip and took a set of rosary beads from the chest. 'Do not mistake these for proof of prayer; heretics use the tools of the good Christian to mock them, to usurp the power of the Church. They play with these, while conducting obscene rituals.'

They were stirring now, whispering; becoming uneasy. Bede handed the Spanish Fly to the bishop. He held up a philtre. 'The poison *she* fed to her husband, and most likely all her husbands before him.'

He had them then. They all gazed at the small flask in his hand. It was time. He nodded to the three monks; it was time to set light to the evil objects. Just as the first torch was about to touch the chest, a man stepped out of the crowd.

'You'll not burn that here!' he declared.

It was Sir Arnold's nephew, Stephen le Poer.

'This is not your jurisdiction,' he continued. 'It is mine and I order you to leave.'

Ledrede grabbed a torch from a nearby monk and set light to the chest. A fire burned for all to see, and the bishop himself threw into its flames all the evil items they had just displayed to the crowd. Someone grabbed his arm, jerked him around. Stephen le Poer pushed his nose close to the bishop's. 'You do not rule in Hightown, Lord Richard – that privilege was granted to the burgesses since time before memory. Move along, back to your own side of the gates.'

'This is a matter of faith –'

'Oh, be quiet! You've got rid of Kytler – are you not satisfied?'

'For all we know, she could be here still, lurking.'

'They were seen, two women fleeing on horseback at dawn, leaving the city and galloping south, no doubt towards the coast and a ship. Now let this matter drop and the citizens of Kilkennie rest.'

The bishop stepped away, nodding to Bede and his men to do likewise. He led them back towards Irishtown, still clutching the philtre. That would be kept as evidence. It must be cleansed first, seared of its evil – he would bless it, exorcize it. Had Le Poer spoken the truth – was Kytler riding south?

If so, Stephen wasn't as loyal to Kytler as his uncle. Of course, the bishop had almost forgotten: he had beaten her son for the position of seneschal. That would've displeased the dame greatly. There was no love lost there. The bishop would send some men south – two troops on good horses, one to New Ross, one to Waterford. He didn't hold much hope; he knew in his heart that his quarry was gone. He looked at the philtre of dark glass and realized all might not be lost.

49. Petronelle

It was dusk and snow blew through the bars. The bearded gaoler pushed old hides under the gate. He behaved kindly but spoke little. I thought of the gaolers as Day and Night. Night was kind; Day was cruel. The bishop was perverse. The outlandish things he accused me of – gaining power from underworld demons. Would I not use this power if I had it? After dawn, I saw the glimmer of candles, as Ledrede approached for another of his hateful inquisitions. After he said his Ave Maria, he began.

'It was *you* taught Dame Kytler magick, not the other way around.'

I closed my eyes, to save myself the sight of this man, with his foul notions. I pictured the orchard, could almost hear the drone from the hives. Chanting came then, from the crowd outside the gaol. I could not make out which prayer they recited. I opened my eyes.

'Witnesses say, and I say – it was you who taught Dame Kytler magick. You're the real witch, the mediatrix between her and the demon world.'

What magick had I to teach Alice? I recalled two girls kneeling, their heads close; sap on their fingers, small knives on the ground. One is whispering: 'You tie this ribbon as such, three times around the whitethorn branch, and with each winding say, "I bind my love to me this night, I bind my love and bind him tight." And then you tether it, like this, see?' 'I bind my love,' the other sang, 'I bind my love . . .'

'You conjured the demon Robin; he taught you all you know –'

'No demon taught me.'

'From whom, then, did you learn about evil and demons?' He bent and looked at me closely.

'From your sermons.'

'The devil is in her.' He grabbed my throat with both hands. 'He controls her tongue!'

'Stop, you will kill her.' Someone pulled the bishop off.

Released, I fell back, gasping for air.

'Come outside and speak to the people,' the same voice said. It was the gaoler. 'A crowd has gathered; they're becoming more and more raucous. This town is on the verge; it depends on you, Lord Bishop, whether it falls or is saved.'

From outside, the voices indeed rose up – yet it was no prayer they chanted but a demand. 'Bring out the sorceress.' Didn't the people know that Alice had escaped?

'Next time, you will confess.'

I heard the gates close behind the bishop, but could not rise from the floor. After a while, his voice carried down between the bars of the window. The real witch, he told the people outside the gaol, was Kytler's maid, not Kytler at all.

The night gaoler came, bringing a small almond pastry and a potent mug of spiced wine. At first, pain came with each swallow, but it soon eased. I was almost asleep when he returned to take the cup away. Later, much later, my head began to ache, a childish whispering filled the darkness, and shadows crept over my skin, small cold hands going *pat, pat, pat* . . . urging me to stand. As I rose from the floor, everything became hazy. The cell gate faded to a trace of itself, and I saw myself travel through it and past the empty cells. How different the gaoler seemed, slumped in sleep. I almost stopped to bid him farewell. The outer gate was shut, but one touch from my hand and it sprang back. The castle grounds were lit with snow. The door in the wall was ajar. Outside, the road was empty but for a hound guarding a chest. I stroked the hound and opened the lid. Inside lay a mantle of grey wolfskin. I lifted it out – it was heavy, full length, my length, so I shrugged it over my shoulders and pinned it closed. I smelt smoke, turned and saw a blaze further down the hill, in front of the Tholsel. The flames were orange, dancing low like those beneath a pot. Lantern joined lantern in the darkness as people made their way towards the bonfire, and gathered around it. I moved towards them. Light flickered across their animal masks, and behind carved-out eyes real eyes blinked. Gloved hands beckoned, welcoming me. A man reached out and caught my wrist. He wore a half-mask, his mouth was full, familiar – that I had tasted it once was all I could remember.

50. The Bishop's Quarters

Another missive had arrived from Fournier, confirming Ledrede's suspicions: Jacques was soon to be made cardinal. Referring to his own inquisition, he boasted that a skilled interrogator did not stoop to torture. The skilled interrogator he had in mind was, of course, his pious self. How easy to be sanctimonious when one had not been tested the way Ledrede had been tested. Since he had captured that creature, the bishop had been subjected to the most depraved visitations at night. A succubus, he was certain of it.

He rubbed his eyes as he read the rest of the letter. Jacques wrote that he was compiling a dossier; he was sure it would prove most invaluable. Ha! Invaluable indeed – time would tell whose records were of most value. And, speaking of value, it was time for Ledrede to claim his due. He smiled at the thought of the fine property in Low Lane with land stretching to the river, of Kytler's rumoured lands in Leix, her furniture, jewels, horses . . . not to mention the money; there must be hoards of it. There was just the matter of the sick man to oust. He, no doubt, would be glad to return to Callan to recover. The bishop had summoned Sir John to Irishtown, to speak privately of the matter.

Sir John stood in the bishop's room, his tossed dark-blond hair longer than it should've been. The scalp above his ears was bald. If the bishop didn't know better, he would have mistaken it for the Irish style. He wore no livery, neither Le Poers' nor Outlawes'. That pleased the bishop. The man appeared much stronger than before. The bishop commented as such.

'Being out of my wife's reach, my health has improved somewhat but I'm far from the man she wed.'

'Why didn't you do something before this?'

'I had no proof till the maid showed me that diabolical chest.'

'I've excommunicated Kytler for her crimes. This means her possessions will be seized – those items, property, land, livestock, household goods and personal artefacts she owned in her own right.'

'She was my wife, Ledrede; all she possessed, I now wholly possess.'

'You weren't married by any priest. I do not recall such a ceremony.'

'Oh, but we were. We swore our oath in front of a priest, and many witnesses. We kissed in the door of Saint Mary's Church. It was very sweet. And now, if you'll forgive me, my strength wanes.'

The bishop watched from his window as John walked down the path towards the arch. A barefoot woman with flaxen braids joined him. They embraced and continued down the lane together. The bishop's quarry had fled, and now a so-called dying knight had just deprived him of his spoils. All he had left after all this work was a maid in Kilkennie Castle Gaol who refused to confess.

51. Petronelle

The first lash knocked me to the ground. The next cut into my shoulder, tearing cloth and flesh. The bishop stood over me, chanting something in Latin. He brought the whip down again, and the blood ran warm.

'God can see,' I whispered, 'and his Holy Mother can see, that whip you wield, the skin you tear off a mother's back.'

He threw down his whip and shouted for me to confess, over and over. To tell him I was something I was not. That I would never do.

'Confess, Petronelle.'

'That is not my name,' I reminded myself. 'It's someone else he torments, and you are safe inside her, safe inside her. *Lollai, lollai, litil child, you are safe inside her.*'

Before dawn, the night gaoler came. He set down his light, opened a small clay crock and beckoned me to move closer to the bars. When I did, he bid me to turn around. He eased the shredded cloth away from my wounds and drizzled something over each cut. I recognized the scent of honey. He told me that his name was Anthony. I kept my head bowed as tears ran down my face. It was almost unbearable, this tenderness.

I said my thanks, and he nodded, shoved a cup under the gate and left me alone again. I reached out to get the drink. Blood trickled down my back as a wound opened afresh. Expecting ale, I was surprised by the taste. It was mead. Seeds caught in my teeth as I swallowed. I remembered my dream of lanterns, the masked people beckoning me to join them, and the man I'd loved, living, breathing and reaching out to me again. There was something in my food, something relieving the pain, giving me reveries. Nevertheless, I drank till all the mead was gone. I did not want to have a clear head.

Ledrede and his scribe returned at sunrise. The day gaoler carried a three-legged stool for Ledrede. The bishop arranged his frock about him as he sat. The scribe stood behind him, his tablet ready. Ledrede looked at me with disgust, as if my wretched condition was someone else's handiwork.

'While you worked in her household, did Dame Kytler journey at night?'

I didn't answer but stared instead at his feet. His toes were clean, the nails neatly clipped. The Franciscan sandals signified poverty but these feet were as manicured as my mistress's hands.

'Answer or I'll fetch the whip.'

'Yes, Dame Kytler journeyed every night.'

'See how efficient torture can be, scribe? Where did Kytler go?'

'To her bed, your grace.'

The bishop reddened. 'Mock once more, and your daughter will also have her back torn.'

'You found her?'

'Look at her terror, scribe; she's afraid of what the girl will tell us.'

'She won't say a word; she cannot.'

'Tell the truth, then, save this daughter of yours. Dame Kytler's nocturnal meetings, what happened, what –'

'There were demons, deals, spells and sorcery, just as you said before.'

I thought it would end there, but he wanted more.

'How did you work your magick?'

'By spells.'

'Cast how? Over a cauldron, gathered together at night?'

'At night, yes.'

'And lit a fire of oak and boiled the intestines of a cockerel mixed with worms and . . . go on, tell.'

'And herbs.'

'And more that you do not say.'

'Yes, more that I do not say.'

'Nails cut from dead bodies.'

'Oh, Lord.'

'Hairs from buttocks . . .'

I laughed. He tipped forward and struck my face. His ring sliced into the corner of my mouth. Ralph showed no shock at what had been said but just wrote on, his mouth set in a smug smile. Oh, the anger I suddenly felt towards that mere boy. It drove me to say ludicrous things, just to appal him.

'You sacrificed to Robin?' asked Ledrede.

'Yes, I sacrificed to him. I was the –'

'Mediatrix.'

'Yes, the mediatrix, between Alice and him.'

'You used sorcery to lure men to her home.'

'Yes, wealthy men with their purses full of silver.'

'And left them with nothing.'

'Not even a pulse, your grace.'

I scarcely recognized the concoctions that spun from my tongue, but I would spin till dawn to be free of this place.

'As for women? What did you do to them?'

'We turned gossips and slatterns into goats, had them slaughtered and skinned. We took their fat for our candles, their meat for our stews, their horns to drink from. Their skins, we sold to the monks, who turned them into parchment.'

The scribe dropped his quill. He chose another from his satchel rather than retrieve it from the ground.

'Oh, evil, evil meddlers! And how did the demon first come to you?'

'He came at night, as all evil things do, while I was in bed after my prayers.'

'After your prayers!'

'He did creep in and I would suffer his presence and praise him.'

'For he is vain.'

'Yes, vain, dark and horned.'

'And he touched you of course.'

'Indeed, all over, and made me promise to keep faithful to him alone.'

'Where? Where first did he touch?'

'My . . . hair – he removed the combs.'

'He is a demon, not a courtly lover. You'd have me think he's a gentleman.'

'He tore the sheets from me.'

'Exposed his lower regions, showed you his snake, and it was monstrous.'

'And then he disappeared in a wisp of smoke.'

'No, then he had carnal knowledge of you, shot his seed between your legs while he whispered his secret spells . . . Take note,' he snapped at the boy, who had paused his writing.

Both were looking at me with a peculiar trust, waiting to hear what I would say next. The bishop had claimed he'd captured Líadan, but I didn't sense her near.

'I don't believe you have my girl.'

He ignored me, asked further questions about crossroads and sacrifices. I didn't answer. I felt exhausted, sickened by the strange and dreadful things I found myself saying. What if I stopped answering? What if I didn't say another word?

Ledrede swept from the cell then, instructing the scribe

to bring out the stool. The boy avoided my gaze as he retrieved his quill and lifted the chair. I felt the knife under my clothes – if only the gaoler wasn't watching.

'Where is my daughter?' I asked Ralph.

He did not answer. After he left, the gaoler secured the padlock.

52. Basilia

It was always night here. There were candles everywhere –
flickering over the stuffed creatures, making the glass eyes
gleam and the dead furs shimmer. I noticed that the trapdoor had been covered with a long mat. It was the one with
the odd blue tree. I ran over and rolled it up. Ulf lifted me
away as if I weighed nothing.

'No,' said Alice, 'let her look. She's waiting; her mother is
coming.'

Ulf tested the heavy handle, pulling to check that it would
lift. It did. I leant over; saw how the ladder disappeared into
the darkness. No sign of anyone. Then Ulf dropped the
door. It lodged higher than the floor; he stood on it, and
walked up and down until it became flush with the earth.

I found my green cushion and sat on it, all the time watching the trapdoor. After a time, there was a knock. Sir Stephen
came in, went over to Alice and touched her shoulder. She
did not shrug him off.

'That must've been Arnold's key,' she said, looking up.

'What key?'

'The one you used to get us into this room. For mine' –
she slipped her hand into the slit in her skirts – 'is still with
me, and there was only one other copy.'

'Ah, yes,' said Stephen. 'He gave it to me, in case –'

'He trusted you.'

Alice's expression was soft – she saw Arnold in his
nephew's face.

Stephen explained how he had misled the bishop and told

him that Alice had ridden south to New Ross, where a boat waited to carry her to England.

'But you'll travel east to Dublin instead – not by road but through the mountains. And then, when the wind is favourable, you'll set sail.'

'I'll not travel at all.' Alice's expression had grown less fond. 'This is my house, my home. Every ounce of timber, eel of fabric and linch of tin is mine; every tun of wine or frail of figs, every crock, every spoon, every stone is mine,' she whispered fiercely. 'I'll not scamper like a coward. Summons be damned – that man must be driven out by a sword if need be. Do you understand, Le Poer?'

'You wish me to end up like my uncle?'

'He died fighting as knights are born to. You're a knight, are you not?'

'Yes, I am.'

Alice glanced around the room and took in Ulf and me, and then Sir Stephen's man, standing off to the side, his hand hovering over his dagger. Confused, her eyes searched each corner of the room. She had forgotten my mother was not with us.

'Dame, you are not safe. Venture upstairs and look outside your beloved front door if you so wish. You'll lose your head in the act. Listen to the plan. In the next day or so, you'll be ushered out the back.'

'And be seized by Ledrede.'

'He'll not be there; he'll be distracted.'

'How so?'

'I'll not say aloud what you must already guess.'

Did they plan to kidnap the bishop? It must have been so, for Alice did not argue further; in fact she hardly spoke at all. Stephen said that no person, besides those present and the constable, knew of her whereabouts, for there were too many turncoats amongst us.

'Will?'

'Not yet.'

'I trust my own son!'

'Yes, but can you trust his friends?'

'Oh, I see.'

'Ulf will guard the door. I'll be back when it's time.'

He went up the steps, opened the door slowly and peered into the cellar before slipping away. When I locked it behind him, the bolt glided smoothly into its ring. It had been oiled.

Alice warmed her hands over the brazier. I carried my cushion over to the trapdoor, yearning to ask how long before my mother joined us. I tried to speak. The words wouldn't come. Instead, a dry cough left my throat. Alice jumped. Had she forgotten I was there?

I waited and watched, but the trapdoor didn't budge. Where was my mother? I remembered the way she had breathed over a dead butterfly, made its wings open, made it flutter to life. Soon, I'd see the trapdoor rising up and my mother's face. And this time, when she called me *Líadan*, I'd answer.

53. The Bishop's Quarters

Fournier's would not be the only chronicle. The bishop worked into the night to document recent events: 'The Kilkennie Sorcery Trial: An Inquisitor's Record'. He might as well stay up. He had been sleeping very badly. The monks had heard him cry out from his chamber – only a night terror, he explained over dinner. Some young priests had exchanged smirks.

'The friars here are no scholars; they have not my knowledge of sorcery. Mine is the only clear eye here. Perhaps this is why she chose me. I've been visited by a succubus and I know her source: we have her trapped in our prison; a powerful witch.'

The succubus had had the look of that maid – not the exact image, but perhaps it wasn't an exact magick. She was tall and narrow with, he knew now, long dark hair and feverish skin. The bishop had been in bed, and all was quiet and very black when he discerned a foetid mix of hair, wool and civet. He was unable to move; it was as if his body were turned to stone. He tried to speak, to cry out, but could not. Yet all his senses were acute, for he heard her breathing or, now that he thought on it, perhaps feigning breath. What use for air has a phantom?

He glimpsed her then, an imitation of a woman – stark naked but for a mass of hair that trailed to her hips. She pulled the blankets from him and elicited a response from his mortal flesh. Ledrede began to pray, as strong a prayer as he had ever prayed, to the Lord, and to Christ, his son.

Though he prayed in silence, the creature moved to the rhythm of his words, splayed herself above his unwilling tumescence, folding back her lips, to reveal innards that glistened with evil. At that, from somewhere, came the strength to release his voice, and he cried out to the Holy Virgin Mother. He fell into a peaceful sleep as soon as those words left his mouth. When the bishop awoke, the demon was gone, but his bedclothes showed evidence of his struggle.

'The devil tries hardest to win he who is righteous,' he wrote, 'sends demons to torment him with their vile bodies, but even in his sleep he defeats them and sends them back out into the night, those whores of Satan, depraved and insatiable.'

Ledrede shivered, not because it was cold as a grave but that she should have set her eye on him while he slept – that succubus, that witch's familiar – and dared to enter a bishop's chamber! He felt a breath – no, a draught was all.

'If they break into the bishop's bedchamber, who knows where else they roam? Not everyone has the strong will of the bishop . . .'

The bishop had noticed a change in the young scribe, how he leant exhausted over his desk yesterday, smudging ink as he transcribed the creature's testimony. The bishop was not blind; he knew what he saw. Ralph tried to hide it, but he was tormented, too.

'Tonight, I will build my defences high,' wrote Ledrede, 'with prayer, and more prayer. And tomorrow I will fix it so the creature cannot travel here.' He sprinkled sand on the page he had finished and set his chronicle aside.

54. Petronelle

They have chained me so I cannot fly at night. I may no longer be able to move, but I can still pray. I prayed for Líadan's safekeeping. It brought none of the solace that prayers usually did. Was it because it was said in this cell, in this place where murderers have waited for the gibbet? The iron fetter bit my ankle when I moved, so I stayed still and tried to keep warm as best I could. My hands made a dry sound when I rubbed them, like leaves whispering. Closing my eyes, I imagined that branches creaked in the wind above me. I raised my face towards the weak light from the window. As a girl waiting for Otto, I'd seek a patch of light on the woodland floor, shut my eyes and lift my face to the warmth and listen for his footsteps.

Ralph was always with Ledrede now, arriving with his wax tablet smooth and ready, leaving with it hatched with marks. The bishop had become intent that every word be recorded. This time he brought proof that he had Líadan. He opened his palm and a length of her hair was coiled there. He shut his fist when I reached to touch it.

'Now tell us. You are a mistress of the black arts. You have power beyond measure, more than your mistress. And Robin is your true master, yes?'

'Yes.'

'And he wears the devil's girdle –'

'Yes, and when the bells ring at prime, nones and vespers he blesses himself backwards. And after curfew, he journeys out beneath a black cloak unseen by watchmen but not by his fellow devil worshippers. He has many disguises. Let me see my daughter.'

'Disguises, such as –'

'He wore masks, once the silver face of an angel and a tunic painted with stars and wings made from the feathers of a swan.'

'He could transform?'

'Yes.'

'And you also, Petronelle de Midia, transformed and flew at night.'

'Yes. We flew right over the walls. Let me see my daughter.'

'And there amongst the wooded slopes you danced naked and chanted, used candles made from stolen wax to concoct potions, recited spells to incite people to love, hate, injure and kill.'

'Yes, I incited you to hate me, to gaol me here, to whip me like a beast and take pleasure in it.'

The bishop stood. 'That's not possible!'

'None of it is; I don't know any demon, no one came to my bed. I mutter only to pray. I am so tired and filthy with it, with what you say. Let me see my daughter.'

'The creature Petronelle denies the truth despite having uttered it. The devil is back in control of her tongue.'

I quelled the desire to tell this strange demented man that I had a name, and it was not the one he used over and over.

As soon as it was dark, Anthony came with a small parcel and cup. He saw my torn and filthy state and did not look away. The package contained a tart of almond and cardamom. My hunger was great but I ate and drank as slowly as I could bear. When I was finished, I lifted my amber bead from beneath the neck of my gown and studied the floating discs trapped inside. They gleamed at certain angles like tiny golden shields. I had shown them to Alice a long time ago. I was eager to share everything in those days, especially my happiness.

'My brother wouldn't give you those,' she'd said. 'You took them!'

'He did give them to me. Look, we're promised.' I pointed to my ivory ring.

Alice reached towards the beads, as if to wrench them from my neck. I skipped backwards.

'You stupid slattern,' Alice shouted. 'He's heir; you have nothing. Our kind make alliances, not love matches.'

He died not long afterwards, but my stomach had already begun to swell, smooth and firm. 'Life pushing forth,' Líthgen had said. Our hut was crammed with baskets of coloured spools; my mother bent close to the loom, her eyes falling shut with tiredness, singing soft songs in Gaelic. She had begun the golden tapestry. Then Jose's manservant came to cast me from the town.

'You cannot banish her; she lives outside the walls,' Líthgen said.

'Like lice on the back of a beast, you live off Flemingstown. Were it not for the work you get from Jose, you would starve.' He pushed my mother backwards. 'The girl will leave, or she'll lose a limb, or worse.'

'My daughter has done nothing wrong.'

'She smuggled ancient amber from the house of Kytler. Mistress Alice is witness.'

'Mistress Alice is a liar,' said Mother.

'More insolence. I could slit her mongrel throat now, and be done with it.'

Watching my mother argue with Jose's man, I felt as if I had already left. I saw us all from above, as if from a great distance, and we were very small, and none of it really mattered.

55. Kytler's

The twins were in their beloved Altar Room. They had filled it with wild saffron, and its purple petals littered the floor as the sisters unpicked each other's yellow crosses with small, sharp blades. Upstairs, in the chamber that used to belong to Jose Kytler, Sir John lounged on the large canopied bed, eating pear fritters. As he licked the brown sugar from his fingers, he assessed the hangings on the wall, the fine strip of carpet that led from the door to the bed, the lustreware on the shelves – all now his.

The door creaked open. The maid Helene stood there, her skin dusty and a cross still stitched to her gown. She did not pirouette as she once did but waited for permission to enter the chamber. She looked almost as poorly as he had before. Had the foolish wretch been gulping from that cursed poison wine, he wondered? He felt a little sorry for the maid, but she could not stay – his love would not tolerate it.

The master waved his hand, indicating that she could come closer. The maid sidled towards his bed, about to issue her thanks, when she noticed the figure at the dressing table. A fair woman was paring her nails with a knife. The woman glanced up. She was the spit of the twins. It dawned on Helene that this was the person who had drawn Sir John so often back to Callan. His first wife – Gráinne Ní Dhuibhne – not dead at all but alive, smiling and now lifting and ringing Alice's small brass bell.

'Ahoy!' John called to the maid.

He loosed his alms purse from his belt and threw it towards her. Despite herself, she was a good catch.

'Now, leave,' he said, 'and do not come back.'

Ulf appeared. Gráinne ceased ringing the bell and nodded towards Helene. Taking his cue, he slung the maid over his shoulder, carried her from the chamber, down the stairs, across the hall where Stephen le Poer and another man played cards by the fire, opened the door and placed her out in the lane. Helene walked over to the steps of Market Slip, and sat. Ulf followed and joined her. They sat together in silence, he with his hands on his head, she with Sir John's purse on her lap.

Stephen slammed the door on the icy cold and cursed the giant for leaving it open. He stamped his feet and went back to playing cards.

'How much do I owe you now?' he asked his companion.

'Almost as much as the town owed the dame.'

'She'll collect no more debts now.'

'Is she really gone?'

'They all think she is,' Stephen whispered, 'except Sir John, the constable and that giant fool. But she's not gone, not yet.'

'So where does she hide?'

'Not far away at all,' Stephen said, smiling at his comrade's sudden frown.

56. Basilia

Alice noticed how I stared at the trapdoor. She came over, and knelt amidst all her skirts on the floor beside me. She moved slowly, placing her hand over mine. Ulf watched from the steps.

'Why so good to a maid's daughter?' he asked.

Alice frowned at the guard's impudence, but his question was a good one. Close though we were, I was not a person of any importance. Alice saw my confusion.

'Otto was my brother, so she's my niece. She belongs to me.'

She smiled at my expression. 'So your mother never said. You really do know nothing.'

Yes, I knew nothing, except that I did not belong to anyone.

Alice leant back and instructed Ulf to light more candles. She said no more of what she had told me. I looked at my mistress. Did we resemble each other, I wondered? I felt a warm kinship towards her; something of my father was here in this room. I felt it as I curled up on my green cushion and shut my eyes.

That night, though maybe it wasn't night at all . . . whether or not, I had a dream, and in it I was running through a stone maze of lanes and alleys, and steep steps, slipping through a series of narrow gates. 'Asylum Lane, Blind Boreen, Gaol Street, Red Lane . . .' a voice chanted, fading beneath a hammer's beat. A glow pulsed in the distance, a smith at his forge. I stopped and caught my breath, then I heard a sound that chilled me: the chime of keys from Alice's girdle. I began to run – the smith was soldering a key, and I must reach it before my mistress did.

When I woke, I saw Alice had dragged a bench over to the brazier. She closed her eyes, but she sat rigid, as if in a proper chair, tapping the gems about her neck. I leant against the cellar door: it was strong, made from thick beams of ash, but clumsily fitted, and there was a gap between it and the earth. From far above, I could hear the murmur of voices. Spoons rasped against tin, a bench creaked. They were in the kitchen. The talk was low, cautious. After some time, the room quietened. They had gone, perhaps back to the hall to guard Kytler's against the bishop and other robbers. A shadow broke the weak line of light beneath the door. A man cleared his throat. It was Ulf, come back down. When his voice came, it was as if we were right next to each other.

'The women have all been released, you know,' he whispered, 'all but your mother . . .'

How did he know it was I who listened, not Alice? Suddenly she was right beside me. She tugged my sleeve.

'Come away,' she snapped, when I didn't move fast enough.

I backed away from the door. Alice didn't look surprised at what Ulf had said but she was white-faced, angry. Through the door she cautioned him for talking. Anyone could be listening, she chided, anyone. We could be captured if he wasn't careful. He pushed a piece of parchment under the door. Alice opened it and read what it said. She lifted her skirts and came back down the steps; held the note over the flames and dropped it in.

She sat and held her head. Why was she crying? What had the message said? Why didn't she ask Ulf about my mother? Would the women come here? Would I soon hear Esme's voice, Helene's? Would I be hiding from them, too? Alice pointed at me, and then patted the bench. I was to sit alongside her. She put her arm around me when I did.

'I mean only to protect.' Her lips were cold against my forehead.

She's your aunt, I thought. I'd never had an aunt. Why, then, had we not visited her sooner, why all those hungry winters in the mountains when I could have been warm, fed? Why did my mother wait till we were desperate? Alice's head drooped as she dozed off. I got up and went to the trapdoor, lifted it up – darkness, cold air. The thud, when it fell back down, roused her.

'Close it; she won't come at this time of night.'

I opened it. If Alice wished, she could shut it herself. Why shouldn't my mother come in the middle of the night? We had. I sat and poked the brazier so the ash fell. I added a piece of wood, watched it catch. Sparks fell to the ground. Alice did not rise from the bench to shut the hatch. The embroidery on her bodice looked jaundiced in the dusk of the cellar. Her locket ring gleamed like an extra knuckle.

57. Petronelle

Anthony brought clean straw and another blanket.

'I'll come before dawn to remove them. The bishop does not know; you must never tell him.'

'I'll pray for you.'

'Don't.'

There was a heated stone inside the blankets. I spread the straw and pulled the covers over me. I lay back slowly, shivering. It still felt as if every inch of my back had been lacerated. If penance frees us from sin, cleanses our souls, surely I must be clean by now. I pictured Alice's armoire of furs in my mind's eye, opened the door and caressed the pelts one by one, furs of deep, dark brown, of blue-black, fox-red and mink-white. I lifted each one over me and lay back under layers of skins, remembering my father, laid out in death, with all his possessions about his remains.

I could end this. I could tear strips from my skirt. I saw myself hanging. Where did that vision come from? Had some demon sneaked in? Was it he, not God, who listened to my prayers? For it did not feel that any god dwelt here. The blanket rippled in the darkness like the skin of a river. I felt a wild longing to scream it all out – the demons, the sorcery, the filth, the evil, the bishop's mouth opening and closing.

I had weakened – for, despite the cold, I was constantly falling asleep, if it could be called sleep; sometimes it was more akin to falling back into life again. Before all this, I had loved Alice's garden. It wasn't just the bees and the orchard but the river, too, how the trees and sky were reflected in the water. It was like a second Kilkennie, an upside-down watery one. Was that where I went in the dreams that felt so real? What if this, all this – the bishop, his mouth moving, his mad eyes – was a night terror? What if that which I had thought was real was the dream? Then nothing Ledrede could do would ever hurt, because sooner or later I must wake up.

The next time Ledrede came, he was alone. There was a change in him. He whispered in an almost confiding manner and addressed me only as 'creature'. He spoke of a monk he saw burn, and his voice slowed as he described how the demons cried out as they had left the man's body.

'Afterwards, there was a great peace. The silence was beautiful. You could tell that God was well pleased.'

He droned on about the frantic movements of the monk's head, the stuttering denials, the pleading, the weeping; the glorious silence.

Was there no one to release me from the relentless hell of Ledrede's imagination? I tried to drown out his words with ones from inside my head – 'I'm not chained to the ground; I am in Alice's house, and sit by her side.' I saw Helene serve steaming pies, black pudding and spiced sausages. The comb on my dish was white with honey; I broke it with my thumb, and, as I ate, its sweetness trickled down my wrist. 'I'm not chained to the ground; I sit by Alice. I smile, and she smiles back. When I reach for my cup, my skin is unbroken, and I am a person. I am a person.'

That night I walked the streets of Kilkennie, my upside-down one. A path appeared beneath my feet: it was riddled with small bones, as if birds had fallen from the sky and been picked clean. I saw a narrow slipway, and sensed it led somewhere safe. I entered – the steps were steep. It was dark, and the way out was not within sight. I heard a splash from above and looked up to see ripples overhead, circles moving outwards, as if the sky were a river. I could not breathe but it did not discomfort me; somehow I was walking under water, and the splash was a pebble thrown by my daughter.

In the morning, the bishop arrived with a scroll and announced that my testimony was complete. As he read, his voice seemed very far away.

'In their unholy art, she, Petronelle, was mistress of the ritual. Yet she was nothing, she claimed, in comparison with Dame Alice, from whom she learnt all she knew. There was no one in the kingdom of England more skilled than Alice, nor was there anyone in the world her equal in the art of witchcraft . . .'

'Those are not my words,' I told him, 'those are not my words and that's not my name.'

'They are and it is. We made a record, it is written. Don't dare look at me as if I were the evil one! You who sent a succubus to a bishop's chambers!'

Ledrede smiled. Small wonder he spared the world his smiles. I did not answer him; I was finished with his kind of talk. He could cut out my tongue if he wanted to – he was welcome to it. He did something strange then, something he hadn't done before: he looked in my eyes.

'It's tonight,' he whispered. 'The pyre is ready.'

A pyre. Fire. He meant to burn me, to burn me. The bishop put his hands over his ears.

'Make her stop, make her stop!' he screamed to the gaoler.

I couldn't stop. The grief cry folded me, put me on all fours, tore my throat.

*

I was alone, the bishop was gone. I tried to pray. The shadows of the sinking day played over my hands – this was all I had left, this body, so wretched, so paltry. I held my hands in front of my face, hands that had wound thread, stitched hems, woven wool, reached out for love. Hands worn with lines, lines read by my mother, lines that told of work and love and a daughter, but not of this. These hands had plucked birds, sliced flesh, wiped tears, ground herbs, carried my child, laid her beside me to rest; folded under my head as I dreamt, all kinds of dreams, but never of this. I looked at them till they seemed to be no longer mine. Could they have done things I did not remember? Held the mane of a horse and ridden out into the night?

I stretched out my arms, held them steady. He thought I could fly, that I could utter incantations and change shape. I changed my shape the only way I could: I crouched small in the corner of the cell. 'I am not here, I am gone, I am not here, I am gone . . . this is a dream I shall wake from' – and I saw myself walk from this place, my bare feet in the snow, hardly feeling the cold. Making footprints all the way to Alice's door, and it opened for me, and, though a crowd of men stood around the fire, they did not notice me or stop their talk. I passed through, a figment of my own making, walked up the stairs and to the door, and pushed it, and entered. Líadan was there, but she was not a girl – she was old, and was standing at the open shutters looking towards the river, and when I reached out to wipe the tears from her face, she did not seem to feel my hand or know I was there.

58. Basilia

Ulf entered with a rush light and fixed it to the wall. He then reappeared with a trencher of food – hard cheese, pickled onions and black bread. Alice picked at it.

'Servant's food,' she muttered. 'What of my husband?'

'Upstairs, making a fine recovery – the Welsh maid showed her face.'

'In my house! So she'll be lilting in my kitchen, while we're trapped here like mice!'

'Oh, if she does any singing you won't hear it, for she went straight up to his chamber.'

Alice picked up the trencher in both hands and tipped the food into the flames. I reached in and caught a piece of bread.

Alice was getting more and more bad-tempered. She ordered me to shut the trapdoor, but I ignored her. I waited, watching the black hole in the ground. It looked like a grave. What delayed Mother? Maybe the next time Ulf came through the door, I'd rush past him, escape and find out what was happening at the gaol. My mistress just sat there; she didn't pace any more.

From above came cries and the sudden clash of blades.

'Plunderers!' Alice cried. She grabbed my arm and dragged me over to the trapdoor. 'Go! Go!' My foot found the top step.

The cellar door opened; light tumbled in. I squinted and Ulf ran towards us.

'Down!' Alice said. 'Go down, Basilia.'

I climbed down as fast as I could. Alice came after, her heels stamping on my fingers in her rush. I saw Ulf's face, his eyes, just before he dropped the trapdoor. I heard him above, thumping on the boards. I prayed he didn't crash in on top of us. Were he not there, to pull the rush mats across the door . . .

Alice rustled and swore soft oaths above me. I dropped suddenly, misjudging the steps. I felt the stone wall against my back. Alice's gown swept my face as she fell, too. She breathed heavily from the ground; perhaps she was injured. I turned, ran my hands along the wall, felt the grooves of the door. I could retrace our way through the underground tunnels, find the passage into the gaol, a way to my mother. Someone pounded directly above us; I feared the boards would shatter. Whoever it was might feel the difference between what was solid and what was hollow beneath his feet and come looking. I hardly dared to breathe.

The cries, and blades clashing, and thumping grew fainter, but every now and again something crashed to the floor above. I thought of the brazier, of the flames. Alice did not rise from the ground. I slipped my hand into my pouch; checked my poppet was in one piece. It was. The noise above ceased. I suddenly began to tremble and could not stop. Bells began to ring and ring. All four cathedral bells, chiming against each other. Alice put her hand on my arm, this time not to give comfort but to find it.

59. Marketplace, Irishtown

Bells tolled to gather the people. It had occurred to the bishop that the dame might attempt to save the creature, might send armed men. If so, they would find the gates locked, guards patrolling the Breagach, and archers aiming from the walls. People gathered around the pyre, tentative, with questions in their eyes.

Ledrede drove her forward with his whip, waiting, when she fell, for her to rise and start again. The bishop wished it were Alice Kytler before him. How well she would have burned, her furs and gowns sizzling to ash, leaving old bones, and gold. But with the dame there would be consequences: her magnates and relatives would take revenge. With an outsider, a servant, there would be no revenge.

The creature stumbled, her gown shredded, her hair loose and uncovered. Dignitaries and clergy craned their necks to catch sight of the stake, the pyre piled high with sticks. The gaoler stepped forward and offered her a cup, and she drank. The bishop approached her.

'Take this chance to properly repent, confess,' he said.

She looked up at him and shook her head.

'See how utterly she refuses?' he proclaimed to the vast crowd.

The threads of the bishop's robe shimmered in the dusk. He stood beside the creature and began the Lord's Prayer, his arms open wide. The crowd recited along. In the silence after Amen, the bishop turned to her, ripped her sleeve and lifted her arm.

They saw that it was discoloured and crossed with deep blue scratches.

'Her demon lover slashed secret symbols into her skin.'

Some blessed themselves, others swore oaths, and someone shouted, 'Shame!' The crowd had waited for her to speak, to cry out, to defend her name, denounce the devil, proclaim her innocence, her guilt, anything. But she did not give them that.

60. Petronelle

It is already dark. The marketplace is crammed, yet my daughter is not there. She can't be, for I saw her in a dream, sitting in a boat that rocked like a cradle in vast blue waters.

Bundles of faggots, logs and branches are stacked around a stake. A high platform, a wooden ladder, wait. My hands are tied, so I stumble, appearing foolish, changed. Not myself, not the woman known to them. Anthony steps forward, offers water I cannot stomach. 'Drink, it will help.' So I drink.

Someone grips my shoulder, guides me step by step up the ladder; catches me when I slip backwards. I do not see his face. The post digs into my back as ropes are pulled across my hips and chest. Whose hands bind them? Do I know him?

'For God's sake,' I whisper, 'throttle me.' He doesn't speak.

The pyre is lit and it smells like autumn. The dry wood crackles. A child runs forward, crying, 'Stop! Stop!' He's pulled back, held fast, legs kicking.

They'll see now what I'm made of underneath my clothes, underneath my skin, when my blistering flesh blackens and falls, when my fat melts to grease. They'll know me to the bone, those that stay till the end. This is their carnival, their miracle play. I am the sacrifice: my hair, my eyes, my tongue, my flesh will turn to ash, will drift on the breeze, will be the air they breathe.

The sky is black and full of stars. The cathedral bells ring on. The fire rises, attacks my ankles, my legs, my thighs, my stomach, flames that bite worse than any wolf. I wonder where souls go, and how they go. Are they winged, do they fly? They must do, to leave earth, to reach Heaven, to soar into the arms of the Mother. I imagine mine, flying from my mouth. I am not afraid to die.

Through the smoke I see my gaoler. Anthony looks at me, and then upwards – I follow his gaze towards the stars, see seeds of silver in the dark. I see fish scales in a blackened pan, the silver skin of Líthgen's wrist as she turns salmon, grass being whipped into a path by running girls, rivulets crossing my stomach as it grows round, my child's eyes opening – and I tumble down, down towards a bed of leaves on a forest floor, tumble down and kiss the silver scar on my lover's lip.

61. Basilia

The bells rang, and rang. Finally they ceased, leaving the whole house in silence. Whatever was happening above was over. Whatever they found and took for their own, it wasn't us. I stood and felt for the door to the underground passage that led to the gaol. I found the latch, and tugged. It did not budge. Maybe I remembered wrong. I pushed, shoved my full weight against it, nothing. I ran my hands along the surface, felt a ridge. A keyhole. I was crying, as I ran my finger over the cold metal slot. All this time I'd been waiting for my mother, the door was sealed against her. I thumped and thumped the wood.

'Stop it, stop it,' whispered Alice. 'You're making a racket. The damn thing is locked. She was never coming.'

A noise loosened my throat. Alice slapped my face, clamped her hand over my mouth. She was shouting but I couldn't hear her words: they didn't reach me, I didn't want them to. She said it again and again, until they did.

'She's dead. Your mother is dead. The bishop did it. It's over. The bells were for her.'

Everything left me then, all sense, all hearing. I was kneeling. Alice crouched beside me. My mother had died, she told me; she didn't survive. Survive what? She was in the cells like us. She was to follow.

'Stop wailing. You must measure and balance, and do what you can, not dwell on that which cannot be altered. I couldn't take her with me, but I could take you. I did that, at least, for her.'

She could've taken her, she could.

Alice hugged me tight. 'We are blood,' she reminded me. 'We are blood.'

I pushed her off me. I didn't want her. I wanted my mother. Alice moved away and climbed the ladder, pushed on the hatch door and stumbled out into the Pledge Room.

It was Alice the bishop had wanted, not me or my mother. Why hadn't she offered herself up? I heard her cross the room above, heard the cold clank of keys as she walked. It was never going to be her the bishop killed – the money-lender with powerful friends. *Measure and balance, and do what you can.* She had hidden down here while my mother was killed. *Those that come here, do not return.*

I took the poppet from my pouch. They said we were witches. They said we could brew up love or hatred, start things and end things. I tore the stitching along the side of the doll's gown, unpeeled the velvet. How perfectly I had finished the small figure. On the stomach were the marks of the blade that had smoothed the bone into shape. It was hard to break, but eventually it snapped.

I climbed up the ladder. Alice sat on the ground beside the wall of furs. She was rubbing her hip as if injured. I took unsteady steps towards her. I put out my hand and she clasped it. I pulled her up easily enough. Without a word, she disappeared through the pelts. I followed her down. Though it was dim, she unlocked the padlock with ease. As she pushed in the heavy door, I heard a noise behind us. I looked over my shoulder and saw Ulf, just his face, for an instant. He had parted the pelts, looked down and then let the furs fall closed again. He could not be seen, but was still there, watching. Alice hadn't noticed. She was bending in and out of the small room, lifting out one bag of coins after another and laying them on the steps about my feet. 'I'll take good care of you,' she was saying. 'With this, we can do anything you want.'

I rammed into her without a single thought, watched as she fell back on to the bags, her leg at a strange angle. I tried to close the door, seal her in with her beloved coins, but she rose to her feet. We pushed from either side of the door, our faces only a hand's width apart. I wrenched the door open and, catching her off guard, shoved her to the ground again. She lay there looking up at me. It was just as I had seen before. The dark clay walls, Alice's terror as she reached out, trying to save herself.

'Basilia,' she begged.

'There's no such person,' I answered. 'There never was.'

Líadan

It didn't take me long to find Jack. He was near the river, covered in frost-white leaves. He was feather-light when I lifted him. He looked up, and it was as if we had known each other for a very long time, as if he had no doubt that I knew what I was doing.

Ulf guided us through the mountains, and eastwards. He was well rewarded when he took his leave of us.

A week later and I am looking at the sea. It lunges towards us in huge waves with gleaming undersides, as if the sky has swooped down and transformed into water.

I remember Bébinn – as she was before. When I was child enough to love her just for being my mother. I see her hair, drawn into a braided nest. The line at her nape is shaped like a bird, wings outstretched. Her fingers uncurl to reveal an amber bead. My smile makes her smile.

There is cinnamon dust on her wrists.

Author's Note

Her Kind is a work of imagination. It is inspired by real events that took place in Kilkenny in 1324.

With regard to the epigraph extracts: some are direct quotations; some are paraphrased; and one is imagined – reflecting the nature of the book itself, a mixture of fact and fiction. Most 'official' sources for a historical case such as this one were written by elite males like Richard Ledrede. These accounts are frequently considered to be reliable vehicles for the truth. The bishop's narrative, for example, is often quoted as unbiased fact. *Her Kind* is a retelling, one in which a healthy disrespect for 'official sources' is vital. It's not their turn to tell the story.

All anyone knows of Petronelle de Midia is her name and the date of her death: 3 November 1324. I've written this novel to explore what may have happened, to give her a voice. It's written in memory of her, and women like her.

Acknowledgements

Thanks are due to the following people. Some generously gave me writing space, some sourced books or gave guided tours, some gave advice and support, or commissioned writing and teaching work: John and Jacinta Scannell, Kate O'Rourke, Noel Fitzpatrick, Catriona Kyles, Sean Hickey, Jennifer Liston, Sarah Barry, Antonia Case, Mary Pat Moloney, Orla Murphy, Catherine Dunne, the Irish Writers' Centre, Words Ireland, Lorraine Murphy Dooley and Sinéad Gleeson.

Thanks to Kilkenny Library's Local Studies Department for access to documents. I also wish to acknowledge the work of L. S. Davidson and J. O Ward, editors of *The Sorcery Trial of Alice Kytler: A Contemporary Account* (Pegasus Press, 2004), which was a vital resource.

Thanks to The Banshees, my brilliant writing group – especially Jennifer Wallace and Caroline Sutherland who read an early draft of this book. Also amazing are Irene Kane, Celine Mescall, Marie Hughes, Caroline Waugh, Helena Duggan, Sylvia Martin, and Tom Hunt whom we miss very much.

To my wonderful agent, Nicola Barr, for her patience and encouragement. To the team at Penguin Ireland, Cliona Lewis, Aislin Reddie, Orla King, Carrie Anderson and especially to my editor, Patricia Deevy. And to Donna Poppy, for being such a fantastic and meticulous copy-editor.

Many thanks are due to my family – to my sister Olivia, for the Kilkenny sessions, and always being supportive; to my parents, Anne and Francis, to whom this book is dedicated; and last but not least, to Rosie, Joshua, Donagh and Paul.

Her Kind – book club extras

> 'Her Kind *is far more than a work of historical fiction, it is
> as searing a critique of our own times as is Arthur Miller's*
> The Crucible'
>
> Judges for EU Prize for Literature

*Here are some questions and observations you might like to consider for
your book club discussion:*

Q. How did you feel towards Alice? Towards Petronelle?
Towards Basilia? Towards Ledrede? Did you prefer one
character over another? Why?

Q. What was Ledrede's real motivation for accusing Alice
Kytler of witchcraft?

> 'In the fourteenth century, the Pope was based in Avignon,
> France. He had a lively fear of sorcery and witchcraft and
> accused members of his own court of sticking pins in his
> waxen likeness. He gave Richard Ledrede, one of his favoured
> clerics, the Bishopric of Ossory. Until then, Richard, an
> Englishman, had never set foot in Ireland' Niamh Boyce

Q. How did Alice's love for her husband drive the story?
To what extent do you think it was her undoing?

Q. What was the real cause of Sir John's illness? Who did you think was behind it?

> *'The characters are part of a world that at times is utterly alien to us, and one of the most haunting aspects of the novel is the depiction of anchoress, the holy woman who has been bricked alive into the walls of St Canice's Cathedral'* Irish Times

> 'The cathedral was where I came across the anchoress's grave. An anchorite or anchoress is a hermit who gives up ordinary life for a solitary life of prayer – they are often sealed in between the walls of a church, with only small "squints" or windows to receive food through. The figure of a nun is carved on to the anchoress's gravestone. Her hands are held in old-style prayer position, palm facing outwards rather than palms together. When I placed my palms over her stone ones, I felt a strange sensation, close to the one that Petronelle describes in *Her Kind*, that of an old truth pushing back – that day the character of Agnes the anchoress came to life' Niamh Boyce

Q. Who do you think the anchoress Agnes really was and why was she locked between the walls?

Q. If there was a point of no return in the book, a point where things were never going to be the same again – where do you think that was?

> *'Sorcery, religion, politics, greed, privilege, power – all pale in comparison to what one finds at the heart of this story: that natural connection, the love of a mother for her child'* Historical Novels Review

Q. What did you think about the relationship between mothers and daughters in the book? How do they differ from such relationships nowadays?

Q. Alice Kytler was a powerful, mature woman. Are older women still sometimes demonized for being independent? How?

Q. The word 'witch' – how is it used nowadays? What labels have the same impact now as 'witch' had in medieval times? Can you still destroy someone's reputation by calling them a name?

Q. What had you expected medieval Ireland to be like? How was it different from the world depicted in *Her Kind*? What resonated?

Q. Medieval Ireland was a melting pot – full of different languages and customs. Were you surprised to learn how diverse Ireland was, that it was a fractured place, full of tribes and walled towns – not one united entity?

Q. Would you have preferred to live outside or inside the walls of Kilkenny City? Why?

Q. On arriving in Hightown, Petronelle and her daughter are given new – non-Irish – names and clothes, and are forbidden to speak their native language. What affect do you think this has on their relationship? On their sense of identity?

Can you see any resonances between how they are treated and how people seeking refuge are treated now?

Q. There is no reference to this trial in the ancient *Liber Primus Kilkennius* (a record of the minutes of meetings of the city's governing corporation), yet it records many less significant cases from the time. Why do you think that might have happened? Could it be that it was undocumented? Or that references were removed from this record of the goings-on in fourteenth-century Kilkenny?

Q. *Her Kind* is a reimagining of the 1324 Sorcery Trial of Dame Alice Kytler. It was a landmark case in the history of witchcraft trials and notorious at the time – many of the annals contain a reference to the case. The trial resulted in Europe's first case of an accused woman being burned as a witch. Had you heard of the case before you read the book? Why do you think Alice's story has remained outside of standard history books?

Q. *Her Kind* is inspired by real events. Did that affect how you felt about the characters and their fates? Have you been inspired to find out more about the (sparse) historical records and compare with what the author has written? What do you think of what she's done with the story? How comfortable are you with an author reimagining real events?

Q. Petronelle's existence is recorded in Judy Chicago's work of art *The Dinner Party* (check it out online). Apart from that there has been no memorial or monument to Petronella de Midia. Yet Bishop Ledrede's effigy can be seen in St Canice's Cathedral to this day. Who do you think decides who gets remembered? What happens to those who are not commemorated, listed, archived, named? Whose names are on the streets of your town? Who is your local bridge named after? If you open a map, what do the names tell you? What do they mean? Is that meaning still alive? Who is mapping our history for us? Do these things matter?

Q. If you were to retrieve a voice from history, whose would it be?

ABOUT THE AUTHOR

Niamh Boyce is a Hennessy award-winning writer whose first novel, *The Herbalist*, a critically acclaimed bestseller, won Sunday Independent Debut of the Year at the Irish Book Awards and was longlisted for the International Dublin Literary Award. *Her Kind* was shortlisted for the EU Prize for Literature. Her poetry collection *Inside the Wolf* (Red Dress Press) was released in 2018. Niamh's writing has been broadcast, adapted for stage and anthologized, most recently in *The Long Gaze Back*, *The Hennessy Book of Irish Fiction 2005–2015* and *Hallelujah for 50 Foot Women*.

Twitter: @NiamhBoyce

He just wanted a decent book to read ...

Not too much to ask, is it? It was in 1935 when Allen Lane, Managing Director of Bodley Head Publishers, stood on a platform at Exeter railway station looking for something good to read on his journey back to London. His choice was limited to popular magazines and poor-quality paperbacks – the same choice faced every day by the vast majority of readers, few of whom could afford hardbacks. Lane's disappointment and subsequent anger at the range of books generally available led him to found a company – and change the world.

'We believed in the existence in this country of a vast reading public for intelligent books at a low price, and staked everything on it'
Sir Allen Lane, 1902–1970, founder of Penguin Books

The quality paperback had arrived – and not just in bookshops. Lane was adamant that his Penguins should appear in chain stores and tobacconists, and should cost no more than a packet of cigarettes.

Reading habits (and cigarette prices) have changed since 1935, but Penguin still believes in publishing the best books for everybody to enjoy. We still believe that good design costs no more than bad design, and we still believe that quality books published passionately and responsibly make the world a better place.

So wherever you see the little bird – whether it's on a piece of prize-winning literary fiction or a celebrity autobiography, political tour de force or historical masterpiece, a serial-killer thriller, reference book, world classic or a piece of pure escapism – you can bet that it represents the very best that the genre has to offer.

Whatever you like to read – trust Penguin.